ABOUT THE AUTHOR

No other writer has presented us with so peculiarly American a vision of loneliness as Sherwood Anderson (1876–1941). And if, in this century, we have come to expect the shock of self-recognition from the American short story, more than from our longer fiction or our poetry, it is in large part because in the 1920s Anderson fashioned the story form as the genre of interiority. He was this country's premier storyteller, the writer who wrested short fiction from the upbeat conventionality of the popular magazines of his day—which repeatedly commissioned stories from him only to reject them—and molded it to express the isolation of individual people.

He published 23 books in his lifetime, mainly short story collections and novels, but also volumes of memoirs, essays, poems, and reportage. Four volumes of stories, *Winesburg, Ohio* (1919), *The Triumph of the Egg* (1921), *Horses and Men* (1923) and *Death in the Woods* (1933) comprise as significant an achievement as has been produced by any American short story writer.

Anderson was from southwestern Ohio. Until mid-life his profession was advertising, where he used his gift for words to sell things like irons and washing machines. He did it well and advanced in this profession. Eventually he moved to Chicago and began to write in earnest. *Windy McPherson's Son* (1916) was his first published book, a novel about a boy's life in an Iowa town. It was followed in 1917 by another novel, *Marching Men*, set in Pennsylvania coal country, and a book of poems, *Mid-American Chants* (1918). In 1920 *Poor White* appeared, arguably his best novel. Other books include the novel *Many Marriages* (1923), and the autobiographically based works, *A Story Teller's Story* (1924) and *Tar: A Midwest Childhood* (1926). In the early '30s he aligned himself with Communism, but his active political period lasted only three years. His last novel was *Kit Brandon* (1936). Publication of his *Memoirs* (1942) and *Letters* (1953) occurred posthumously.

"Yes, undoubtedly," according to his friend Gertrude Stein, "Sherwood Anderson had a sweetness, and sweetness is rare." "He had," said Alice B. Toklas, "an all-inclusive heart."

THE
TRIUMPH
OF THE EGG

THE
TRIUMPH
OF THE EGG

by
Sherwood Anderson

Four Walls Eight Windows
New York

Copyright 1921 by B.W. Huebsch, Inc.
Copyright renewed 1948 by Eleanor C. Anderson.
Introduction copyright © 1988 by Herbert Gold.
The Sound in the Stream: Copyright 1942 by Eleanor Copenhaver Anderson.
Copyright © renewed 1970.

First Four Walls Eight Windows Edition published 1988 by Four Walls Eight
Windows, Inc., New York

Library of Congress Cataloging-in-Publication Data
Anderson, Sherwood, 1876-1941.
    Triumph of the egg / by Sherwood Anderson.
        p. cm.
    ISBN 0-941423-11-5 (pbk.) : $8.95
    I. Title.
PS3501.N4T75 1988
813'.52—dc 19   87-35411
                                                                  CIP

Four Walls Eight Windows
P.O. Box 548
Village Station
New York, N.Y. 10014

Printed in the U.S.A.

CONTENTS

THE
TRIUMPH
OF THE EGG

Tales are people who sit on the doorstep of the house of my mind.
It is cold outside and they sit waiting.
I look out at a window.

        The tales have cold hands,
        Their hands are freezing.

A short thickly-built tale arises and threshes his arms about.
His nose is red and he has two gold teeth.

There is an old female tale sitting hunched up in a cloak.

Many tales come to sit for a few moments on the doorstep and then
      go away.
It is too cold for them outside.
The street before the door of the house of my mind is filled with tales.
They murmur and cry out, they are dying of cold and hunger.

I am a helpless man—my hands tremble.
I should be sitting on a bench like a tailor.
I should be weaving warm cloth out of the threads of thought.
The tales should be clothed.
They are freezing on the doorstep of the house of my mind.

I am a helpless man—my hands tremble.
I feel in the darkness but cannot find the doorknob.
I look out at a window.
Many tales are dying in the street before the house of my mind.

IMPRESSIONS IN CLAY

BY

Tennessee Mitchell

Labor

"They are squarer with kids,
I don't know why."

For I WANT TO KNOW WHY

She worked her way through college

Well-to-do

The Old Scholar

For THE EGG

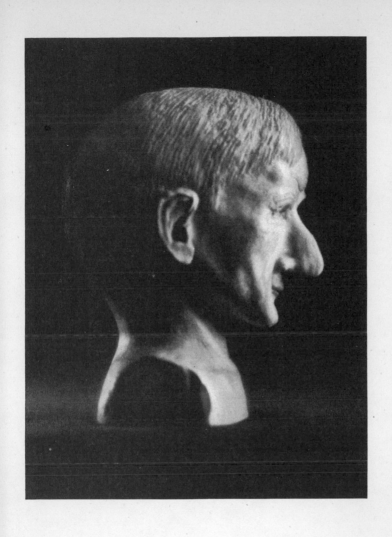

Melville Stoner

For OUT OF NOWHERE INTO NOTHING

INTRODUCTION

The Purity and Cunning
of Sherwood Anderson

THE OLD charges against Anderson remain: elements of the mawkish, the maudlin, of self-display, carrying the unhealed wound of adolescence into middle age and beyond. In different ways, the same accusation can be made against Walt Whitman, William Faulkner, Thomas Wolfe, J. D. Salinger, and especially against the Ernest Hemingway who so ungratefully ridiculed his elder friend and patron. The poet is a child in the body of a grownup, Francois Mauriac said; both good and bad poets share this habit of unlicensed occupancy.

There should be a bit of midwestern sincerity in all Americans. When Anderson speaks the obvious, he often enough has the poet's talent for making us see it afresh. Sincere may be out of fashion; my graffiti says: *Sincere Lives*! Anderson writes in "The Egg": "Something happened to the two people. They became ambitious. The American passion for getting up in the world took possession of them." Yet it's not a lecture. In the story we see a family's taciturn isolation in the getting-up world. A title like "I Want to Know Why" utters the fact of the case without shame: metaphysical yearnings must infest the writer's enterprise. He wants to know why sex, why age, why loneliness, why loss, why failure, why death. Why love and why not-love? The questions are still new and unanswerable.

The elegy for human possibility not only reminds us of what we lose but also of what we still precariously require for clinging purposes. "In October leaves should be carried away, out over the plains, in a wind. They should go dancing away."

For these moments, this remembrance, surely we can forgive the hurt self-dramatization of the "poetic" interludes, as in: "I said that life was life, that men in streets and cities might build temples to their souls." Allegedly it's "the man with the trumpet" making this appeal, but it's really, as we know, the weary self-appointed prophet at the end of his book. Let us forgive: all prophets are self-appointed, and Anderson is right, even if the expression makes us squirm. When the expression comes filtered through images of barns, farmhouses, lonely men in cities, silent women, a child "with her back against the tree on warm bright afternoons," the lamentation and prophecy holds us in its thrall.

Sherwood Anderson was never in fashion and cannot be forgotten. He makes vivid an America beneath both the willed satisfaction and the willed discontent. He is not in the business of fabricating images; he lets the longing and turmoil reveal itself in particular lives then and now. Even his flaw—a kind of bachelor desire in the unrequited love of country—fits the case of what it is to be an American. Perhaps even more appropriately today than in his lifetime.

Rereading *The Triumph of the Egg* after all these years, I remember the words of another poet, Rachel Auerbach, naming losses which Sherwood Anderson could not have imagined because no one can properly imagine the holocaust:

> Let us not mourn them,
> But love them as if they were among us.

It's a treasure to which Sherwood Anderson returns us: the dearness of our souls and the souls of others, here and departed.

1. "A Little Worm in the Fair Apple of Progress."

He said it of himself. He saw himself curled up, busily feeding on midwestern America, sheltered, destructive, loving his host, and needed by this age and place in order that they could get some sense of buoyancy and carry within them the richness of growth. He recognized his own childish self-absorption, great even for an artist, a breed accused by everyone of being childishly self-absorbed. Therefore he wrote about death with praise because "it will in any case give us escape from this disease of self." Self-love is surely the beginning of the love of others, but it is only the beginning. Sherwood Anderson, an old child, suffered a merely erratic love of himself, therefore writhed with a tormented love of others. All his stories are bound up in this sense of the self's isolation, seen as glory and sickness, as sickness and glory. He is one of the purest, most intense poets of loneliness—the loneliness of being buffeted in the current, the loneliness of isolation and that of being swallowed. One type represents the traditional retreat into the self for self-possession; the other, and its adversary at times, arises out of the angry resentment of a sensible man in an assemblyline civilization. Anderson's work is a manual of the ways in which loneliness can be used. It was his nourishment and sometimes his poison.

"I pour a dream over it .... I want to write beautifully, create beautifully, not outside but in this thing in which I am born, in this place where, in the midst of ugly towns, cities, Fords, moving pictures, I have always lived, must always live." Yet he fled it

always. He fled in order to find himself, then prayed
to flee that disease of self, to become "beautiful and
clear . . . plangent and radiant." He felt that he loved
only the midwestern land and people, but was still
fleeing when he died—in the Panama Canal Zone.

In his photographs he often showed his hair hanging over his eyes. The affectation means a great deal:
first mere arty affectation (how he loved the "free
spirits" of Greenwich Village and New Orleans!),
then something feminine and wanting to be pretty
and lovable for prettiness, and then of course the
blurring of sight when you try to see through your
own hair. What do you see? A world organized by
your hair. "I must snap my finger at the world I
have thought of everyone and everything." His sympathy and his oceanic feelings alternate with arrogant
despair in which the arrogance can deceive no one. So
desperately hurt he is, trying so hard to convince the
"word-fellows" to admire him. But then his nostalgia
gives us the mood he sought to force: " . . . old fellows in my home town speaking feelingly of an evening spent on the big, empty plains. It has taken the
shrillness out of them. They had learned the trick of
quiet. It affected their whole lives. It made them
significant."

We understand him at last!

And then again the helpless bombast: "At my best,
brother, I am like a great mother bird . . . . " He

exuded through his pores the ferocious longing of a
giant of loneliness. The typical chords from his letters sound under the changing heroes of the stories:

Youth not given a break—youth licked before it starts.

Filled with sadness that you weren't there.

I have a lot I want to tell you if I can. . . . Anyway you
know what I mean when we talked of a man working in
the small, trying to save a little of the feeling of man for
man.

    The romantic sentimentalist held up his mirror to
look at his world, peered deeply, saw himself instead,
of course; wrote painfully about what he saw; and it
turned out that he was writing about the world after
all, squeezing it by this palpitating midwestern
honesty out of his grandiose sorrows and longings.
Sometimes, anyway. He was not a pure man; he had a
kind of farmer cunning, plus his groaning artiness
and pretense, with which he hoped to convince the
"word-fellows" and the pretty girls that he was a Poet
although not a young one. What he really wanted was
to be alone in that succession of gray furnished rooms
he talked about so eloquently, making immortal the
quiet noise and gentle terror of his childhood. "I try
to believe in beauty and innocence in the midst of the
most terrible clutter." But clutter too was the truth of

his life; he fed on it; how else does a poet take the measure of his need for "beauty and innocence"? He must have remained an optimist, too, amidst all his disillusion. He married four times. To the end of his life he went on believing, and marrying.

Anderson the writer arouses a poking curiosity about Anderson the man even in the most resolute critic. The implication of confession is always with us: Here I am, it's good that you know!

His paragraphs are soaked in the groping of speech. He repeats, cries out, harangues, pleads. All his work, the abysmal failures and the successes which have helped to construct the vision Americans have of themselves, represents an innocent, factitious, improvised, schemed reflection and elaboration of the elements of his own life. He turns the private into the public and then back into the private again. His mystery as a man remains despite his childish longing to reveal himself—the mystery of a man who looks at a man with a beard and a scar in a conference room and sees, instead, a lover fleeing his girl's brothers through the fields. (They had knives and slashed—could this be the same man? he asks himself.) Anderson confounds us with bombast and wit, tenderness and softheadedness, rant and exquisite delicacy.

The best of his work is what matters.

Let's look at what the worm made of his apple.

2. *"My Feet Are Cold and Wet."*

He loved to create, he loved his fantasy as the lonely boy does. In his best work, the fantasy is most controlled, or if not exactly controlled, simplified, given a single lyrical line. The novels had trouble passing the test of the adult imagination, being wild proliferations of daydream. But his simple stories join Sherwood Anderson with the reader's sense of wonder and despair at the pathetic in his own past—childish hope of love, failed ambition, weakness and loneliness. As music can do, such stories liberate the fantasies of our secret lives. However, musicians will agree that music is for listening, not to be used as a stimulus for fantasy. We must attend to the song itself, not take advantage of it and make it the instrument of our dreaming. In the same way, the great writers hope to arouse and lead the reader's imagination toward a strong individual perspective on experience. Sherwood Anderson, however, was not of that company, despite his personal hobby of eccentric Bohemianism. Rather, he was the dreamy, sad, romantic within each of us, evoking with nostalgia and grief the bitter moments of recognition which have formed him— formed all of us in our lonely America.

James Joyce used the word "epiphany" to name that moment of revelation when words and acts come together to manifest something new, familiar, timeless, a deep summation of meaning. The lyric tales of Anderson give this wonderful rapt coming-forth, time and time again.

In "The Untold Lie," for example, in his best-known collection, *Winesburg, Ohio*, two men tenderly meet in order to talk about whether one, the younger, should marry the girl he has made pregnant. The older man, unhappy in his own marriage, wants to see the young man's life free and charged with powerful action as his own has never been. But it is revealed to him—revelation almost always climaxes Anderson's stories—that life without wife and children is impossible and that one man's sorrows cannot be used by him to prevent another man from choosing the same sorrows. The life of conjugal sorrows is not merely a life of conjugal sorrows: the story finally breathes the sadness, the beauty, the necessary risks of grownup desire. "Whatever I told him would have been a lie," he decides. Each man has to make his own decisions, live out his chosen failures of ideal freedom.

Many of Anderson's stories deploy circumstances which have a grandiose folkish quality; many of both the most impressive and the most mawkish are concerned with an archetypical experience of civilization: the test which, successfully passed, commands manhood. The end sought is manliness, that new clean and free life; failure is seen as a process of being made effeminate, or falling into old patterns of feeling and action. At his best in these stories, there is a physical joy in triumph which is fresh, clean, genial—we think of Mark Twain, although a Twain without the robust humor; at his weak moments, we may also think of the sentimental sick Twain or the maundering moping of a prettified Thomas Wolfe.

The line between the subjects of Anderson's stories and Sherwood Anderson himself is barely drawn. His relation to his material, as shaper of his material, is as intense and personal as that of any modern writer. Unlike most writing dealing with the unhappy and frustrated, Anderson's work is absolutely authentic in the double sense—not merely communicating the feeling of these people as people, but also convincing us that the author shares both their bitter frustration and their evanescent occasional triumphs. By comparison with Sherwood Anderson, Dostoevsky is a monument of cool detachment. His identification sometimes verges upon the morbid: "Everyone in the world is Christ and they are all crucified." He has a primitive idealism, a spoiled romanticism like that of Rousseau: we could be all innocent and pure in our crafts if the machines of America and the fates that bring machines did not cripple us.

This romantic idealism can be illustrated again by his treatment of another theme, marriage, in the story "Loneliness," in which he writes of Enoch Robinson: "Two children were born to the woman he married,"—just as if they did not happen to Robinson at all, which is indeed the truth about the self-isolated personality he describes. "He dismissed the essence of things," Anderson can write, "and played with realities." Again the romantic Platonist sees a conflict between the deepest meaning and the fact of our lives, between what we do and what we "really" are. With a kind of purity and cunning, Anderson seems to thrive on this curiously boyish notion the limitations of which most of us quickly learn. We work and love because there is no other way to be ourselves than in relation to the rest of the world. The kind man is the man who performs kind acts; the generous man is one who behaves generously; we distrust the "essential" generosity sometimes claimed for the soul of a man who selfishly watches out only for himself. And yet we can be reminded by Anderson's conviction in his boyish dream of isolated personality that there is something totally private, untouchable, beyond appearance and action, in all of us. The observation is a familiar one, but the experience can be emotionally crucial.

His characters, abstracted people playing out their time in a fragmentary society, these "heroes" are isolated, as Anderson himself was isolated, by art or unfulfilled love or religion—by the unsurmounted challenge of finding the self within relationship with others. It was the deep trouble of Anderson's own life that he saw his self, which could be realized only by that monstrous thing, the Life of Art, as flourishing in opposition to decent connections with others. Marriage, work, friendship were beautiful things; but the gray series of furnished slum rooms, in which he wrote, enough rooms to fill a city, were his real home. Writing letters and brooding behind his locked door, he idealized love, he idealized friendship. He withdrew to the company of phantom creatures. He hoped to guard his integrity. He kept himself the sort of child-man he described with such comprehending sympathy.

In many writers dealing with the grim facts of our lives, the personal sense of triumph at encompassing the material adds a note of confidence which is at variance with the story itself. Hemingway is a good example; his heroes go down to defeat, but Papa Hemingway the chronicler springs eternal. In Anderson this external note of confidence and pride in craft is lacking, except in some of the specious, overwilled novels. Generally he does not import his poetry into the work—he allows only the poetry that is *there*— nor does his independent life as a creator come to change the tone of these sad tales. The stories are unselfconsciously committed to him as he is sworn true to them; the identification—a variety of loyalty—is complete; he is related to his material with a love that lacks esthetic detachment and often lacks the control which comes with that detachment. This is what gives them their sometimes embarrassing, often unforgettable folk quality. Still they are not folktales but, rather, pseudofolktales. The romantic longing and grieving is not characteristic of the folktale, despite the other elements: a matter-of-fact storytelling, a colloquial American language (complicated by chivalry and the Bible, but at its best not "literary"), and the authority of Anderson's priestly devotion to his lives and people. Later, of course, the romantic judgment culminated in rebellion, sometimes in a kind of esthetic rant against the way things are.

In "The Strength of God," the Reverend Curtis Hartman (as in a parable, Heart-man) "wondered if the flame of the spirit really burned in him and dreamed of a day when a strong sweet current of power would come like a great wind into his voice and his soul and the people would tremble before the spirit of God made manifest in him. 'I am a poor stick and that will never really happen to me,' he mused dejectedly, and then a patient smile lit up his features. 'Oh well, I suppose I'm doing well enough,' he added philosophically."

These, as *The New Yorker* would put it, are musings that never got mused and philosophic additions that never got philosophically added. They have an archaic directness that amounts to a kind of stylization. The simplicity itself is a sophisticated manner. As the officer of the Pharisees said, "Never man spake like this man." It recalls to us the days of storytellers who suggested the broad line of an action and allowed us to give our imaginations to it. Nowadays we demand detail upon detail, and the phrase "I am a poor stick" might require a whole book of exposition.

The pathos of the pious man's temptation by the flesh has a flavor beautifully evocative of adolescence. We no longer think of "carnal temptation" as Anderson did. But we remember our fears and guilts; we are reminded of ourselves. Hartman's silent, secret battle with himself over Kate Swift is given part of its bite by her own story—this pimply, passionate young school teacher who strikes beauty without knowing it and can find no one to speak to her. Her story is told with a delicacy that reflects Anderson's reticence about women. Enoch Robinson, he says, "tried to have an affair with a woman of the town met on the sidewalk before his lodging house." To have an affair! (The boy got frightened and ran away; the woman roared with laughter and picked up someone else.)

Except for the poetic schoolteacher and a very few others, women are not women in Anderson's stories. There are the girls who suffer under the kind of sensitivity, passion, and lonely burning which was Anderson's own lot; and then there are the Women. For Anderson women have a holy power; they are earth-mothers, ectoplasmic spirits, sometimes succubi, rarely individual living creatures. The berry-picking "maidens" gambol while the boys are "boisterous," and the hero flutters in his tormented realm between the sexes.

In a tormented realm, Sherwood Anderson also abode. American cities, as he wrote, are "noisy and terrible," and they fascinated him. He got much of the noise and terror into his writing about big cities, and the quiet noise and gentle terror of little towns into his stories about them. And among the frights, he continually rediscovered these minor beauties which made life possible for him—the moment of love, of friendship, of self-realization. That they were but moments is not entirely the fault of his own character.

3. "The Air of a Creator."

Sherwood Anderson "added to the confusion of men," as he said of the great financiers and industrialists, the Morgans, Goulds, Carnegies, Vanderbilts, "by taking on the air of a creator." He has helped to create the image we have of ourselves as

Americans. His characters haunt us as do our neighbors, our friends, our own secret selves which we first met one springtime in childhood.

Herbert Gold

San Francisco
February, 1988

THE DUMB MAN

THERE is a story.—I cannot tell it.—I have no
   words.
The story is almost forgotten but sometimes I remember.

The story concerns three men in a house in a street.
If I could say the words I would sing the story.
I would whisper it into the ears of women, of mothers.
I would run through the streets saying it over and over.
My tongue would be torn loose—it would rattle
   against my teeth.

The three men are in a room in the house.
One is young and dandified.
He continually laughs.

There is a second man who has a long white beard.
He is consumed with doubt but occasionally his doubt
   leaves him and he sleeps.

A third man there is who has wicked eyes and who
   moves nervously about the room rubbing his
   hands together.
The three men are waiting—waiting.

Upstairs in the house there is a woman standing with her back to a wall, in half darkness by a window.

That is the foundation of my story and everything I will ever know is distilled in it.

I remember that a fourth man came to the house, a white silent man.
Everything was as silent as the sea at night.
His feet on the stone floor of the room where the three men were made no sound.

The man with the wicked eyes became like a boiling liquid—he ran back and forth like a caged animal.
The old grey man was infected by his nervousness— he kept pulling at his beard.

The fourth man, the white one, went upstairs to the woman.

There she was—waiting.

How silent the house was—how loudly all the clocks in the neighborhood ticked.
The woman upstairs craved love. That must have been the story. She hungered for love with her whole being. She wanted to create in love.
When the white silent man came into her presence she sprang forward.

Her lips were parted.
There was a smile on her lips.

The white one said nothing.
In his eyes there was no rebuke, no question.
His eyes were as impersonal as stars.

Down stairs the wicked one whined and ran back and
    forth like a little lost hungry dog.
The grey one tried to follow him about but presently
    grew tired and lay down on the floor to sleep.
He never awoke again.

The dandified fellow lay on the floor too.
He laughed and played with his tiny black mustache.

I have no words to tell what happened in my story.
I cannot tell the story.

The white silent one may have been Death.

The waiting eager woman may have been Life.

Both the old grey bearded man and the wicked one
    puzzle me.
I think and think but cannot understand them.
Most of the time however I do not think of them at
    all.
I keep thinking about the dandified man who laughed
    all through my story.

If I could understand him I could understand everything.
I could run through the world telling a wonderful
story.
I would no longer be dumb.

Why was I not given words?
Why am I dumb?

I have a wonderful story to tell but know no way to
tell it.

I WANT TO KNOW WHY

WE GOT up at four in the morning, that first day in the east. On the evening before we had climbed off a freight train at the edge of town, and with the true instinct of Kentucky boys had found our way across town and to the race track and the stables at once. Then we knew we were all right. Hanley Turner right away found a nigger we knew. It was Bildad Johnson who in the winter works at Ed Becker's livery barn in our home town, Beckersville. Bildad is a good cook as almost all our niggers are and of course he, like everyone in our part of Kentucky who is anyone at all, likes the horses. In the spring Bildad begins to scratch around. A nigger from our country can flatter and wheedle anyone into letting him do most anything he wants. Bildad wheedles the stable men and the trainers from the horse farms in our country around Lexington. The trainers come into town in the evening to stand around and talk and maybe get into a poker game. Bildad gets in with them. He is always doing little favors and telling about things to eat, chicken browned in a pan, and how is the best way to cook sweet potatoes and corn bread. It makes your mouth water to hear him.

5

When the racing season comes on and the horses go to the races and there is all the talk on the streets in the evenings about the new colts, and everyone says when they are going over to Lexington or to the spring meeting at Churchhill Downs or to Latonia, and the horsemen that have been down to New Orleans or maybe at the winter meeting at Havana in Cuba come home to spend a week before they start out again, at such a time when everything talked about in Beckersville is just horses and nothing else and the outfits start out and horse racing is in every breath of air you breathe, Bildad shows up with a job as cook for some outfit. Often when I think about it, his always going all season to the races and working in the livery barn in the winter where horses are and where men like to come and talk about horses, I wish I was a nigger. It's a foolish thing to say, but that's the way I am about being around horses, just crazy. I can't help it.

Well, I must tell you about what we did and let you in on what I'm talking about. Four of us boys from Beckersville, all whites and sons of men who live in Beckersville regular, made up our minds we were going to the races, not just to Lexington or Louisville, I don't mean, but to the big eastern track we were always hearing our Beckersville men talk about, to Saratoga. We were all pretty young then. I was just turned fifteen and I was the oldest of the four. It was my scheme.

I admit that and I talked the others into trying it.
There was Hanley Turner and Henry Rieback and
Tom Tumberton and myself. I had thirty-seven dollars I had earned during the winter working nights
and Saturdays in Enoch Myer's grocery. Henry Rieback had eleven dollars and the others, Hanley and
Tom had only a dollar or two each. We fixed it all
up and laid low until the Kentucky spring meetings
were over and some of our men, the sportiest ones, the
ones we envied the most, had cut out—then we cut
out too.

I won't tell you the trouble we had beating our way
on freights and all. We went through Cleveland and
Buffalo and other cities and saw Niagara Falls. We
bought things there, souvenirs and spoons and cards
and shells with pictures of the falls on them for our
sisters and mothers, but thought we had better not
send any of the things home. We didn't want to put
the folks on our trail and maybe be nabbed.

We got into Saratoga as I said at night and went
to the track. Bildad fed us up. He showed us a place
to sleep in hay over a shed and promised to keep
still. Niggers are all right about things like that.
They won't squeal on you. Often a white man you
might meet, when you had run away from home like
that, might appear to be all right and give you a quarter
or a half dollar or something, and then go right and
give you away. White men will do that, but not a

nigger. You can trust them. They are squarer with kids. I don't know why.

At the Saratoga meeting that year there were a lot of men from home. Dave Williams and Arthur Mulford and Jerry Myers and others. Then there was a lot from Louisville and Lexington Henry Rieback knew but I didn't. They were professional gamblers and Henry Rieback's father is one too. He is what is called a sheet writer and goes away most of the year to tracks. In the winter when he is home in Beckersville he don't stay there much but goes away to cities and deals faro. He is a nice man and generous, is always sending Henry presents, a bicycle and a gold watch and a boy scout suit of clothes and things like that.

My own father is a lawyer. He's all right, but don't make much money and can't buy me things and anyway I'm getting so old now I don't expect it. He never said nothing to me against Henry, but Hanley Turner and Tom Tumberton's fathers did. They said to their boys that money so come by is no good and they didn't want their boys brought up to hear gamblers' talk and be thinking about such things and maybe embrace them.

That's all right and I guess the men know what they are talking about, but I don't see what it's got to do with Henry or with horses either. That's what I'm writing this story about. I'm puzzled. I'm getting to be a man and want to think straight and be O. K., and there's something I saw at the race meeting at the eastern track I can't figure out.

I can't help it, I'm crazy about thoroughbred horses. I've always been that way. When I was ten years old and saw I was growing to be big and couldn't be a rider I was so sorry I nearly died. Harry Hellinfinger in Beckersville, whose father is Postmaster, is grown up and too lazy to work, but likes to stand around in the street and get up jokes on boys like sending them to a hardware store for a gimlet to bore square holes and other jokes like that. He played one on me. He told me that if I would eat a half a cigar I would be stunted and not grow any more and maybe could be a rider. I did it. When father wasn't looking I took a cigar out of his pocket and gagged it down some way. It made me awful sick and the doctor had to be sent for, and then it did no good. I kept right on growing. It was a joke. When I told what I had done and why most fathers would have whipped me but mine didn't.

Well, I didn't get stunted and didn't die. It serves Harry Hellinfinger right. Then I made up my mind I would like to be a stable boy, but had to give that up too. Mostly niggers do that work and I knew father wouldn't let me go into it. No use to ask him.

If you've never been crazy about thoroughbreds it's because you've never been around where they are much and don't know any better. They're beautiful. There isn't anything so lovely and clean and full of spunk and honest and everything as some race horses. On the big horse farms that are all around our town Beckersville there are tracks and the horses run in the early morning. More than a thousand times I've got out of bed before daylight and walked two or three miles to the tracks. Mother wouldn't of let me go but father always says, "Let him alone," So I got some bread out of the bread box and some butter and jam, gobbled it and lit out.

At the tracks you sit on the fence with men, whites and niggers, and they chew tobacco and talk, and then the colts are brought out. It's early and the grass is covered with shiny dew and in another field a man is plowing and they are frying things in a shed where the track niggers sleep, and you know how a nigger can giggle and laugh and say things that make you laugh. A white man can't do it and some niggers can't but a track nigger can every time.

And so the colts are brought out and some are just galloped by stable boys, but almost every morning on a big track owned by a rich man who lives maybe in New York, there are always, nearly every morning, a few colts and some of the old race horses and geldings and mares that are cut loose.

It brings a lump up into my throat when a horse runs. I don't mean all horses but some. I can pick them nearly every time. It's in my blood like in the blood of race track niggers and trainers. Even when they just go slop-jogging along with a little nigger on their backs I can tell a winner. If my throat hurts and it's hard for me to swallow, that's him. He'll run like Sam Hill when you let him out. If he don't win every time it'll be a wonder and because they've got him in a pocket behind another or he was pulled or got off bad at the post or something. If I wanted to be a gambler like Henry Rieback's father I could get rich. I know I could and Henry says so too. All I would have to do is to wait 'til that hurt comes when I see a horse and then bet every cent. That's what I would do if I wanted to be a gambler, but I don't.

When you're at the tracks in the morning—not the race tracks but the training tracks around Beckersville —you don't see a horse, the kind I've been talking about, very often, but it's nice anyway. Any thorough-bred, that is sired right and out of a good mare and trained by a man that knows how, can run. If he couldn't what would he be there for and not pulling a plow?

Well, out of the stables they come and the boys are on their backs and it's lovely to be there. You hunch down on top of the fence and itch inside you. Over in the sheds the niggers giggle and sing. Bacon is being fried and coffee made. Everything smells lovely. Nothing smells better than coffee and manure and horses and niggers and bacon frying and pipes being smoked out of doors on a morning like that. It just gets you, that's what it does.

But about Saratoga. We was there six days and not a soul from home seen us and everything came off just as we wanted it to, fine weather and horses and races and all. We beat our way home and Bildad gave us a basket with fried chicken and bread and other eatables in, and I had eighteen dollars when we got back to Beckersville. Mother jawed and cried but Pop didn't say much. I told everything we done except one thing. I did and saw that alone. That's what I'm writing about. It got me upset. I think about it at night. Here it is.

At Saratoga we laid up nights in the hay in the shed Bildad had showed us and ate with the niggers early and at night when the race people had all gone away. The men from home stayed mostly in the grandstand and betting field, and didn't come out around the places where the horses are kept except to the paddocks just before a race when the horses are saddled. At Saratoga they don't have paddocks under an open shed as at Lexington and Churchill Downs and other tracks down in our country, but saddle the horses right out in an open place under trees on a lawn as smooth and nice as Banker Bohon's front yard here in Beckersville. It's lovely. The horses are sweaty and nervous and shine and the men come out and smoke cigars and look at them and the trainers are there and the owners, and your heart thumps so you can hardly breathe.

Then the bugle blows for post and the boys that ride come running out with their silk clothes on and you run to get a place by the fence with the niggers.

I always am wanting to be a trainer or owner, and at the risk of being seen and caught and sent home I went to the paddocks before every race. The other boys didn't but I did.

We got to Saratoga on a Friday and on Wednesday the next week the big Mullford Handicap was to be run. Middlestride was in it and Sunstreak. The weather was fine and the track fast. I couldn't sleep the night before.

What had happened was that both these horses are the kind it makes my throat hurt to see. Middlestride is long and looks awkward and is a gelding. He belongs to Joe Thompson, a little owner from home who only has a half dozen horses. The Mullford Handicap is for a mile and Middlestride can't untrack fast. He goes away slow and is always way back at the half, then he begins to run and if the race is a mile and a quarter he'll just eat up everything and get there.

Sunstreak is different. He is a stallion and nervous and belongs on the biggest farm we've got in our country, the Van Riddle place that belongs to Mr. Van Riddle of New York. Sunstreak is like a girl you think about sometimes but never see. He is hard all over and lovely too. When you look at his head you want to kiss him. He is trained by Jerry Tillford who knows me and has been good to me lots of times, lets me walk into a horse's stall to look at him close and other things. There isn't anything as sweet as that horse. He stands at the post quiet and not letting on, but he is just burning up inside. Then when the barrier goes up he is off like his name, Sunstreak. It makes you ache to see him. It hurts you. He just lays down and runs like a bird dog. There can't anything I ever see run like him except Middlestride when he gets untracked and stretches himself.

Gee! I ached to see that race and those two horses run, ached and dreaded it too. I didn't want to see either of our horses beaten. We had never sent a pair like that to the races before. Old men in Beckersville said so and the niggers said so. It was a fact.

Before the race I went over to the paddocks to see. I looked a last look at Middlestride, who isn't such a much standing in a paddock that way, then I went to see Sunstreak.

It was his day. I knew when I see him. I forgot all about being seen myself and walked right up. All the men from Beckersville were there and no one noticed me except Jerry Tillford. He saw me and something happened. I'll tell you about that.

I was standing looking at that horse and aching. In some way, I can't tell how, I knew just how Sunstreak felt inside. He was quiet and letting the niggers rub his legs and Mr. Van Riddle himself put the saddle on, but he was just a raging torrent inside. He was like the water in the river at Niagara Falls just before its goes plunk down. That horse wasn't thinking about running. He don't have to think about that. He was just thinking about holding himself back 'til the time for the running came. I knew that. I could just in a way see right inside him. He was going to do some awful running and I knew it. He wasn't bragging or letting on much or prancing or making a fuss, but just waiting. I knew it and Jerry Tillford his trainer knew. I looked up and then that man and I looked into each other's eyes. Something happened to me. I guess I loved the man as much as I did the horse because he knew what I knew. Seemed to me there wasn't anything in the world but that man and the horse and me. I cried and Jerry Tillford had a shine in his eyes. Then I came away to the fence to wait for the race. The horse was better than me, more steadier, and now I know better than Jerry. He was the quietest and he had to do the running.

Sunstreak ran first of course and he busted the world's record for a mile. I've seen that if I never see anything more. Everything came out just as I expected. Middlestride got left at the post and was way back and closed up to be second, just as I knew he would. He'll get a world's record too some day. They can't skin the Beckersville country on horses.

I watched the race calm because I knew what would happen. I was sure. Hanley Turner and Henry Rieback and Tom Tumberton were all more excited than me.

A funny thing had happened to me. I was thinking about Jerry Tillford the trainer and how happy he was all through the race. I liked him that afternoon even more than I ever liked my own father. I almost forgot the horses thinking that way about him. It was because of what I had seen in his eyes as he stood in the paddocks beside Sunstreak before the race started. I knew he had been watching and working with Sunstreak since the horse was a baby colt, had taught him to run and be patient and when to let himself out and not to quit, never. I knew that for him it was like a mother seeing her child do something brave or wonderful. It was the first time I ever felt for a man like that.

After the race that night I cut out from Tom and Hanley and Henry. I wanted to be by myself and I wanted to be near Jerry Tillford if I could work it. Here is what happened.

The track in Saratoga is near the edge of town. It

is all polished up and trees around, the evergreen kind, and grass and everything painted and nice. If you go past the track you get to a hard road made of asphalt for automobiles, and if you go along this for a few miles there is a road turns off to a little rummy-looking farm house set in a yard.

That night after the race I went along that road because I had seen Jerry and some other men go that way in an automobile. I didn't expect to find them. I walked for a ways and then sat down by a fence to think. It was the direction they went in. I wanted to be as near Jerry as I could. I felt close to him. Pretty soon I went up the side road—I don't know why—and came to the rummy farm house. I was just lonesome to see Jerry, like wanting to see your father at night when you are a young kid. Just then an automobile came along and turned in. Jerry was in it and Henry Rieback's father, and Arthur Bedford from home, and Dave Williams and two other men I didn't know. They got out of the car and went into the house, all but Henry Rieback's father who quar- reled with them and said he wouldn't go. It was only about nine o'clock, but they were all drunk and the rummy looking farm house was a place for bad women to stay in. That's what it was. I crept up along a fence and looked through a window and saw.

It's what give me the fantods. I can't make it out. The women in the house were all ugly mean-looking women, not nice to look at or be near. They were homely too, except one who was tall and looked a little like the gelding Middlestride, but not clean like him, but with a hard ugly mouth. She had red hair. I saw everything plain. I got up by an old rose bush by an open window and looked. The women had on loose dresses and sat around in chairs. The men came in and some sat on the women's laps. The place smelled rotten and there was rotten talk, the kind a kid hears around a livery stable in a town like Beckersville in the winter but don't ever expect to hear talked when there are women around. It was rotten. A nigger wouldn't go into such a place.

I looked at Jerry Tillford. I've told you how I had been feeling about him on account of his knowing what was going on inside of Sunstreak in the minute before he went to the post for the race in which he made a world's record.

Jerry bragged in that bad woman house as I know Sunstreak wouldn't never have bragged. He said that he made that horse, that it was him that won the race and made the record. He lied and bragged like a fool. I never heard such silly talk.

And then, what do you suppose he did! He looked at the woman in there, the one that was lean and hard-mouthed and looked a little like the gelding Middlestride, but not clean like him, and his eyes began to shine just as they did when he looked at me and at

Sunstreak in the paddocks at the track in the after-noon. I stood there by the window—gee!—but I wished I hadn't gone away from the tracks, but had stayed with the boys and the niggers and the horses. The tall rotten looking woman was between us just as Sunstreak was in the paddocks in the afternoon.

Then, all of a sudden, I began to hate that man. I wanted to scream and rush in the room and kill him. I never had such a feeling before. I was so mad clean through that I cried and my fists were doubled up so my finger nails cut my hands.

And Jerry's eyes kept shining and he waved back and forth, and then he went and kissed that woman and I crept away and went back to the tracks and to bed and didn't sleep hardly any, and then next day I got the other kids to start home with me and never told them anything I seen.

I been thinking about it ever since. I can't make it out. Spring has come again and I'm nearly sixteen and go to the tracks mornings same as always, and I see Sunstreak and Middlestride and a new colt named Strident I'll bet will lay them all out, but no one thinks so but me and two or three niggers.

But things are different. At the tracks the air don't taste as good or smell as good. It's because a man like Jerry Tillford, who knows what he does, could see a horse like Sunstreak run, and kiss a woman like that the same day. I can't make it out. Darn him, what did he want to do like that for? I keep thinking about it and it spoils looking at horses and smelling things and hearing niggers laugh and everything. Sometimes I'm so mad about it I want to fight someone. It gives me the fantods. What did he do it for? I want to know why.

SEEDS

HE WAS a small man with a beard and was very nervous. I remember how the cords of his neck were drawn taut.

For years he had been trying to cure people of illness by the method called psychoanalysis. The idea was the passion of his life. "I came here because I am tired," he said dejectedly. "My body is not tired but something inside me is old and worn-out. I want joy. For a few days or weeks I would like to forget men and women and the influences that make them the sick things they are."

There is a note that comes into the human voice by which you may know real weariness. It comes when one has been trying with all his heart and soul to think his way along some difficult road of thought. Of a sudden he finds himself unable to go on. Something within him stops. A tiny explosion takes place. He bursts into words and talks, perhaps foolishly. Little side currents of his nature he didn't know were there run out and get themselves expressed. It is at such times that a man boasts, uses big words, makes a fool of himself in general.

And so it was the doctor became shrill. He jumped

21

up from the steps where we had been sitting, talking and walked about. "You come from the West. You have kept away from people. You have preserved yourself—damn you! I haven't—" His voice had indeed become shrill. "I have entered into lives. I have gone beneath the surface of the lives of men and women. Women especially I have studied—our own women, here in America."

"You have loved them?" I suggested.

"Yes," he said. "Yes—you are right there. I have done that. It is the only way I can get at things. I have to try to love. You see how that is? It's the only way. Love must be the beginning of things with me."

I began to sense the depths of his weariness. "We will go swim in the lake," I urged.

"I don't want to swim or do any damn plodding thing. I want to run and shout," he declared. "For awhile, for a few hours, I want to be like a dead leaf blown by the winds over these hills. I have one desire and one only—to free myself."

We walked in a dusty country road. I wanted him to know that I thought I understood, so I put the case in my own way.

When he stopped and stared at me I talked. "You are no more and no better than myself," I declared. "You are a dog that has rolled in offal, and because you are not quite a dog you do not like the smell of your own hide."

In turn my voice became shrill. "You blind fool," I cried impatiently. "Men like you are fools. You cannot go along that road. It is given to no man to venture far along the road of lives."

I became passionately in earnest. "The illness you pretend to cure is the universal illness," I said. "The thing you want to do cannot be done. Fool—do you expect love to be understood?"

We stood in the road and looked at each other. The suggestion of a sneer played about the corners of his mouth. He put a hand on my shoulder and shook me. "How smart we are— how aptly we put things!"

He spat the words out and then turned and walked a little away. "You think you understand, but you don't understand," he cried. "What you say can't be done can be done. You're a liar. You cannot be so definite without missing something vague and fine. You miss the whole point. The lives of people are like young trees in a forest. They are being choked by climbing vines. The vines are old thoughts and beliefs planted by dead men. I am myself covered by crawling creeping vines that choke me."

He laughed bitterly. "And that's why I want to run and play," he said. "I want to be a leaf blown by the wind over hills. I want to die and be born again, and I am only a tree covered with vines and slowly dying. I am, you see, weary and want to be made clean. I am an amateur venturing timidly into lives," he concluded. "I am weary and want to be made clean. I am covered by creeping crawling things."

*   *   *

A woman from Iowa came here to Chicago and took a room in a house on the west-side. She was about twenty-seven years old and ostensibly she came to the city to study advanced methods for teaching music.

A certain young man also lived in the west-side house. His room faced a long hall on the second floor of the house and the one taken by the woman was across the hall facing his room.

In regard to the young man—there is something very sweet in his nature. He is a painter but I have often wished he would decide to become a writer. He tells things with understanding and he does not paint brilliantly.

And so the woman from Iowa lived in the west-side house and came home from the city in the evening. She looked like a thousand other women one sees in the streets every day. The only thing that at all made her stand out among the women in the crowds was that she was a little lame. Her right foot was slightly deformed and she walked with a limp. For three months she lived in the house—where she was the only woman except the landlady—and then a feeling in regard to her began to grow up among the men of the house.

The men all said the same thing concerning her. When they met in the hallway at the front of the house they stopped, laughed and whispered. "She wants a lover," they said and winked. "She may not know it but a lover is what she needs."

One knowing Chicago and Chicago men would think that an easy want to be satisfied. I laughed when my friend—whose name is LeRoy—told me the story, but he did not laugh. He shook his head. "It wasn't so easy," he said. "There would be no story were the matter that simple."

LeRoy tried to explain. "Whenever a man approached her she became alarmed," he said. Men kept smiling and speaking to her. They invited her to dinner and to the theatre, but nothing would induce her to walk in the streets with a man. She never went into the streets at night. When a man stopped and tried to talk with her in the hallway she turned her eyes to the floor and then ran into her room. Once a young drygoods clerk who lived there induced her to sit with him on the steps before the house.

He was a sentimental fellow and took hold of her hand. When she began to cry he was alarmed and arose. He put a hand on her shoulder and tried to explain, but under the touch of his fingers her whole body shook with terror. "Don't touch me," she cried, "don't let your hands touch me!" She began to scream and people passing in the street stopped to listen. The drygoods clerk was alarmed and ran up-stairs to his own room. He bolted the door and stood listening. "It is a trick," he declared in a trembling voice. "She is trying to make trouble. I did nothing to her. It was an accident and anyway what's the matter? I only touched her arm with my fingers."

Perhaps a dozen times LeRoy has spoken to me of the experience of the Iowa woman in the west-side house. The men there began to hate her. Although she would have nothing to do with them she would not let them alone. In a hundred ways she continually invited approaches that when made she repelled. When she stood naked in the bathroom facing the hallway where the men passed up and down she left the door slightly ajar. There was a couch in the living room down stairs, and when men were present she would sometimes enter and without saying a word throw her-self down before them. On the couch she lay with lips drawn slightly apart. Her eyes stared at the ceiling. Her whole physical being seemed to be waiting for something. The sense of her filled the room. The men standing about pretended not to see. They talked loudly. Embarrassment took possession of them and one by one they crept quietly away.

One evening the woman was ordered to leave the house. Someone, perhaps the drygoods clerk, had talked to the landlady and she acted at once. "If you leave tonight I shall like it that much better," LeRoy heard the elder woman's voice saying. She stood in the hallway before the Iowa woman's room. The landlady's voice rang through the house.

LeRoy the painter is tall and lean and his life has been spent in devotion to ideas. The passions of his brain have consumed the passions of his body. His income is small and he has not married. Perhaps he has never had a sweetheart. He is not without physical desire but he is not primarily concerned with desire.

On the evening when the Iowa woman was ordered to leave the west-side house, she waited until she thought the landlady had gone down stairs, and then went into LeRoy's room. It was about eight o'clock and he sat by a window reading a book. The woman did not knock but opened the door. She said nothing but ran across the floor and knelt at his feet. LeRoy said that her twisted foot made her run like a wounded bird, that her eyes were burning and that her breath came in little gasps. "Take me," she said, putting her face down upon his knees and trembling violently. "Take me quickly. There must be a beginning to things. I can't stand the waiting. You must take me at once."

You may be quite sure LeRoy was perplexed by all this. From what he has said I gathered that until that evening he had hardly noticed the woman. I suppose that of all the men in the house he had been the most indifferent to her. In the room something happened. The landlady followed the woman when she ran to Le-Roy, and the two women confronted him. The woman from Iowa knelt trembling and frightened at his feet. The landlady was indignant. LeRoy acted on impulse. An inspiration came to him. Putting his hand on the kneeling woman's shoulder he shook her violently. "Now behave yourself," he said quickly. "I will keep my promise." He turned to the landlady and smiled. "We have been engaged to be married," he said. "We have quarreled. She came here to be near me. She has been unwell and excited. I will take her away. Please don't let yourself be annoyed. I will take her away."

When the woman and LeRoy got out of the house she stopped weeping and put her hand into his. Her fears had all gone away. He found a room for her in another house and then went with her into a park and sat on a bench.

*   *   *

Everything LeRoy has told me concerning this woman strengthens my belief in what I said to the man that day in the mountains. You cannot venture along the road of lives. On the bench he and the woman talked until midnight and he saw and talked with her many times later. Nothing came of it. She went back, I suppose, to her place in the West.

In the place from which she had come the woman
had been a teacher of music. She was one of four
sisters, all engaged in the same sort of work and, Le-
Roy says, all quiet capable women. Their father had
died when the eldest girl was not yet ten, and five years
later the mother died also. The girls had a house and
a garden.

In the nature of things I cannot know what the lives
of the women were like but of this one may be quite
certain—they talked only of women's affairs, thought
only of women's affairs. No one of them ever had a
lover. For years no man came near the house.

Of them all only the youngest, the one who came to
Chicago, was visibly affected by the utterly feminine
quality of their lives. It did something to her. All
day and every day she taught music to young girls
and then went home to the women. When she was
twenty-five she began to think and to dream of men.
During the day and through the evening she talked
with women of women's affairs, and all the time she
wanted desperately to be loved by a man. She went
to Chicago with that hope in mind. LeRoy explained
her attitude in the matter and her strange behavior in
the west-side house by saying she had thought too
much and acted too little. "The life force within her
became decentralized," he declared. "What she
wanted she could not achieve. The living force within
could not find expression. When it could not get ex-

pressed in one way it took another. Sex spread itself out over her body. It permeated the very fibre of her being. At the last she was sex personified, sex become condensed and impersonal. Certain words, the touch of a man's hand, sometimes even the sight of a man passing in the street did something to her."

*   *   *

Yesterday I saw LeRoy and he talked to me again of the woman and her strange and terrible fate.

We walked in the park by the lake. As we went along the figure of the woman kept coming into my mind. An idea came to me.

"You might have been her lover," I said. "That was possible. She was not afraid of you."

LeRoy stopped. Like the doctor who was so sure of his ability to walk into lives he grew angry and scolded. For a moment he stared at me and then a rather odd thing happened. Words said by the other man in the dusty road in the hills came to LeRoy's lips and were said over again. The suggestion of a sneer played about the corners of his mouth. "How smart we are. How aptly we put things," he said.

The voice of the young man who walked with me in the park by the lake in the city became shrill. I sensed the weariness in him. Then he laughed and said quietly and softly, "It isn't so simple. By being sure of yourself you are in danger of losing all of the romance of life. You miss the whole point. Noth-

ing in life can be settled so definitely. The woman—
you see—was like a young tree choked by a climbing
vine. The thing that wrapped her about had shut
out the light. She was a grotesque as many trees in
the forest are grotesques. Her problem was such a
difficult one that thinking of it has changed the whole
current of my life. At first I was like you. I was
quite sure. I thought I would be her lover and settle
the matter."

LeRoy turned and walked a little away. Then he
came back and took hold of my arm. A passionate
earnestness took possession of him. His voice
trembled. "She needed a lover, yes, the men in the
house were quite right about that," he said. "She
needed a lover and at the same time a lover was not
what she needed. The need of a lover was, after
all, a quite secondary thing. She needed to be loved,
to be long and quietly and patiently loved. To be
sure she is a grotesque, but then all the people in the
world are grotesques. We all need to be loved. What
would cure her would cure the rest of us also. The
disease she had is, you see, universal. We all want
to be loved and the world has no plan for creating
our lovers."

LeRoy's voice dropped and he walked beside me in
silence. We turned away from the lake and walked
under trees. I looked closely at him. The cords of
his neck were drawn taut. "I have seen under the

shell of life and I am afraid," he mused. "I am myself like the woman. I am covered with creeping crawling vine-like things. I cannot be a lover. I am not subtle or patient enough. I am paying old debts. Old thoughts and beliefs—seeds planted by dead men —spring up in my soul and choke me."

For a long time we walked and LeRoy talked, voicing the thoughts that came into his mind. I listened in silence. His mind struck upon the refrain voiced by the man in the mountains. "I would like to be a dead dry thing," he muttered looking at the leaves scattered over the grass. "I would like to be a leaf blown away by the wind." He looked up and his eyes turned to where among the trees we could see the lake in the distance. "I am weary and want to be made clean. I am a man covered by creeping crawling things. I would like to be dead and blown by the wind over limitless waters," he said. "I want more than anything else in the world to be clean."

THE OTHER WOMAN

"I AM in love with my wife," he said—a super-
flous remark, as I had not questioned his attach-
ment to the woman he had married. We walked for
ten minutes and then he said it again. I turned to look
at him. He began to talk and told me the tale I am
now about to set down.

The thing he had on his mind happened during what
must have been the most eventful week of his life. He
was to be married on Friday afternoon. On Friday of
the week before he got a telegram announcing his ap-
pointment to a government position. Something else
happened that made him very proud and glad. In
secret he was in the habit of writing verses and during
the year before several of them had been printed in
poetry magazines. One of the societies that give
prizes for what they think the best poems published
during the year put his name at the head of its list.
The story of his triumph was printed in the newspapers
of his home city and one of them also printed his picture.

As might have been expected he was excited and in
a rather highly strung nervous state all during that
week. Almost every evening he went to call on his
fiancée, the daughter of a judge. When he got there

the house was filled with people and many letters, tele-
grams and packages were being received. He stood a
little to one side and men and women kept coming up
to speak to him. They congratulated him upon his
success in getting the government position and on his
achievement as a poet. Everyone seemed to be prais-
ing him and when he went home and to bed he could not
sleep. On Wednesday evening he went to the theatre
and it seemed to him that people all over the house
recognized him. Everyone nodded and smiled. After
the first act five or six men and two women left their
seats to gather about him. A little group was formed.
Strangers sitting along the same row of seats stretched
their necks and looked. He had never received so
much attention before, and now a fever of expectancy
took possession of him.

As he explained when he told me of his experience,
it was for him an altogether abnormal time. He felt
like one floating in air. When he got into bed after
seeing so many people and hearing so many words of
praise his head whirled round and round. When he
closed his eyes a crowd of people invaded his room.
It seemed as though the minds of all the people of his
city were centred on himself. The most absurd
fancies took possession of him. He imagined himself
riding in a carriage through the streets of a city.
Windows were thrown open and people ran out at
the doors of houses. "There he is. That's him,"

they shouted, and at the words a glad cry arose. The carriage drove into a street blocked with people. A hundred thousand pairs of eyes looked up at him. "There you are! What a fellow you have managed to make of yourself!" the eyes seemed to be saying.

My friend could not explain whether the excitement of the people was due to the fact that he had written a new poem or whether, in his new government position, he had performed some notable act. The apartment where he lived at that time was on a street perched along the top of a cliff far out at the edge of his city, and from his bedroom window he could look down over trees and factory roofs to a river. As he could not sleep and as the fancies that kept crowding in upon him only made him more excited, he got out of bed and tried to think.

As would be natural under such circumstances, he tried to control his thoughts, but when he sat by the window and was wide awake a most unexpected and humiliating thing happened. The night was clear and fine. There was a moon. He wanted to dream of the woman who was to be his wife, to think out lines for noble poems or make plans that would affect his career. Much to his surprise his mind refused to do anything of the sort.

At a corner of the street where he lived there was a small cigar store and newspaper stand run by a fat man of forty and his wife, a small active woman with bright grey eyes. In the morning he stopped there to buy a paper before going down to the city. Sometimes he saw only the fat man, but often the man had disappeared and the woman waited on him. She was, as he assured me at least twenty times in telling me his tale, a very ordinary person with nothing special or notable about her, but for some reason he could not explain, being in her presence stirred him profoundly. During that week in the midst of his distraction she was the only person he knew who stood out clear and distinct in his mind. When he wanted so much to think noble thoughts he could think only of her. Before he knew what was happening his imagination had taken hold of the notion of having a love affair with the woman.

"I could not understand myself," he declared, in telling me the story. "At night, when the city was quiet and when I should have been asleep, I thought about her all the time. After two or three days of that sort of thing the consciousness of her got into my daytime thoughts. I was terribly muddled. When I went to see the woman who is now my wife I found that my love for her was in no way affected by my vagrant thoughts. There was but one woman in the world I wanted to live with and to be my comrade in undertaking to improve my own character and my position in the world, but for the moment, you see, I wanted this other woman to be in my arms. She had worked

her way into my being. On all sides people were
saying I was a big man who would do big things, and
there I was. That evening when I went to the theatre
I walked home because I knew I would be unable to
sleep, and to satisfy the annoying impulse in myself I
went and stood on the sidewalk before the tobacco
shop. It was a two story building, and I knew the
woman lived upstairs with her husband. For a long
time I stood in the darkness with my body pressed
against the wall of the building, and then I thought of
the two of them up there and no doubt in bed together.
That made me furious.

"Then I grew more furious with myself. I went
home and got into bed, shaken with anger. There are
certain books of verse and some prose writings that
have always moved me deeply, and so I put several
books on a table by my bed.

"The voices in the books were like the voices of the
dead. I did not hear them. The printed words would
not penetrate into my consciousness. I tried to think
of the woman I loved, but her figure had also become
something far away, something with which I for the
moment seemed to have nothing to do. I rolled and
tumbled about in the bed. It was a miserable experience.

"On Thursday morning I went into the store. There
stood the woman alone. I think she knew how I felt.
Perhaps she had been thinking of me as I had been

thinking of her. A doubtful hesitating smile played about the corners of her mouth. She had on a dress made of cheap cloth and there was a tear on the shoulder. She must have been ten years older than myself. When I tried to put my pennies on the glass counter, behind which she stood, my hand trembled so that the pennies made a sharp rattling noise. When I spoke the voice that came out of my throat did not sound like anything that had ever belonged to me. It barely arose above a thick whisper. 'I want you,' I said. 'I want you very much. Can't you run away from your husband? Come to me at my apartment at seven tonight.'

"The woman did come to my apartment at seven. That morning she didn't say anything at all. For a minute perhaps we stood looking at each other. I had forgotten everything in the world but just her. Then she nodded her head and I went away. Now that I think of it I cannot remember a word I ever heard her say. She came to my apartment at seven and it was dark. You must understand this was in the month of October. I had not lighted a light and I had sent my servant away.

"During that day I was no good at all. Several men came to see me at my office, but I got all muddled up in trying to talk with them. They attributed my rattle-headedness to my approaching marriage and went away laughing.

"It was on that morning, just the day before my marriage, that I got a long and very beautiful letter from my fiancée. During the night before she also had been unable to sleep and had got out of bed to write the letter. Everything she said in it was very sharp and real, but she herself, as a living thing, seemed to have receded into the distance. It seemed to me that she was like a bird, flying far away in distant skies, and that I was like a perplexed bare-footed boy standing in the dusty road before a farm house and looking at her receding figure. I wonder if you will understand what I mean?

"In regard to the letter. In it she, the awakening woman, poured out her heart. She of course knew nothing of life, but she was a woman. She lay, I suppose, in her bed feeling nervous and wrought up as I had been doing. She realized that a great change was about to take place in her life and was glad and afraid too. There she lay thinking of it all. Then she got out of bed and began talking to me on the bit of paper. She told me how afraid she was and how glad too. Like most young women she had heard things whispered. In the letter she was very sweet and fine. 'For a long time, after we are married, we will forget we are a man and woman,' she wrote. 'We will be human beings. You must remember that I am ignorant and often I will be very stupid. You must love me and be very patient and kind. When I know more, when after a long time you have taught me the way of life, I will try to repay you. I will love you tenderly and passionately. The possibility of that is in me or I would not want to marry at all. I am afraid but I am also happy. O, I am so glad our marriage time is near at hand!'

"Now you see clearly enough what a mess I was in. In my office, after I had read my fiancée's letter, I became at once very resolute and strong. I remember that I got out of my chair and walked about, proud of the fact that I was to be the husband of so noble a woman. Right away I felt concerning her as I had been feeling about myself before I found out what a weak thing I was. To be sure I took a strong resolution that I would not be weak. At nine that evening I had planned to run in to see my fiancée. 'I'm all right now', I said to myself. 'The beauty of her character has saved me from myself. I will go home now and send the other woman away.' In the morning I had telephoned to my servant and told him that I did not want him to be at the apartment that evening and I now picked up the telephone to tell him to stay at home.

"Then a thought came to me. 'I will not want him there in any event,' I told myself. 'What will he think when he sees a woman coming in my place on the evening before the day I am to be married?' I put the telephone down and prepared to go home. 'If I want my servant out of the apartment it is because I do not want him to hear me talk with the woman. I cannot be rude to her. I will have to make some kind of an explanation,' I said to myself.

"The woman came at seven o'clock, and, as you may have guessed, I let her in and forgot the resolution I had made. It is likely I never had any intention of doing anything else. There was a bell on my door, but she did not ring, but knocked very softly. It seems to me that everything she did that evening was soft and quiet, but very determined and quick. Do I make myself clear? When she came I was standing just within the door where I had been standing and waiting for a half hour. My hands were trembling as they had trembled in the morning when her eyes looked at me and when I tried to put the pennies on the counter in the store. When I opened the door she stepped quickly in and I took her into my arms. We stood together in the darkness. My hands no longer trembled. I felt very happy and strong.

"Although I have tried to make everything clear I have not told you what the woman I married is like. I have emphasized, you see, the other woman. I make the blind statement that I love my wife, and to a man of your shrewdness that means nothing at all. To tell the truth, had I not started to speak of this matter I would feel more comfortable. It is inevitable that I give you the impression that I am in love with the

tobacconist's wife. That's not true. To be sure I
was very conscious of her all during the week before
my marriage, but after she had come to me at my
apartment she went entirely out of my mind.

"Am I telling the truth? I am trying very hard to
tell what happened to me. I am saying that I have
not since that evening thought of the woman who
came to my apartment. Now, to tell the facts of the
case, that is not true. On that evening I went to my
fiancée at nine, as she had asked me to do in her
letter. In a kind of way I cannot explain the other
woman went with me. This is what I mean—you see
I had been thinking that if anything happened between
me and the tobacconist's wife I would not be able to
go through with my marriage. 'It is one thing or the
other with me,' I had said to myself.

"As a matter of fact I went to see my beloved on
that evening filled with a new faith in the outcome of
our life together. I am afraid I muddle this matter
in trying to tell it. A moment ago I said the other
woman, the tobacconist's wife, went with me. I do
not mean she went in fact. What I am trying to say
is that something of her faith in her own desires and
her courage in seeing things through went with me.
Is that clear to you? When I got to my fiancée's house
there was a crowd of people standing about. Some
were relatives from distant places I had not seen before. She looked up quickly when I came into the

room. My face must have been radiant. I never saw her so moved. She thought her letter had affected me deeply, and of course it had. Up she jumped and ran to meet me. She was like a glad child. Right before the people who turned and looked inquiringly at us, she said the thing that was in her mind. 'O, I am so happy,' she cried. 'You have understood. We will be two human beings. We will not have to be husband and wife.'

"As you may suppose everyone laughed, but I did not laugh. The tears came into my eyes. I was so happy I wanted to shout. Perhaps you understand what I mean. In the office that day when I read the letter my fiancée had written I had said to myself, 'I will take care of the dear little woman.' There was something smug, you see, about that. In her house when she cried out in that way, and when everyone laughed, what I said to myself was something like this: 'We will take care of ourselves.' I whispered something of the sort into her ears. To tell you the truth I had come down off my perch. The spirit of the other woman did that to me. Before all the people gathered about I held my fiancée close and we kissed. They thought it very sweet of us to be so affected at the sight of each other. What they would have thought had they known the truth about me God only knows!

"Twice now I have said that after that evening I

never thought of the other woman at all. That is partially true but, sometimes in the evening when I am walking alone in the street or in the park as we are walking now, and when evening comes softly and quickly as it has come to-night, the feeling of her comes sharply into my body and mind. After that one meeting I never saw her again. On the next day I was married and I have never gone back into her street. Often however as I am walking along as I am doing now, a quick sharp earthy feeling takes possession of me. It is as though I were a seed in the ground and the warm rains of the spring had come. It is as though I were not a man but a tree.

"And now you see I am married and everything is all right. My marriage is to me a very beautiful fact. If you were to say that my marriage is not a happy one I could call you a liar and be speaking the absolute truth. I have tried to tell you about this other woman. There is a kind of relief in speaking of her. I have never done it before. I wonder why I was so silly as to be afraid that I would give you the impression I am not in love with my wife. If I did not instinctively trust your understanding I would not have spoken. As the matter stands I have a little stirred myself up. To-night I shall think of the other woman. That sometimes occurs. It will happen after I have gone to bed. My wife sleeps in the next room to mine and the door is always left open. There will be a moon to-night, and when there is a moon long streaks of light fall on her bed. I shall awake at midnight to-night. She will be lying asleep with one arm thrown over her head.

"What is it that I am now talking about? A man does not speak of his wife lying in bed. What I am trying to say is that, because of this talk, I shall think of the other woman to-night. My thoughts will not take the form they did during the week before I was married. I will wonder what has become of the woman. For a moment I will again feel myself holding her close. I will think that for an hour I was closer to her than I have ever been to anyone else. Then I will think of the time when I will be as close as that to my wife. She is still, you see, an awakening woman. For a moment I will close my eyes and the quick, shrewd, determined eyes of that other woman will look into mine. My head will swim and then I will quickly open my eyes and see again the dear woman with whom I have undertaken to live out my life. Then I will sleep and when I awake in the morning it will be as it was that evening when I walked out of my dark apartment after having had the most notable experience of my life. What I mean to say, you understand is that, for me, when I awake, the other woman will be utterly gone."

THE EGG

M Y FATHER was, I am sure, intended by nature to be a cheerful, kindly man. Until he was thirty-four years old he worked as a farm-hand for a man named Thomas Butterworth whose place lay near the town of Bidwell, Ohio. He had then a horse of his own and on Saturday evenings drove into town to spend a few hours in social intercourse with other farm-hands. In town he drank several glasses of beer and stood about in Ben Head's saloon—crowded on Saturday evenings with visiting farm-hands. Songs were sung and glasses thumped on the bar. At ten o'clock father drove home along a lonely country road, made his horse comfortable for the night and himself went to bed, quite happy in his position in life. He had at that time no notion of trying to rise in the world.

It was in the spring of his thirty-fifth year that father married my mother, then a country school-teacher, and in the following spring I came wriggling and crying into the world. Something happened to the two people. They became ambitious. The American passion for getting up in the world took possession of them.

It may have been that mother was responsible. Being a school-teacher she had no doubt read books and magazines. She had, I presume, read of how Garfield, Lincoln, and other Americans rose from poverty to fame and greatness and as I lay beside her—in the days of her lying-in—she may have dreamed that I would some day rule men and cities. At any rate she induced father to give up his place as a farm-hand, sell his horse and embark on an independent enterprise of his own. She was a tall silent woman with a long nose and troubled grey eyes. For herself she wanted nothing. For father and myself she was incurably ambitious.

The first venture into which the two people went turned out badly. They rented ten acres of poor stony land on Griggs's Road, eight miles from Bidwell, and launched into chicken raising. I grew into boyhood on the place and got my first impressions of life there. From the beginning they were impressions of disaster and if, in my turn, I am a gloomy man inclined to see the darker side of life, I attribute it to the fact that what should have been for me the happy joyous days of childhood were spent on a chicken farm.

One unversed in such matters can have no notion of the many and tragic things that can happen to a chicken. It is born out of an egg, lives for a few weeks as a tiny fluffy thing such as you will see pictured on Easter cards, then becomes hideously naked, eats quan-

tities of corn and meal bought by the sweat of your
father's brow, gets diseases called pip, cholera, and
other names, stands looking with stupid eyes at the
sun, becomes sick and dies. A few hens and now and
then a rooster, intended to serve God's mysterious
ends, struggle through to maturity. The hens lay eggs
out of which come other chickens and the dreadful
cycle is thus made complete. It is all unbelievably
complex. Most philosophers must have been raised on
chicken farms. One hopes for so much from a chicken
and is so dreadfully disillusioned. Small chickens,
just setting out on the journey of life, look so bright
and alert and they are in fact so dreadfully stupid.
They are so much like people they mix one up in one's
judgments of life. If disease does not kill them they
wait until your expectations are thoroughly aroused
and then walk under the wheels of a wagon—to go
squashed and dead back to their maker. Vermin infest their youth, and fortunes must be spent for cura-
tive powders. In later life I have seen how a literature
has been built up on the subject of fortunes to be made
out of the raising of chickens. It is intended to be
read by the gods who have just eaten of the tree of
the knowledge of good and evil. It is a hopeful literature and declares that much may be done by simple
ambitious people who own a few hens. Do not be led
astray by it. It was not written for you. Go hunt for
gold on the frozen hills of Alaska, put your faith in

the honesty of a politician, believe if you will that the
world is daily growing better and that good will triumph over evil, but do not read and believe the literature that is written concerning the hen.   It was not
written for you.

I, however, digress. My tale does not primarily con-
cern itself with the hen. If correctly told it will centre
on the egg.   For ten years my father and mother struggled to make our chicken farm pay and then they gave
up that struggle and began another.   They moved into
the town of Bidwell, Ohio and embarked in the restaurant business.   After ten years of worry with in-
cubators that did not hatch, and with tiny—and in
their own way lovely   balls of fluff that passed on into
semi-naked pullethood and from that into dead henhood, we threw all aside and packing our belongings
on a wagon drove down Griggs's Road toward Bidwell, a tiny caravan of hope looking for a new place
from which to start on our upward journey through
life.

We must have been a sad looking lot, not, I fancy,
unlike refugees fleeing from a battlefield.   Mother and
I walked in the road.   The wagon that contained our
goods had been borrowed for the day from Mr. Albert
Griggs, a neighbor.   Out of its sides stuck the legs of
cheap chairs and at the back of the pile of beds, tables,
and boxes filled with kitchen utensils was a crate of
live chickens, and on top of that the baby carriage in

which I had been wheeled about in my infancy. Why we stuck to the baby carriage I don't know. It was unlikely other children would be born and the wheels were broken. People who have few possessions cling tightly to those they have. That is one of the facts that make life so discouraging.

Father rode on top of the wagon. He was then a bald-headed man of forty-five, a little fat and from long association with mother and the chickens he had become habitually silent and discouraged. All during our ten years on the chicken farm he had worked as a laborer on neighboring farms and most of the money he had earned had been spent for remedies to cure chicken diseases, on Wilmer's White Wonder Cholera Cure or Professor Bidlow's Egg Producer or some other preparations that mother found advertised in the poultry papers. There were two little patches of hair on father's head just above his ears. I remember that as a child I used to sit looking at him when he had gone to sleep in a chair before the stove on Sunday afternoons in the winter. I had at that time already begun to read books and have notions of my own and the bald path that led over the top of his head was, I fancied, something like a broad road, such a road as Caesar might have made on which to lead his legions out of Rome and into the wonders of an unknown world. The tufts of hair that grew above father's ears were, I thought, like forests. I fell into a half-sleeping, half-waking state and dreamed I was a tiny thing going along the road into a far beautiful place where there were no chicken farms and where life was a happy eggless affair.

One might write a book concerning our flight from the chicken farm into town. Mother and I walked the entire eight miles—she to be sure that nothing fell from the wagon and I to see the wonders of the world. On the seat of the wagon beside father was his greatest treasure. I will tell you of that.

On a chicken farm where hundreds and even thousands of chickens come out of eggs surprising things sometimes happen. Grotesques are born out of eggs as out of people. The accident does not often occur—perhaps once in a thousand births. A chicken is, you see, born that has four legs, two pairs of wings, two heads or what not. The things do not live. They go quickly back to the hand of their maker that has for a moment trembled. The fact that the poor little things could not live was one of the tragedies of life to father. He had some sort of notion that if he could but bring into henhood or roosterhood a five-legged hen or a two-headed rooster his fortune would be made. He dreamed of taking the wonder about to county fairs and of growing rich by exhibiting it to other farm-hands.

At any rate he saved all the little monstrous things that had been born on our chicken farm. They were preserved in alcohol and put each in its own glass bottle. These he had carefully put into a box and on our journey into town it was carried on the wagon seat beside him. He drove the horses with one hand and with the other clung to the box. When we got to our destination the box was taken down at once and the bottles removed. All during our days as keepers of a restaurant in the town of Bidwell, Ohio, the grotesques in their little glass bottles sat on a shelf back of the counter. Mother sometimes protested but father was a rock on the subject of his treasure. The grotesques were, he declared, valuable. People, he said, liked to look at strange and wonderful things.

Did I say that we embarked in the restaurant business in the town of Bidwell, Ohio? I exaggerated a little. The town itself lay at the foot of a low hill and on the shore of a small river. The railroad did not run through the town and the station was a mile away to the north at a place called Pickleville. There had been a cider mill and pickle factory at the station, but before the time of our coming they had both gone out of business. In the morning and in the evening busses came down to the station along a road called Turner's Pike from the hotel on the main street of Bidwell. Our going to the out of the way place to embark in the restaurant business was mother's idea. She talked of it for a year and then one day went off and rented an empty store building opposite the railroad station. It was her idea that the restaurant would be profitable. Travelling men, she said, would be always waiting around to take trains out of town and town people would come to the station to await incoming trains. They would come to the restaurant to buy pieces of pie and drink coffee. Now that I am older I know that she had another motive in going. She was ambitious for me. She wanted me to rise in the world, to get into a town school and become a man of the towns.

At Pickleville father and mother worked hard as they always had done. At first there was the necessity of putting our place into shape to be a restaurant. That took a month. Father built a shelf on which he put tins of vegetables. He painted a sign on which he put his name in large red letters. Below his name was the sharp command—"EAT HERE"—that was so seldom obeyed. A show case was bought and filled with cigars and tobacco. Mother scrubbed the floor and the walls of the room. I went to school in the town and was glad to be away from the farm and from the presence of the discouraged, sad-looking chickens. Still I was not very joyous. In the evening I walked home from school along Turner's Pike and remembered the children I had seen playing in the town school yard. A troop of little girls had gone hopping about and singing. I tried that. Down along the frozen road I went hopping solemnly on one leg. "Hippity

Hop To The Barber Shop," I sang shrilly. Then I stopped and looked doubtfully about. I was afraid of being seen in my gay mood. It must have seemed to me that I was doing a thing that should not be done by one who, like myself, had been raised on a chicken farm where death was a daily visitor.

Mother decided that our restaurant should remain open at night. At ten in the evening a passenger train went north past our door followed by a local freight. The freight crew had switching to do in Pickleville and when the work was done they came to our restaurant for hot coffee and food. Sometimes one of them ordered a fried egg. In the morning at four they returned north-bound and again visited us. A little trade began to grow up. Mother slept at night and during the day tended the restaurant and fed our boarders while father slept. He slept in the same bed mother had occupied during the night and I went off to the town of Bidwell and to school. During the long nights, while mother and I slept, father cooked meats that were to go into sandwiches for the lunch baskets of our boarders. Then an idea in regard to getting up in the world came into his head. The American spirit took hold of him. He also became ambitious.

In the long nights when there was little to do father had time to think. That was his undoing. He decided that he had in the past been an unsuccessful man because he had not been cheerful enough and that in the future he would adopt a cheerful outlook on life. In the early morning he came upstairs and got into bed with mother. She woke and the two talked. From my bed in the corner I listened.

It was father's idea that both he and mother should try to entertain the people who came to eat at our restaurant. I cannot now remember his words, but he gave the impression of one about to become in some obscure way a kind of public entertainer. When people, particularly young people from the town of Bidwell, came into our place, as on very rare occasions they did, bright entertaining conversation was to be made. From father's words I gathered that something of the jolly inn-keeper effect was to be sought. Mother must have been doubtful from the first, but she said nothing discouraging. It was father's notion that a passion for the company of himself and mother would spring up in the breasts of the younger people of the town of Bidwell. In the evening bright happy groups would come singing down Turner's Pike. They would troop shouting with joy and laughter into our place. There would be song and festivity. I do not mean to give the impression that father spoke so elaborately of the matter. He was as I have said an uncommunicative man. "They want some place to go. I tell you they want some place to go," he said over and over. That was as far as he got. My own imagination has filled in the blanks.

For two or three weeks this notion of father's invaded our house. We did not talk much, but in our daily lives tried earnestly to make smiles take the place of glum looks. Mother smiled at the boarders and I, catching the infection, smiled at our cat. Father became a little feverish in his anxiety to please. There was no doubt, lurking somewhere in him, a touch of the spirit of the showman. He did not waste much of his ammunition on the railroad men he served at night but seemed to be waiting for a young man or woman from Bidwell to come in to show what he could do. On the counter in the restaurant there was a wire basket kept always filled with eggs, and it must have been before his eyes when the idea of being entertaining was born in his brain. There was something pre-natal about the way eggs kept themselves connected with the development of his idea. At any rate an egg ruined his new impulse in life. Late one night I was awakened by a roar of anger coming from father's throat. Both mother and I sat upright in our beds. With trembling hands she lighted a lamp that stood on a table by her head. Downstairs the front door of our restaurant went shut with a bang and in a few minutes father tramped up the stairs. He held an egg in his hand and his hand trembled as though he were having a chill. There was a half insane light in his eyes. As he stood glaring at us I was sure he intended throwing the egg at either mother or me. Then he laid it gently on the table beside the lamp and dropped on his knees beside mother's bed. He began to cry like a boy and I, carried away by his grief, cried with him. The two of us filled the little upstairs room with our wailing voices. It is ridiculous, but of the picture we made I can remember only the fact that mother's hand continually stroked the bald path that ran across the top of his head. I have forgotten what mother said to him and how she induced him to tell her of what had happened downstairs. His explanation also has gone out of my mind. I remember only my own grief and fright and the shiny path over father's head glowing in the lamp light as he knelt by the bed.

As to what happened downstairs. For some unexplainable reason I know the story as well as though I had been a witness to my father's discomfiture. One in time gets to know many unexplainable things. On that evening young Joe Kane, son of a merchant of Bidwell, came to Pickleville to meet his father, who was expected on the ten o'clock evening train from the South. The train was three hours late and Joe came into our place to loaf about and to wait for its arrival. The local freight train came in and the freight crew were fed. Joe was left alone in the restaurant with father.

From the moment he came into our place the Bidwell young man must have been puzzled by my father's actions. It was his notion that father was angry at him for hanging around. He noticed that the restaurant keeper was apparently disturbed by his presence and he thought of going out. However, it began to rain and he did not fancy the long walk to town and back. He bought a five-cent cigar and ordered a cup of coffee. He had a newspaper in his pocket and took it out and began to read. "I'm waiting for the evening train. It's late," he said apologetically.

For a long time father, whom Joe Kane had never seen before, remained silently gazing at his visitor. He was no doubt suffering from an attack of stage fright. As so often happens in life he had thought so much and so often of the situation that now confronted him that he was somewhat nervous in its presence.

For one thing, he did not know what to do with his hands. He thrust one of them nervously over the counter and shook hands with Joe Kane. "How-de-do," he said. Joe Kane put his newspaper down and stared at him. Father's eye lighted on the basket of eggs that sat on the counter and he began to talk. "Well," he began hesitatingly, "well, you have heard of Christopher Columbus, eh?" He seemed to be angry. "That Christopher Columbus was a cheat," he declared emphatically. "He talked of making an egg stand on its end. He talked, he did, and then he went and broke the end of the egg."

My father seemed to his visitor to be beside himself
at the duplicity of Christopher Columbus. He muttered and swore. He declared it was wrong to teach
children that Christopher Columbus was a great man
when, after all, he cheated at the critical moment. He
had declared he would make an egg stand on end and
then when his bluff had been called he had done a
trick. Still grumbling at Columbus, father took an
egg from the basket on the counter and began to walk
up and down. He rolled the egg between the palms
of his hands. He smiled genially. He began to
mumble words regarding the effect to be produced on
an egg by the electricity that comes out of the human
body. He declared that without breaking its shell
and by virtue of rolling it back and forth in his hands
he could stand the egg on its end. He explained that
the warmth of his hands and the gentle rolling movement he gave the egg created a new centre of gravity,
and Joe Kane was mildly interested. "I have handled
thousands of eggs," father said. "No one knows more
about eggs than I do."

He stood the egg on the counter and it fell on its
side. He tried the trick again and again, each time
rolling the egg between the palms of his hands and
saying the words regarding the wonders of electricity
and the laws of gravity. When after a half hour's effort he did succeed in making the egg stand for a
moment he looked up to find that his visitor was no

longer watching. By the time he had succeeded in calling Joe Kane's attention to the success of his effort the egg had again rolled over and lay on its side.

Afire with the showman's passion and at the same time a good deal disconcerted by the failure of his first effort, father now took the bottles containing the poultry monstrosities down from their place on the shelf and began to show them to his visitor. "How would you like to have seven legs and two heads like this fellow?" he asked, exhibiting the most remarkable of his treasures. A cheerful smile played over his face. He reached over the counter and tried to slap Joe Kane on the shoulder as he had seen men do in Ben Head's saloon when he was a young farm-hand and drove to town on Saturday evenings. His visitor was made a little ill by the sight of the body of the terribly deformed bird floating in the alcohol in the bottle and got up to go. Coming from behind the counter father took hold of the young man's arm and led him back to his seat. He grew a little angry and for a moment had to turn his face away and force himself to smile. Then he put the bottles back on the shelf. In an outburst of generosity he fairly compelled Joe Kane to have a fresh cup of coffee and another cigar at his expense. Then he took a pan and filling it with vinegar, taken from a jug that sat beneath the counter, he declared himself about to do a new trick. "I will heat this egg in this pan of vinegar," he said. "Then I will put it through the neck of a bottle without breaking the shell. When the egg is inside the bottle it will resume its normal shape and the shell will become hard again. Then I will give the bottle with the egg in it to you. You can take it about with you wherever you go. People will want to know how you got the egg in the bottle. Don't tell them. Keep them guessing. That is the way to have fun with this trick."

Father grinned and winked at his visitor. Joe Kane decided that the man who confronted him was mildly insane but harmless. He drank the cup of coffee that had been given him and began to read his paper again. When the egg had been heated in vinegar father carried it on a spoon to the counter and going into a back room got an empty bottle. He was angry because his visitor did not watch him as he began to do his trick, but nevertheless went cheerfully to work. For a long time he struggled, trying to get the egg to go through the neck of the bottle. He put the pan of vinegar back on the stove, intending to reheat the egg, then picked it up and burned his fingers. After a second bath in the hot vinegar the shell of the egg had been softened a little but not enough for his purpose. He worked and worked and a spirit of desperate determination took possession of him. When he thought that at last the trick was about to be consummated the delayed train came in at the station and Joe Kane started to go nonchalantly out at the door. Father made a last desperate effort to conquer the egg and make it do the thing that would establish his reputation as one who knew how to entertain guests who came into his restaurant. He worried the egg. He attempted to be somewhat rough with it. He swore and the sweat stood out on his forehead. The egg broke under his hand. When the contents spurted over his clothes, Joe Kane, who had stopped at the door, turned and laughed.

A roar of anger rose from my father's throat. He danced and shouted a string of inarticulate words. Grabbing another egg from the basket on the counter, he threw it, just missing the head of the young man as he dodged through the door and escaped.

Father came upstairs to mother and me with an egg in his hand. I do not know what he intended to do. I imagine he had some idea of destroying it, of destroying all eggs, and that he intended to let mother and me see him begin. When, however, he got into the presence of mother something happened to him. He laid the egg gently on the table and dropped on his knees by the bed as I have already explained. He later decided to close the restaurant for the night and to come upstairs and get into bed. When he did so he blew out the light and after much muttered conversation both he and mother went to sleep. I suppose I went to sleep also, but my sleep was troubled.

I awoke at dawn and for a long time looked at the egg that lay on the table. I wondered why eggs had to be and why from the egg came the hen who again laid the egg. The question got into my blood. It has stayed there, I imagine, because I am the son of my father. At any rate, the problem remains unsolved in my mind. And that, I conclude, is but another evidence of the complete and final triumph of the egg— at least as far as my family is concerned.

UNLIGHTED LAMPS

MARY COCHRAN went out of the rooms where she lived with her father, Doctor Lester Cochran, at seven o'clock on a Sunday evening. It was June of the year nineteen hundred and eight and Mary was eighteen years old. She walked along Tremont to Main Street and across the railroad tracks to Upper Main, lined with small shops and shoddy houses, a rather quiet cheerless place on Sundays when there were few people about. She had told her father she was going to church but did not intend doing anything of the kind. She did not know what she wanted to do. "I'll get off by myself and think," she told herself as she walked slowly along. The night she thought promised to be too fine to be spent sitting in a stuffy church and hearing a man talk of things that had apparently nothing to do with her own problem. Her own affairs were approaching a crisis and it was time for her to begin thinking seriously of her future.

The thoughtful serious state of mind in which Mary found herself had been induced in her by a conversation had with her father on the evening before. Without any preliminary talk and quite suddenly and abruptly he had told her that he was a victim of heart

64

disease and might die at any moment. He had made the announcement as they stood together in the Doctor's office, back of which were the rooms in which the father and daughter lived.

It was growing dark outside when she came into the office and found him sitting alone. The office and living rooms were on the second floor of an old frame building in the town of Huntersburg, Illinois, and as the Doctor talked he stood beside his daughter near one of the windows that looked down into Tremont Street. The hushed murmur of the town's Saturday night life went on in Main Street just around a corner, and the evening train, bound to Chicago fifty miles to the east, had just passed. The hotel bus came rattling out of Lincoln Street and went through Tremont toward the hotel on Lower Main. A cloud of dust kicked up by the horses' hoofs floated on the quiet air. A straggling group of people followed the bus and the row of hitching posts on Tremont Street was already lined with buggies in which farmers and their wives had driven into town for the evening of shopping and gossip.

After the station bus had passed three or four more buggies were driven into the street. From one of them a young man helped his sweetheart to alight. He took hold of her arm with a certain air of tenderness, and a hunger to be touched thus tenderly by a man's hand, that had come to Mary many times before, returned at almost the same moment her father made the announcement of his approaching death.

As the Doctor began to speak Barney Smithfield, who owned a livery barn that opened into Tremont Street directly opposite the building in which the Cochrans lived, came back to his place of business from his evening meal. He stopped to tell a story to a group of men gathered before the barn door and a shout of laughter arose. One of the loungers in the street, a strongly built young man in a checkered suit, stepped away from the others and stood before the liveryman. Having seen Mary he was trying to attract her attention. He also began to tell a story and as he talked he gesticulated, waved his arms and from time to time looked over his shoulder to see if the girl still stood by the window and if she were watching.

Doctor Cochran had told his daughter of his approaching death in a cold quiet voice. To the girl it had seemed that everything concerning her father must be cold and quiet. "I have a disease of the heart," he said flatly, "have long suspected there was something of the sort the matter with me and on Thursday when I went into Chicago I had myself examined. The truth is I may die at any moment. I would not tell you but for one reason—I will leave little money and you must be making plans for the future."

The Doctor stepped nearer the window where his daughter stood with her hand on the frame. The announcement had made her a little pale and her hand trembled. In spite of his apparent coldness he was touched and wanted to reassure her. "There now," he said hesitatingly, "it'll likely be all right after all. Don't worry. I haven't been a doctor for thirty years without knowing there's a great deal of nonsense about these pronouncements on the part of experts. In a matter like this, that is to say when a man has a disease of the heart, he may putter about for years." He laughed uncomfortably. "I've even heard it said that the best way to insure a long life is to contract a disease of the heart."

With these words the Doctor had turned and walked out of his office, going down a wooden stairway to the street. He had wanted to put his arm about his daughter's shoulder as he talked to her, but never having shown any feeling in his relations with her could not sufficiently release some tight thing in himself.

Mary had stood for a long time looking down into the street. The young man in the checkered suit, whose name was Duke Yetter, had finished telling his tale and a shout of laughter arose. She turned to look toward the door through which her father had passed and dread took possession of her. In all her life there had never been anything warm and close. She shivered although the night was warm and with a quick girlish gesture passed her hand over her eyes.

The gesture was but an expression of a desire to brush away the cloud of fear that had settled down upon her but it was misinterpreted by Duke Yetter who now stood a little apart from the other men before the livery barn. When he saw Mary's hand go up he smiled and turning quickly to be sure he was unobserved began jerking his head and making motions with his hand as a sign that he wished her to come down into the street where he would have an opportunity to join her.

*   *   *

On the Sunday evening Mary, having walked through Upper Main, turned into Wilmott, a street of workmens' houses. During that year the first sign of the march of factories westward from Chicago into the prairie towns had come to Huntersburg. A Chicago manufacturer of furniture had built a plant in the sleepy little farming town, hoping thus to escape the labor organizations that had begun to give him trouble in the city. At the upper end of town, in Wilmott, Swift, Harrison and Chestnut Streets and in cheap, badly-constructed frame houses, most of the factory workers lived. On the warm summer evening they were gathered on the porches at the front of the houses and a mob of children played in the dusty streets. Red-faced men in white shirts and without collars and coats slept in chairs or lay sprawled on strips of grass or on the hard earth before the doors of the houses.

The laborers' wives had gathered in groups and stood gossiping by the fences that separated the yards. Occasionally the voice of one of the women arose sharp and distinct above the steady flow of voices that ran like a murmuring river through the hot little streets.

In the roadway two children had got into a fight. A thick-shouldered red-haired boy struck another boy who had a pale sharp-featured face, a blow on the shoulder. Other children came running. The mother of the red-haired boy brought the promised fight to an end. "Stop it Johnny, I tell you to stop it. I'll break your neck if you don't," the woman screamed.

The pale boy turned and walked away from his antagonist. As he went slinking along the sidewalk past Mary Cochran his sharp little eyes, burning with hatred, looked up at her.

Mary went quickly along. The strange new part of her native town with the hubbub of life always stirring and asserting itself had a strong fascination for her. There was something dark and resentful in her own nature that made her feel at home in the crowded place where life carried itself off darkly, with a blow and an oath. The habitual silence of her father and the mystery concerning the unhappy married life of her father and mother, that had affected the attitude toward her of the people of the town, had made her own life a lonely one and had encouraged in her a rather dogged determination to in some way think her own way through the things of life she could not understand.

And back of Mary's thinking there was an intense curiosity and a courageous determination toward adventure. She was like a little animal of the forest that has been robbed of its mother by the gun of a sportsman and has been driven by hunger to go forth and seek food. Twenty times during the year she had walked alone at evening in the new and fast growing factory district of her town. She was eighteen and had begun to look like a woman, and she felt that other girls of the town of her own age would not have dared to walk in such a place alone. The feeling made her somewhat proud and as she went along she looked boldly about.

Among the workers in Wilmott Street, men and women who had been brought to town by the furniture manufacturer, were many who spoke in foreign tongues. Mary walked among them and liked the sound of the strange voices. To be in the street made her feel that she had gone out of her town and on a voyage into a strange land. In Lower Main Street or in the residence streets in the eastern part of town where lived the young men and women she had always known and where lived also the merchants, the clerks, the lawyers and the more well-to-do American workmen of Huntersburg, she felt always a secret antagonism to herself. The antagonism was not due to anything in her own character. She was sure of that. She had kept so much to herself that she was in fact but little known. "It is because I am the daughter of my mother," she told herself and did not walk often in the part of town where other girls of her class lived.

Mary had been so often in Wilmott Street that many of the people had begun to feel acquainted with her. "She is the daughter of some farmer and has got into the habit of walking into town," they said. A red-haired, broad-hipped woman who came out at the front door of one of the houses nodded to her. On a narrow strip of grass beside another house sat a young man with his back against a tree. He was smoking a pipe, but when he looked up and saw her he took the pipe from his mouth. She decided he must be an Italian, his hair and eyes were so black. "Ne bella! si fai un onore a passare di qua," he called waving his hand and smiling.

Mary went to the end of Wilmott Street and came out upon a country road. It seemed to her that a long time must have passed since she left her father's presence although the walk had in fact occupied but a few minutes. By the side of the road and on top of a small hill there was a ruined barn, and before the barn a great hole filled with the charred timbers of what had once been a farmhouse. A pile of stones lay beside the hole and these were covered with creeping vines. Between the site of the house and the barn there was an old orchard in which grew a mass of tangled weeds.

Pushing her way in among the weeds, many of which were covered with blossoms, Mary found herself a seat on a rock that had been rolled against the trunk of an old apple tree. The weeds half concealed her and from the road only her head was visible. Buried away thus in the weeds she looked like a quail that runs in the tall grass and that on hearing some un-usual sound, stops, throws up its head and looks sharply about.

The doctor's daughter had been to the decayed old orchard many times before. At the foot of the hill on which it stood the streets of the town began, and as she sat on the rock she could hear faint shouts and cries coming out of Wilmott Street. A hedge separated the orchard from the fields on the hillside. Mary in-tended to sit by the tree until darkness came creep-ing over the land and to try to think out some plan regarding her future. The notion that her father was soon to die seemed both true and untrue, but her mind was unable to take hold of the thought of him as physically dead. For the moment death in relation to her father did not take the form of a cold inanimate body that was to be buried in the ground, instead it seemed to her that her father was not to die but to go away somewhere on a journey. Long ago her mother had done that. There was a strange hesitating sense of relief in the thought. "Well," she told herself, "when the time comes I also shall be setting out, I shall get out of here and into the world." On several occasions Mary had gone to spend a day with her father in Chicago and she was fascinated by the thought that soon she might be going there to live. Before her mind's eye floated a vision of long streets filled with thousands of people all strangers to herself. To go into such streets and to live her life among strangers would be like coming out of a waterless desert and into a cool forest carpeted with tender young grass.

In Huntersburg she had always lived under a cloud and now she was becoming a woman and the close stuffy atmosphere she had always breathed was becoming constantly more and more oppressive. It was true no direct question had ever been raised touching her own standing in the community life, but she felt that a kind of prejudice against her existed. While she was still a baby there had been a scandal involving her father and mother. The town of Huntersburg had rocked with it and when she was a child people had sometimes looked at her with mocking sympathetic eyes. "Poor child! It's too bad," they said. Once, on a cloudy summer evening when her father had driven off to the country and she sat alone in the darkness by his office window, she heard a man and

woman in the street mention her name. The couple
stumbled along in the darkness on the sidewalk below
the office window. "That daughter of Doc Cochran's
is a nice girl," said the man. The woman laughed.
"She's growing up and attracting men's attention now.
Better keep your eyes in your head. She'll turn out
bad. Like mother, like daughter," the woman replied.

For ten or fifteen minutes Mary sat on the stone beneath the tree in the orchard and thought of the attitude of the town toward herself and her father.
"It should have drawn us together," she told herself,
and wondered if the approach of death would do what
the cloud that had for years hung over them had not
done. It did not at the moment seem to her cruel that
the figure of death was soon to visit her father. In a
way Death had become for her and for the time a lovely and gracious figure intent upon good. The hand of
death was to open the door out of her father's house
and into life. With the cruelty of youth she thought
first of the adventurous possibilities of the new life.

Mary sat very still. In the long weeds the insects
that had been disturbed in their evening song began
to sing again. A robin flew into the tree beneath
which she sat and struck a clear sharp note of alarm.
The voices of people in the town's new factory district
came softly up the hillside. They were like bells of
distant cathedrals calling people to worship. Some-

thing within the girl's breast seemed to break and putting her head into her hands she rocked slowly back and forth. Tears came accompanied by a warm tender impulse toward the living men and women of Huntersburg.

And then from the road came a call. "Hello there kid," shouted a voice, and Mary sprang quickly to her feet. Her mellow mood passed like a puff of wind and in its place hot anger came.

In the road stood Duke Yetter who from his loafing place before the livery barn had seen her set out for the Sunday evening walk and had followed. When she went through Upper Main Street and into the new factory district he was sure of his conquest. "She doesn't want to be seen walking with me," he had told himself, "that's all right. She knows well enough I'll follow but doesn't want me to put in an appearance until she is well out of sight of her friends. She's a little stuck up and needs to be brought down a peg, but what do I care? She's gone out of her way to give me this chance and maybe she's only afraid of her dad."

Duke climbed the little incline out of the road and came into the orchard, but when he reached the pile of stones covered by vines he stumbled and fell. He arose and laughed. Mary had not waited for him to reach her but had started toward him, and when his laugh broke the silence that lay over the orchard she sprang forward and with her open hand struck him a sharp blow on the cheek. Then she turned and as he stood with his feet tangled in the vines ran out to the road. "If you follow or speak to me I'll get someone to kill you," she shouted.

Mary walked along the road and down the hill toward Wilmott Street. Broken bits of the story concerning her mother that had for years circulated in town had reached her ears. Her mother, it was said, had disappeared on a summer night long ago and a young town rough, who had been in the habit of loitering before Barney Smithfield's Livery Barn, had gone away with her. Now another young rough was trying to make up to her. The thought made her furious.

Her mind groped about striving to lay hold of some weapon with which she could strike a more telling blow at Duke Yetter. In desperation it lit upon the figure of her father already broken in health and now about to die. "My father just wants the chance to kill some such fellow as you," she shouted, turning to face the young man, who having got clear of the mass of vines in the orchard, had followed her into the road. "My father just wants to kill someone because of the lies that have been told in this town about mother."

Having given way to the impulse to threaten Duke Yetter Mary was instantly ashamed of her outburst and walked rapidly along, the tears running from her eyes. With hanging head Duke walked at her heels. "I didn't mean no harm, Miss Cochran," he pleaded. "I didn't mean no harm. Don't tell your father. I was only funning with you. I tell you I didn't mean no harm."

* * *

The light of the summer evening had begun to fall and the faces of the people made soft little ovals of light as they stood grouped under the dark porches or by the fences in Wilmott Street. The voices of the children had become subdued and they also stood in groups. They became silent as Mary passed and stood with upturned faces and staring eyes. "The lady doesn't live very far. She must be almost a neighbor," she heard a woman's voice saying in English. When she turned her head she saw only a crowd of dark-skinned men standing before a house. From within the house came the sound of a woman's voice singing a child to sleep.

The young Italian, who had called to her earlier in the evening and who was now apparently setting out of his own Sunday evening's adventures, came along the sidewalk and walked quickly away into the darkness. He had dressed himself in his Sunday clothes and had put on a black derby hat and a stiff white collar, set off by a red necktie. The shining whiteness of the collar made his brown skin look almost black. He smiled boyishly and raised his hat awkwardly but did not speak.

Mary kept looking back along the street to be sure

Duke Yetter had not followed but in the dim light could see nothing of him. Her angry excited mood went away.

She did not want to go home and decided it was too late to go to church. From Upper Main Street there was a short street that ran eastward and fell rather sharply down a hillside to a creek and a bridge that marked the end of the town's growth in that direction. She went down along the street to the bridge and stood in the failing light watching two boys who were fishing in the creek.

A broad-shouldered man dressed in rough clothes came down along the street and stopping on the bridge spoke to her. It was the first time she had ever heard a citizen of her home town speak with feeling of her father. "You are Doctor Cochran's daughter?" he asked hesitatingly. "I guess you don't know who I am but your father does." He pointed toward the two boys who sat with fishpoles in their hands on the weed-grown bank of the creek. "Those are my boys and I have four other children," he explained. "There is another boy and I have three girls. One of my daughters has a job in a store. She is as old as yourself." The man explained his relations with Doctor Cochran. He had been a farm laborer, he said, and had but recently moved to town to work in the furniture factory. During the previous winter he had been ill for a long time and had no money. While he lay in bed one of his boys fell out of a barn loft and there was a terrible cut in his head.

"Your father came every day to see us and he sewed up my Tom's head." The laborer turned away from Mary and stood with his cap in his hand looking toward the boys. "I was down and out and your father not only took care of me and the boys but he gave my old woman money to buy the things we had to have from the stores in town here, groceries and medicines." The man spoke in such low tones that Mary had to lean forward to hear his words. Her face almost touched the laborer's shoulder. "Your father is a good man and I don't think he is very happy," he went on. "The boy and I got well and I got work here in town but he wouldn't take any money from me. 'You know how to live with your children and with your wife. You know how to make them happy. Keep your money and spend it on them,' that's what he said to me."

The laborer went on across the bridge and along the creek bank toward the spot where his two sons sat fishing and Mary leaned on the railing of the bridge and looked at the slow moving water. It was almost black in the shadows under the bridge and she thought that it was thus her father's life had been lived. "It has been like a stream running always in shadows and never coming out into the sunlight," she thought, and fear that her own life would run on in darkness gripped her. A great new love for her father swept over her and in fancy she felt his arms about her. As a child she had continually dreamed of caresses received at her father's hands and now the dream came back. For a long time she stood looking at the stream and she resolved that the night should not pass without an effort on her part to make the old dream come true. When she again looked up the laborer had built a little fire of sticks at the edge of the stream. "We catch bullheads here," he called. "The light of the fire draws them close to the shore. If you want to come and try your hand at fishing the boys will lend you one of the poles."

"O, I thank you, I won't do it tonight," Mary said, and then fearing she might suddenly begin weeping and that if the man spoke to her again she would find herself unable to answer, she hurried away. "Good bye!" shouted the man and the two boys. The words came quite spontaneously out of the three throats and created a sharp trumpet-like effect that rang like a glad cry across the heaviness of her mood.

*   *   *

When his daughter Mary went out for her evening walk Doctor Cochran sat for an hour alone in his office. It began to grow dark and the men who all afternoon had been sitting on chairs and boxes before the livery barn across the street went home for the evening meal. The noise of voices grew faint and sometimes for five or ten minutes there was silence.

Then from some distant street came a child's cry. Presently church bells began to ring.

The Doctor was not a very neat man and sometimes for several days he forgot to shave. With a long lean hand he stroked his half grown beard. His illness had struck deeper than he had admitted even to himself and his mind had an inclination to float out of his body. Often when he sat thus his hands lay in his lap and he looked at them with a child's absorption. It seemed to him they must belong to someone else. He grew philosophic. "It's an odd thing about my body. Here I've lived in it all these years and how little use I have had of it. Now it's going to die and decay never having been used. I wonder why it did not get another tenant." He smiled sadly over this fancy but went on with it. "Well I've had thoughts enough concerning people and I've had the use of these lips and a tongue but I've let them lie idle. When my Ellen was here living with me I let her think me cold and unfeeling while something within me was straining and straining trying to tear itself loose."

He remembered how often, as a young man, he had sat in the evening in silence beside his wife in this same office and how his hands had ached to reach across the narrow space that separated them and touch her hands, her face, her hair.

Well, everyone in town had predicted his marriage would turn out badly! His wife had been an actress with a company that came to Huntersburg and got stranded there. At the same time the girl became ill and had no money to pay for her room at the hotel. The young doctor had attended to that and when the girl was convalescent took her to ride about the country in his buggy. Her life had been a hard one and the notion of leading a quiet existence in the little town appealed to her.

And then after the marriage and after the child was born she had suddenly found herself unable to go on living with the silent cold man. There had been a story of her having run away with a young sport, the son of a saloon keeper who had disappeared from town at the same time, but the story was untrue. Lester Cochran had himself taken her to Chicago where she got work with a company going into the far western states. Then he had taken her to the door of her hotel, had put money into her hands and in silence and without even a farewell kiss had turned and walked away.

The Doctor sat in his office living over that moment and other intense moments when he had been deeply stirred and had been on the surface so cool and quiet. He wondered if the woman had known. How many times he had asked himself that question. After he left her that night at the hotel door she never wrote. "Perhaps she is dead," he thought for the thousandth time.

A thing happened that had been happening at odd moments for more than a year. In Doctor Cochran's mind the remembered figure of his wife became confused with the figure of his daughter. When at such moments he tried to separate the two figures, to make them stand out distinct from each other, he was unsuccessful. Turning his head slightly he imagined he saw a white girlish figure coming through a door out of the rooms in which he and his daughter lived. The door was painted white and swung slowly in a light breeze that came in at an open window. The wind ran softly and quietly through the room and played over some papers lying on a desk in a corner. There was a soft swishing sound as of a woman's skirts. The doctor arose and stood trembling. "Which is it? Is it you Mary or is it Ellen?" he asked huskily.

On the stairway leading up from the street there was the sound of heavy feet and the outer door opened. The doctor's weak heart fluttered and he dropped heavily back into his chair.

A man came into the room. He was a farmer, one of the doctor's patients, and coming to the centre of the room he struck a match, held it above his head and shouted. "Hello!" he called. When the doctor arose from his chair and answered he was so startled that the match fell from his hand and lay burning faintly at his feet.

The young farmer had sturdy legs that were like two

pillars of stone supporting a heavy building, and the little flame of the match that burned and fluttered in the light breeze on the floor between his feet threw dancing shadows along the walls of the room. The doctor's confused mind refused to clear itself of his fancies that now began to feed upon this new situation.

He forgot the presence of the farmer and his mind raced back over his life as a married man. The flickering light on the wall recalled another dancing light. One afternoon in the summer during the first year after his marriage his wife Ellen had driven with him into the country. They were then furnishing their rooms and at a farmer's house Ellen had seen an old mirror, no longer in use, standing against a wall in a shed. Because of something quaint in the design the mirror had taken her fancy and the farmer's wife had given it to her. On the drive home the young wife had told her husband of her pregnancy and the doctor had been stirred as never before. He sat holding the mirror on his knees while his wife drove and when she announced the coming of the child she looked away across the fields.

How deeply etched, that scene in the sick man's mind! The sun was going down over young corn and oat fields beside the road. The prairie land was black and occasionally the road ran through short lanes of trees that also looked black in the waning light.

The mirror on his knees caught the rays of the departing sun and sent a great ball of golden light dancing across the fields and among the branches of trees. Now as he stood in the presence of the farmer and as the little light from the burning match on the floor recalled that other evening of dancing lights, he thought he understood the failure of his marriage and of his life. On that evening long ago when Ellen had told him of the coming of the great adventure of their marriage he had remained silent because he had thought no words he could utter would express what he felt. There had been a defense for himself built up. "I told myself she should have understood without words and I've all my life been telling myself the same thing about Mary. I've been a fool and a coward. I've always been silent because I've been afraid of expressing myself—like a blundering fool. I've been a proud man and a coward.

"Tonight I'll do it. If it kills me I'll make myself talk to the girl," he said aloud, his mind coming back to the figure of his daughter.

"Hey! What's that?" asked the farmer who stood with his hat in his hand waiting to tell of his mission.

The doctor got his horse from Barney Smithfield's livery and drove off to the country to attend the farmer's wife who was about to give birth to her first child. She was a slender narrow-hipped woman and the child was large, but the doctor was feverishly strong. He worked desperately and the woman, who was fright-

ened, groaned and struggled.   Her husband kept coming in and going out of the room and two neighbor
women appeared and stood silently about waiting to be
of service.   It was past ten o'clock when everything
was done and the doctor was ready to depart for town.

The farmer hitched his horse and brought it to the
door and the doctor drove off feeling strangely weak
and at the same time strong.   How simple now seemed
the thing he had yet to do.   Perhaps when he got home
his daughter would have gone to bed but he would ask
her to get up and come into the office.   Then he would
tell the whole story of his marriage and its failure spar-
ing himself no humiliation.   "There was something very
dear and beautiful in my Ellen and I must make Mary
understand that.   It will help her to be a beautiful
woman," he thought, full of confidence in the strength
of his resolution.

He got to the door of the livery barn at eleven
o'clock and Barney Smithfield with young Duke Yetter
and two other men sat talking there.   The liveryman
took his horse away into the darkness of the barn and
the doctor stood for a moment leaning against the wall
of the building.   The town's night watchman stood
with the group by the barn door and a quarrel broke
out between him and Duke Yetter, but the doctor did
not hear the hot words that flew back and forth or
Duke's loud laughter at the night watchman's anger.
A queer hesitating mood had taken possession of him.

There was something he passionately desired to do but
could not remember. Did it have to do with his wife
Ellen or Mary his daughter? The figures of the two
women were again confused in his mind and to add to
the confusion there was a third figure, that of the
woman he had just assisted through child birth. Everything was confusion. He started across the street
toward the entrance of the stairway leading to his
office and then stopped in the road and stared about.
Barney Smithfield having returned from putting his
horse in the stall shut the door of the barn and a hanging lantern over the door swung back and forth. It
threw grotesque dancing shadows down over the faces
and forms of the men standing and quarreling beside
the wall of the barn.

*   *   *

Mary sat by a window in the doctor's office awaiting
his return. So absorbed was she in her own thoughts
that she was unconscious of the voice of Duke Yetter
talking with the men in the street.

When Duke had come into the street the hot anger
of the early part of the evening had returned and she
again saw him advancing toward her in the orchard
with the look of arrogant male confidence in his eyes
but presently she forgot him and thought only of her
father. An incident of her childhood returned to haunt
her. One afternoon in the month of May when she
was fifteen her father had asked her to accompany him

on an evening drive into the country. The doctor went
to visit a sick woman at a farmhouse five miles from
town and as there had been a great deal of rain the
roads were heavy. It was dark when they reached the
farmer's house and they went into the kitchen and ate
cold food off a kitchen table. For some reason her
father had, on that evening, appeared boyish and almost gay. On the road he had talked a little. Even
at that early age Mary had grown tall and her figure
was becoming womanly. After the cold supper in the
farm kitchen he walked with her around the house and
she sat on a narrow porch. For a moment her father
stood before her. He put his hands into his trouser
pockets and throwing back his head laughed almost
heartily. "It seems strange to think you will soon be a
woman," he said. "When you do become a woman
what do you suppose is going to happen, eh? What
kind of a life will you lead? What will happen to
you?"

The doctor sat on the porch beside the child and for
a moment she had thought he was about to put his arm
around her. Then he jumped up and went into the
house leaving her to sit alone in the darkness.

As she remembered the incident Mary remembered
also that on that evening of her childhood she had met
her father's advances in silence. It seemed to her that
she, not her father, was to blame for the life they had
led together. The farm laborer she had met on the

bridge had not felt her father's coldness. That was because he had himself been warm and generous in his attitude toward the man who had cared for him in his hour of sickness and misfortune. Her father had said that the laborer knew how to be a father and Mary remembered with what warmth the two boys fishing by the creek had called to her as she went away into the darkness. "Their father has known how to be a father because his children have known how to give themselves," she thought guiltily. She also would give herself. Before the night had passed she would do that. On that evening long ago and as she rode home beside her father he had made another unsuccessful effort to break through the wall that separated them. The heavy rains had swollen the streams they had to cross and when they had almost reached town he had stopped the horse on a wooden bridge. The horse danced nervously about and her father held the reins firmly and occasionally spoke to him. Beneath the bridge the swollen stream made a great roaring sound and beside the road in a long flat field there was a lake of flood water. At that moment the moon had come out from behind clouds and the wind that blew across the water made little waves. The lake of flood water was covered with dancing lights. "I'm going to tell you about your mother and myself," her father said huskily, but at that moment the timbers of the bridge began to crack dangerously and the horse plunged for-

ward.   When her father had regained control of the
frightened beast they were in the streets of the town
and his diffident silent nature had reasserted itself.

Mary sat in the darkness by the office window and
saw her father drive into the street.   When his horse
had been put away he did not, as was his custom, come
at once up the stairway to the office but lingered in the
darkness before the barn door.   Once he started to
cross the street and then returned into the darkness.

Among the men who for two hours had been sitting
and talking quietly a quarrel broke out.   Jack Fisher
the town nightwatchman had been telling the others
the story of a battle in which he had fought during the
Civil War and Duke Yetter had begun bantering him.
The nightwatchman grew angry.   Grasping his night-
stick he limped up and down.   The loud voice of Duke
Yetter cut across the shrill angry voice of the victim of
his wit.   "You ought to a flanked the fellow, I tell you
Jack.   Yes sir 'ee, you ought to a flanked that reb and
then when you got him flanked you ought to a knocked
the stuffings out of the cuss.   That's what I would a
done," Duke shouted, laughing boisterously.   "You
would a raised hell, you would," the night watchman
answered, filled with ineffectual wrath.

The old soldier went off along the street followed
by the laughter of Duke and his companions and Barney Smithfield, having put the doctor's horse away,
came out and closed the barn door.   A lantern hanging

above the door swung back and forth. Doctor Cochran again started across the street and when he had reached the foot of the stairway turned and shouted to the men. "Good night," he called cheerfully. A strand of hair was blown by the light summer breeze across Mary's cheek and she jumped to her feet as though she had been touched by a hand reached out to her from the darkness. A hundred times she had seen her father return from drives in the evening but never before had he said anything at all to the loiterers by the barn door. She became half convinced that not her father but some other man was now coming up the stairway.

The heavy dragging footsteps rang loudly on the wooden stairs and Mary heard her father set down the little square medicine case he always carried. The strange cheerful hearty mood of the man continued but his mind was in a confused riot. Mary imagined she could see his dark form in the doorway. "The woman has had a baby," said the hearty voice from the landing outside the door. "Who did that happen to? Was it Ellen or that other woman or my little Mary?"

A stream of words, a protest came from the man's lips. "Who's been having a baby? I want to know. Who's been having a baby? Life doesn't work out. Why are babies always being born?" he asked.

A laugh broke from the doctor's lips and his daughter leaned forward and gripped the arms of her chair.

"A babe has been born," he said again. "It's strange eh, that my hands should have helped a baby be born while all the time death stood at my elbow?"

Doctor Cochran stamped upon the floor of the landing. "My feet are cold and numb from waiting for life to come out of life," he said heavily "The woman struggled and now I must struggle."

Silence followed the stamping of feet and the tired heavy declaration from the sick man's lips. From the street below came another loud shout of laughter from Duke Yetter.

And then Doctor Cochran fell backward down the narrow stairs to the street. There was no cry from him, just the clatter of his shoes upon the stairs and the terrible subdued sound of the body falling.

Mary did not move from her chair. With closed eyes she waited. Her heart pounded. A weakness complete and overmastering had possession of her and from feet to head ran little waves of feeling as though tiny creatures with soft hair-like feet were playing upon her body.

It was Duke Yetter who carried the dead man up the stairs and laid him on a bed in one of the rooms back of the office. One of the men who had been sitting with him before the door of the barn followed lifting his hands and dropping them nervously. Between his fingers he held a forgotten cigarette the light from which danced up and down in the darkness.

SENILITY

HE WAS an old man and he sat on the steps of the railroad station in a small Kentucky town.

A well dressed man, some traveler from the city, approached and stood before him.

The old man became self-conscious.

His smile was like the smile of a very young child. His face was all sunken and wrinkled and he had a huge nose.

"Have you any coughs, colds, consumption or bleeding sickness?" he asked. In his voice there was a pleading quality.

The stranger shook his head. The old man arose.

"The sickness that bleeds is a terrible nuisance," he said. His tongue protruded from between his teeth and he rattled it about. He put his hand on the stranger's arm and laughed.

"Bully, pretty," he exclaimed. "I cure them all—coughs, colds, consumption and the sickness that bleeds. I take warts from the hand—I cannot explain how I do it—it is a mystery—I charge nothing—my name is Tom—do you like me?"

The stranger was cordial. He nodded his head. The old man became reminiscent.

"My father was a hard man," he declared. "He was like me, a blacksmith by trade, but he wore a plug hat. When the corn was high he said to the poor, 'go into the fields and pick' but when the war came he made a rich man pay five dollars for a bushel of corn."

"I married against his will. He came to me and he said, 'Tom I do not like that girl.' "

" 'But I love her,' I said.

" 'I don't,' he said.

"My father and I sat on a log. He was a pretty man and wore a plug hat. 'I will get the license,' I said.

" 'I will give you no money,' he said.

"My marriage cost me twenty-one dollars—I worked in the corn—it rained and the horses were blind—the clerk said, 'Are you over twenty-one?' I said 'yes' and she said 'yes.' We had chalked it on our shoes. My father said, 'I give you your freedom.' We had no money. My marriage cost twenty-one dollars. She is dead."

The old man looked at the sky. It was evening and the sun had set. The sky was all mottled with grey clouds. "I paint beautiful pictures and give them away," he declared. "My brother is in the penitentiary. He killed a man who called him an ugly name."

The decrepit old man held his hands before the face of the stranger. He opened and shut them. They were black with grime. "I pick out warts," he explained plaintively. "They are as soft as your hands."

"I play on an accordion. You are thirty-seven years old. I sat beside my brother in the penitentiary. He is a pretty man with pompadour hair. 'Albert,' I said, 'are you sorry you killed a man?' 'No,' he said, 'I am not sorry. I would kill ten, a hundred, a thousand!' "

The old man began to weep and to wipe his hands with a soiled handkerchief. He attempted to take a chew of tobacco and his false teeth became displaced. He covered his mouth with his hands and was ashamed.

"I am old. You are thirty-seven years old but I am older than that," he whispered.

"My brother is a bad man—he is full of hate—he is pretty and has pompadour hair, but he would kill and kill. I hate old age—I am ashamed that I am old.

"I have a pretty new wife. I wrote her four letters and she replied. She came here and we married—I love to see her walk—O, I buy her pretty clothes.

"Her foot is not straight—it is twisted—my first wife is dead—I pick warts off the hand with my fingers and no blood comes—I cure coughs, colds, consumption and the sickness that bleeds—people can write to me and I answer the letters—if they send me no money it is no matter—all is free."

Again the old man wept and the stranger tried to comfort him. "You are a happy man?" the stranger asked.

"Yes," said the old man, "and a good man too. Ask everywhere about me—my name is Tom, a blacksmith —my wife walks prettily although she has a twisted foot—I have bought her a long dress—she is thirty and I am seventy-five—she has many pairs of shoes— I have bought them for her, but her foot is twisted—I buy straight shoes—

"She thinks I do not know—everybody thinks Tom does not know—I have bought her a long dress that comes down to the ground—my name is Tom, a blacksmith—I am seventy-five and I hate old age—I take warts off the hands and no blood comes—people may write to me and I answer the letters—all is free."

THE MAN IN THE BROWN COAT

Napoleon went down into a battle riding on a horse.
Alexander went down into a battle riding on a horse.
General Grant got off a horse and walked in a wood.
General Hindenburg stood on a hill.
The moon came up out of a clump of bushes.

*   *   *

I AM writing a history of the things men do. I have written three such histories and I am but a young man. Already I have written three hundred, four hundred thousand words.

My wife is somewhere in this house where for hours now I have been sitting and writing. She is a tall woman with black hair, turning a little grey. Listen, she is going softly up a flight of stairs. All day she goes softly about, doing the housework in our house.

I came here to this town from another town in the state of Iowa. My father was a workman, a house painter. He did not rise in the world as I have done. I worked my way through college and became an historian. We own this house in which I sit. This is my room in which I work. Already I have written three histories of peoples. I have told how states were formed and battles fought. You may see my books standing straight up on the shelves of libraries. They stand up like sentries.

I am tall like my wife and my shoulders are a little stooped. Although I write boldly I am a shy man. I like being at work alone in this room with the door closed. There are many books here. Nations march back and forth in the books. It is quiet here but in the books a great thundering goes on.

*   *   *

Napoleon rides down a hill and into a battle.
General Grant walks in a wood.
Alexander rides down a hill and into a battle.

*   *   *

My wife has a serious, almost stern look. Sometimes the thoughts I have concerning her frighten me. In the afternoon she leaves our house and goes for a walk. Sometimes she goes to stores, sometimes to visit a neighbor. There is a yellow house opposite our house. My wife goes out at a side door and passes along the street between our house and the yellow house.

The side door of our house bangs. There is a moment of waiting. My wife's face floats across the yellow background of a picture.

*   *   *

General Pershing rode down a hill and into a battle.
Alexander rode down a hill and into a battle.

*   *   *

Little things are growing big in my mind. The window before my desk makes a little framed place like a picture. Every day I sit staring. I wait with an odd sensation of something impending. My hand trembles. The face that floats through the picture does something I don't understand. The face floats, then it stops. It goes from the right hand side to the left hand side, then it stops.

The face comes into my mind and goes out—the face floats in my mind. The pen has fallen from my fingers. The house is silent. The eyes of the floating face are turned away from me.

My wife is a girl who came here to this town from another town in the state of Ohio. We keep a servant but my wife often sweeps the floors and she sometimes makes the bed in which we sleep together. We sit together in the evening but I do not know her. I cannot shake myself out of myself. I wear a brown coat and I cannot come out of my coat. I cannot come out of myself. My wife is very gentle and she speaks softly but she cannot come out of herself.

My wife has gone out of the house. She does not know that I know every little thought of her life. I know what she thought when she was a child and walked in the streets of an Ohio town. I have heard the voices of her mind. I have heard the little voices. I heard the voice of fear crying when she was first overtaken with passion and crawled into my arms. Again I heard the voices of fear when her lips said words of courage to me as we sat together on the first evening after we were married and moved into this house.

It would be strange if I could sit here, as I am doing now, while my own face floated across the picture made by the yellow house and the window. It would be strange and beautiful if I could meet my wife, come into her presence.

The woman whose face floated across my picture just now knows nothing of me. I know nothing of her. She has gone off, along a street. The voices of her mind are talking. I am here in this room, as alone as ever any man God made.

It would be strange and beautiful if I could float my face across my picture. If my floating face could come into her presence, if it could come into the presence of any man or any woman—that would be a strange and beautiful thing to have happen.

* * *

Napoleon went down into a battle riding on a horse.
General Grant went into a wood.
Alexander went down into a battle riding on a horse.

* * *

I'll tell you what—sometimes the whole life of this world floats in a human face in my mind. The unconscious face of the world stops and stands still before me.

Why do I not say a word out of myself to the others? Why, in all our life together, have I never been able to break through the wall to my wife?

Already I have written three hundred, four hundred thousand words. Are there no words that lead into life? Some day I shall speak to myself. Some day I shall make a testament unto myself.

BROTHERS

I AM at my house in the country and it is late October. It rains. Back of my house is a forest and in front there is a road and beyond that open fields. The country is one of low hills, flattening suddenly into plains. Some twenty miles away, across the flat country, lies the huge city Chicago.

On this rainy day the leaves of the trees that line the road before my window are falling like rain, the yellow, red and golden leaves fall straight down heavily. The rain beats them brutally down. They are denied a last golden flash across the sky. In October leaves should be carried away, out over the plains, in a wind. They should go dancing away.

Yesterday morning I arose at daybreak and went for a walk. There was a heavy fog and I lost myself in it. I went down into the plains and returned to the hills, and everywhere the fog was as a wall before me. Out of it trees sprang suddenly, grotesquely, as in a city street late at night people come suddenly out of the darkness into the circle of light under a street lamp. Above there was the light of day forcing itself slowly into the fog. The fog moved slowly. The tops of trees moved slowly. Under the trees the fog was dense, purple. It was like smoke lying in the streets of a factory town.

An old man came up to me in the fog. I know him well. The people here call him insane. "He is a little cracked," they say. He lives alone in a little house buried deep in the forest and has a small dog he carries always in his arms. On many mornings I have met him walking on the road and he has told me of men and women who are his brothers and sisters, his cousins, aunts, uncles, brothers-in-law. It is confusing. He cannot draw close to people near at hand so he gets hold of a name out of a newspaper and his mind plays with it. On one morning he told me he was a cousin to the man named Cox who at the time when I write is a candidate for the presidency. On another morning he told me that Caruso the singer had married a woman who was his sister-in-law. "She is my wife's sister," he said, holding the little dog close. His grey watery eyes looked appealing up to me. He wanted me to believe. "My wife was a sweet slim girl," he declared. "We lived together in a big house and in the morning walked about arm in arm. Now her sister has married Caruso the singer. He is of my family now."

As someone had told me the old man had never married, I went away wondering. One morning in early September I came upon him sitting under a tree beside a path near his house. The dog barked at me

and then ran and crept into his arms. At that time
the Chicago newspapers were filled with the story of
a millionaire who had got into trouble with his wife
because of an intimacy with an actress. The old man
told me that the actress was his sister. He is sixty
years old and the actress whose story appeared in the
newspapers is twenty but he spoke of their childhood
together. "You would not realize it to see us now
but we were poor then," he said. "It's true. We
lived in a little house on the side of a hill. Once when
there was a storm, the wind nearly swept our house
away. How the wind blew! Our father was a carpenter and he built strong houses for other people
but our own house he did not build very strong!" He
shook his head sorrowfully. "My sister the actress
has got into trouble. Our house is not built very
strongly," he said as I went away along the path.

*   *   *

For a month, two months, the Chicago newspapers,
that are delivered every morning in our village, have
been filled with the story of a murder. A man there
has murdered his wife and there seems no reason for
the deed. The tale runs something like this—

The man, who is now on trial in the courts and will
no doubt be hanged, worked in a bicycle factory where
he was a foreman and lived with his wife and his
wife's mother in an apartment in Thirty-second Street.
He loved a girl who worked in the office of the fac-

tory where he was employed. She came from a town in Iowa and when she first came to the city lived with her aunt who has since died. To the foreman, a heavy stolid looking man with grey eyes, she seemed the most beautiful woman in the world. Her desk was by a window at an angle of the factory, a sort of wing of the building, and the foreman, down in the shop had a desk by another window. He sat at his desk making out sheets containing the record of the work done by each man in his department. When he looked up he could see the girl sitting at work at her desk. The notion got into his head that she was peculiarly lovely. He did not think of trying to draw close to her or of winning her love. He looked at her as one might look at a star or across a country of low hills in October when the leaves of the trees are all red and yellow gold. "She is a pure, virginal thing," he thought vaguely. "What can she be thinking about as she sits there by the window at work."

In fancy the foreman took the girl from Iowa home with him to his apartment in Thirty-second Street and into the presence of his wife and his mother-in-law. All day in the shop and during the evening at home he carried her figure about with him in his mind. As he stood by a window in his apartment and looked out toward the Illinois Central railroad tracks and beyond the tracks to the lake, the girl was there beside him. Down below women walked in the street and in every woman he saw there was something of the Iowa girl. One woman walked as she did, another made a gesture with her hand that reminded of her. All the women he saw except his wife and his mother-in-law were like the girl he had taken inside himself.

The two women in his own house puzzled and confused him. They became suddenly unlovely and commonplace. His wife in particular was like some strange unlovely growth that had attached itself to his body.

In the evening after the day at the factory he went home to his own place and had dinner. He had always been a silent man and when he did not talk no one minded. After dinner he with his wife went to a picture show. There were two children and his wife expected another. They came into the apartment and sat down. The climb up two flights of stairs had wearied his wife. She sat in a chair beside her mother groaning with weariness.

The mother-in-law was the soul of goodness. She took the place of a servant in the home and got no pay. When her daughter wanted to go to a picture show she waved her hand and smiled. "Go on," she said. "I don't want to go. I'd rather sit here." She got a book and sat reading. The little boy of nine awoke and cried. He wanted to sit on the po-po. The mother-in-law attended to that.

After the man and his wife came home the three
people sat in silence for an hour or two before bed
time. The man pretended to read a newspaper. He
looked at his hands. Although he had washed them
carefully grease from the bicycle frames left dark
stains under the nails. He thought of the Iowa girl
and of her white quick hands playing over the keys of
a typewriter. He felt dirty and uncomfortable.

The girl at the factory knew the foreman had
fallen in love with her and the thought excited her a
little. Since her aunt's death she had gone to live in
a rooming house and had nothing to do in the evening.
Although the foreman meant nothing to her she could
in a way use him. To her he became a symbol. Sometimes he came into the office and stood for a moment
by the door. His large hands were covered with black
grease. She looked at him without seeing. In his
place in her imagination stood a tall slender young
man. Of the foreman she saw only the grey eyes that
began to burn with a strange fire. The eyes expressed
eagerness, a humble and devout eagerness. In the
presence of a man with such eyes she felt she need not
be afraid.

She wanted a lover who would come to her with
such a look in his eyes. Occasionally, perhaps once in
two weeks, she stayed a little late at the office, pretending to have work that must be finished. Through
the window she could see the foreman waiting. When

everyone had gone she closed her desk and went into the street. At the same moment the foreman came out at the factory door.

They walked together along the street a half dozen blocks to where she got aboard her car. The factory was in a place called South Chicago and as they went along evening was coming on. The streets were lined with small unpainted frame houses and dirty faced children ran screaming in the dusty roadway. They crossed over a bridge. Two abandoned coal barges lay rotting in the stream.

He went by her side walking heavily and striving to conceal his hands. He had scrubbed them carefully before leaving the factory but they seemed to him like heavy dirty pieces of waste matter hanging at his side. Their walking together happened but a few times and during one summer. "It's hot," he said. He never spoke to her of anything but the weather. "It's hot," he said. "I think it may rain."

She dreamed of the lover who would some time come, a tall fair young man, a rich man owning houses and lands. The workingman who walked beside her had nothing to do with her conception of love. She walked with him, stayed at the office until the others had gone to walk unobserved with him because of his eyes, because of the eager thing in his eyes that was at the same time humble, that bowed down to her. In his presence there was no danger, could be no danger.

He would never attempt to approach too closely, to touch her with his hands. She was safe with him.

In his apartment in the evening the man sat under the electric light with his wife and his mother-in-law. In the next room his two children were asleep. In a short time his wife would have another child. He had been with her to a picture show and in a short time they would get into bed together.

He would lie awake thinking, would hear the creaking of the springs of a bed where, in another room, his mother-in-law was crawling between the sheets. Life was too intimate. He would lie awake eager, expectant—expecting, what?

Nothing. Presently one of the children would cry. It wanted to get out of bed and sit on the po-po. Nothing strange or unusual or lovely would or could happen. Life was too close, intimate. Nothing that could happen in the apartment could in any way stir him; the things his wife might say, her occasional half-hearted outbursts of passion, the goodness of his mother-in-law who did the work of a servant without pay—

He sat in the apartment under the electric light pretending to read a newspaper—thinking. He looked at his hands. They were large, shapeless, a working-man's hands.

The figure of the girl from Iowa walked about the room. With her he went out of the apartment and walked in silence through miles of streets. It was not necessary to say words. He walked with her by a sea, along the crest of a mountain. The night was clear and silent and the stars shone. She also was a star. It was not necessary to say words.

Her eyes were like stars and her lips were like soft hills rising out of dim, star lit plains. "She is unattainable, she is far off like the stars," he thought. "She is unattainable like the stars but unlike the stars she breathes, she lives, like myself she has being."

One evening, some six weeks ago, the man who worked as foreman in the bicycle factory killed his wife and he is now in the courts being tried for murder. Every day the newspapers are filled with the story. On the evening of the murder he had taken his wife as usual to a picture show and they started home at nine. In Thirty-second Street, at a corner near their apartment building, the figure of a man darted suddenly out of an alleyway and then darted back again. The incident may have put the idea of killing his wife into the man's head.

They got to the entrance to the apartment building and stepped into a dark hallway. Then quite suddenly and apparently without thought the man took a knife out of his pocket. "Suppose that man who darted into the alleyway had intended to kill us," he thought. Opening the knife he whirled about and struck at his wife. He struck twice, a dozen times—madly. There was a scream and his wife's body fell.

The janitor had neglected to light the gas in the lower hallway. Afterwards, the foreman decided, that was the reason he did it, that and the fact that the dark slinking figure of a man darted out of an alleyway and then darted back again. "Surely," he told himself, "I could never have done it had the gas been lighted."

He stood in the hallway thinking. His wife was dead and with her had died her unborn child. There was a sound of doors opening in the apartments above. For several minutes nothing happened. His wife and her unborn child were dead—that was all.

He ran upstairs thinking quickly. In the darkness on the lower stairway he had put the knife back into his pocket and, as it turned out later, there was no blood on his hands or on his clothes. The knife he later washed carefully in the bathroom, when the excitement had died down a little. He told everyone the same story. "There has been a holdup," he explained. "A man came slinking out of an alleyway and followed me and my wife home. He followed us into the hallway of the building and there was no light. The janitor has neglected to light the gas." Well—there had been a struggle and in the darkness his wife had been killed. He could not tell how it had happened. "There was no light. The janitor has neglected to light the gas," he kept saying.

For a day or two they did not question him specially and he had time to get rid of the knife. He took a long walk and threw it away into the river in South Chicago where the two abandoned coal barges lay rotting under the bridge, the bridge he had crossed when on the summer evenings he walked to the street car with the girl who was virginal and pure, who was far off and unattainable, like a star and yet not like a star.

And then he was arrested and right away he confessed—told everything. He said he did not know why he killed his wife and was careful to say nothing of the girl at the office. The newspapers tried to discover the motive for the crime. They are still trying. Someone had seen him on the few evenings when he walked with the girl and she was dragged into the affair and had her picture printed in the papers. That has been annoying for her as of course she has been able to prove she had nothing to do with the man.

* * *

Yesterday morning a heavy fog lay over our village here at the edge of the city and I went for a long walk in the early morning. As I returned out of the lowlands into our hill country I met the old man whose family has so many and such strange ramifications. For a time he walked beside me holding the little dog in his arms. It was cold and the dog whined and shivered. In the fog the old man's face was indistinct. It moved slowly back and forth with the fog banks of the upper air and with the tops of trees. He spoke of the man who has killed his wife and whose name is being shouted in the pages of the city newspapers that come to our village each morning. As he walked beside me he launched into a long tale concerning a life he and his brother, who has now become a murderer, once lived together. "He is my brother," he said over and over, shaking his head. He seemed afraid I would not believe. There was a fact that must be established. "We were boys together that man and I," he began again. "You see we played together in a barn back of our father's house. Our father went away to sea in a ship. That is the way our names became confused. You understand that. We have different names, but we are brothers. We had the same father. We played together in a barn back of our father's house. For hours we lay together in the hay in the barn and it was warm there."

In the fog the slender body of the old man became like a little gnarled tree. Then it became a thing suspended in air. It swung back and forth like a body hanging on the gallows. The face beseeched me to believe the story the lips were trying to tell. In my mind everything concerning the relationship of men and women became confused, a muddle. The spirit of the man who had killed his wife came into the body of the little old man there by the roadside.

It was striving to tell me the story it would never be able to tell in the court room in the city, in the presence of the judge. The whole story of mankind's loneliness, of the effort to reach out to unattainable beauty tried to get itself expressed from the lips of a mumbling old man, crazed with loneliness, who stood by the side of a country road on a foggy morning holding a little dog in his arms.

The arms of the old man held the dog so closely that it began to whine with pain. A sort of convulsion shook his body. The soul seemed striving to wrench itself out of the body, to fly away through the fog, down across the plain to the city, to the singer, the politician, the millionaire, the murderer, to its brothers, cousins, sisters, down in the city. The intensity of the old man's desire was terrible and in sympathy my body began to tremble. His arms tightened about the body of the little dog so that it cried with pain. I stepped forward and tore the arms away and the dog fell to the ground and lay whining. No doubt it had been injured. Perhaps ribs had been crushed. The old man stared at the dog lying at his feet as in the hallway of the apartment building the worker from the bicycle factory had stared at his dead wife. "We are brothers," he said again. "We have different names but we are brothers. Our father you understand went off to sea."

*   *   *

I am sitting in my house in the country and it rains. Before my eyes the hills fall suddenly away and there are the flat plains and beyond the plains the city. An hour ago the old man of the house in the forest went past my door and the little dog was not with him. It may be that as we talked in the fog he crushed the life out of his companion. It may be that the dog like the workman's wife and her unborn child is now dead. The leaves of the trees that line the road before my window are falling like rain—the yellow, red and golden leaves fall straight down, heavily. The rain beat them brutally down. They are denied a last golden flash across the sky. In October leaves should be carried away, out over the plains, in a wind. They should go dancing away.

THE DOOR OF THE TRAP

WINIFRED WALKER understood some things clearly enough. She understood that when a man is put behind iron bars he is in prison. Marriage was marriage to her.

It was that to her husband Hugh Walker, too, as he found out. Still he didn't understand. It might have been better had he understood, then he might at least have found himself. He didn't. After his marriage five or six years passed like shadows of wind blown trees playing on a wall. He was in a drugged, silent state. In the morning and evening every day he saw his wife. Occasionally something happened within him and he kissed her. Three children were born. He taught mathematics in the little college at Union Valley, Illinois, and waited.

For what? He began to ask himself that question. It came to him at first faintly like an echo. Then it became an insistent question. "I want answering," the question seemed to say. "Stop fooling along. Give your attention to me."

Hugh walked through the streets of the Illinois town. "Well, I'm married. I have children," he muttered.

He went home to his own house. He did not have
to live within his income from the little college, and
so the house was rather large and comfortably furnished. There was a negro woman who took care of
the children and another who cooked and did the housework. One of the women was in the habit of crooning
low soft negro songs. Sometimes Hugh stopped at the
house door and listened. He could see through the
glass in the door into the room where his family was
gathered. Two children played with blocks on the
floor. His wife sat sewing. The old negress sat in a
rocking chair with his youngest child, a baby, in her
arms. The whole room seemed under the spell of the
crooning voice. Hugh fell under the spell. He
waited in silence. The voice carried him far away
somewhere, into forests, along the edges of swamps.
There was nothing very definite about his thinking.
He would have given a good deal to be able to be
definite.

He went inside the house. "Well, here I am," his
mind seemed to say, "here I am. This is my house,
these are my children."

He looked at his wife Winifred. She had grown
a little plump since their marriage. "Perhaps it is
the mother in her coming out, she has had three children," he thought.

The crooning old negro woman went away, taking
the youngest child with her. He and Winifred held

a fragmentary conversation. "Have you been well to-day, dear?" she asked. "Yes," he answered.

If the two older children were intent on their play his chain of thought was not broken. His wife never broke it as the children did when they came running to pull and tear at him. Throughout the early evening, after the children went to bed, the surface of the shell of him was not broken at all. A brother college professor and his wife came in or he and Winifred went to a neighbor's house. There was talk. Even when he and Winifred were alone together in the house there was talk. "The shutters are becoming loose," she said. The house was an old one and had green shutters. They were continually coming loose and at night blew back and forth on their hinges making a loud banging noise.

Hugh made some remark. He said he would see a carpenter about the shutters. Then his mind began playing away, out of his wife's presence, out of the house, in another sphere. "I am a house and my shutters are loose," his mind said. He thought of himself as a living thing inside a shell, trying to break out. To avoid distracting conversation he got a book and pretended to read. When his wife had also begun to read he watched her closely, intently. Her nose was so and so and her eyes so and so. She had a little habit with her hands. When she became lost in the pages of a book the hand crept up to her cheek, touched it and then was put down again. Her hair was not in very good order. Since her marriage and the coming of the children she had not taken good care of her body. When she read her body slumped down in the chair. It became bag-like. She was one whose race had been run.

Hugh's mind played all about the figure of his wife but did not really approach the woman who sat before him. It was so with his children. Sometimes, just for a moment, they were living things to him, things as alive as his own body. Then for long periods they seemed to go far away like the crooning voice of the negress.

It was odd that the negress was always real enough. He felt an understanding existed between himself and the negress. She was outside his life. He could look at her as at a tree. Sometimes in the evening when she had been putting the children to bed in the upper part of the house and when he sat with a book in his hand pretending to read, the old black woman came softly through the room, going toward the kitchen. She did not look at Winifred, but at Hugh. He thought there was a strange, soft light in her old eyes. "I understand you, my son," her eyes seemed to say.

Hugh was determined to get his life cleaned up if he could manage it. "All right, then," he said, as though speaking to a third person in the room. He was quite sure there was a third person there and that the third person was within himself, inside his body. He addressed the third person.

"Well, there is this woman, this person I married, she has the air of something accomplished," he said, as though speaking aloud. Sometimes it almost seemed to him he had spoken aloud and he looked quickly and sharply at his wife. She continued reading, lost in her book. "That may be it," he went on. "She has had these children. They are accomplished facts to her. They came out of her body, not out of mine. Her body has done something. Now it rests. If she is becoming a little bag-like, that's all right."

He got up and making some trivial excuse got out of the room and out of the house. In his youth and young manhood the long periods of walking straight ahead through the country, that had come upon him like visitations of some recurring disease, had helped. Walking solved nothing. It only tired his body, but when his body was tired he could sleep. After many days of walking and sleeping something occurred. The reality of life was in some queer way re-established in his mind. Some little thing happened. A man walking in the road before him threw a stone at a dog that ran barking out of a farm-house. It was evening perhaps, and he walked in a country of low hills. Suddenly he came out upon the top of one of the hills. Before him the road dipped down into darkness but to the west, across fields, there was a farm-house. The sun had gone down, but a faint glow lit the western horizon. A woman came out of the farmhouse and went toward a barn. He could not see her figure distinctly. She seemed to be carrying something, no doubt a milk pail; she was going to a barn to milk a cow.

The man in the road who had thrown the stone at the farm dog had turned and seen Hugh in the road behind him. He was a little ashamed of having been afraid of the dog. For a moment he seemed about to wait and speak to Hugh, and then was overcome with confusion and hurried away. He was a middle-aged man, but quite suddenly and unexpectedly he looked like a boy.

As for the farm woman, dimly seen going toward a distant barn, she also stopped and looked toward him. It was impossible she should have seen him. She was dressed in white and he could see her but dimly against the blackish green of the trees of an orchard behind her. Still she stood looking and seemed to look directly into his eyes. He had a queer sensation of her having been lifted by an unseen hand and brought to him. It seemed to him he knew all about her life, all about the life of the man who had thrown the stone at the dog.

In his youth, when life had stepped out of his grasp, Hugh had walked and walked until several such things had occurred and then suddenly he was all right again and could again work and live among men.

After his marriage and after such an evening at home he started walking rapidly as soon as he left the house. As quickly as possible he got out of town and struck out along a road that led over the rolling prairie. "Well, I can't walk for days and days as I did once," he thought. "There are certain facts in life and I must face facts. Winifred, my wife, is a fact, and my children are facts. I must get my fingers on facts. I must live by them and with them. It's the way lives are lived."

Hugh got out of town and on to a road that ran between cornfields. He was an athletic looking man and wore loose fitting clothes. He went along distraught and puzzled. In a way he felt like a man capable of taking a man's place in life and in another way he didn't at all.

The country spread out, wide, in all directions. It was always night when he walked thus and he could not see, but the realization of distances was always with him. "Everything goes on and on but I stand still," he thought. He had been a professor in the little college for six years. Young men and women had come into a room and he had taught them. It was nothing. Words and figures had been played with. An effort had been made to arouse minds.

For what?

There was the old question, always coming back,

always wanting answering as a little animal wants food. Hugh gave up trying to answer. He walked rapidly, trying to grow physically tired. He made his mind attend to little things in the effort to forget distances. One night he got out of the road and walked completely around a cornfield. He counted the stalks in each hill of corn and computed the number of stalks in a whole field. "It should yield twelve hundred bushels of corn, that field," he said to himself dumbly, as though it mattered to him. He pulled a little handful of cornsilk out of the top of an ear of corn and played with it. He tried to fashion himself a yellow moustache. "I'd be quite a fellow with a trim yellow moustache," he thought.

One day in his class-room Hugh suddenly began to look with new interest at his pupils. A young girl attracted his attention. She sat beside the son of a Union Valley merchant and the young man was writing something on the back of a book. She looked at it and then turned her head away. The young man waited.

It was winter and the merchant's son had asked the girl to go with him to a skating party. Hugh, however, did not know that. He felt suddenly old. When he asked the girl a question she was confused. Her voice trembled.

When the class was dismissed an amazing thing happened. He asked the merchant's son to stay for a moment and, when the two were alone together in the room, he grew suddenly and furiously angry. His voice was, however, cold and steady. "Young man," he said, " you do not come into this room to write on the back of a book and waste your time. If I see anything of the kind again I'll do something you don't expect. I'll throw you out through a window, that's what I'll do."

Hugh made a gesture and the young man went away, white and silent. Hugh felt miserable. For several days he thought about the girl who had quite accidentally attracted his attention. "I'll get acquainted with her. I'll find out about her," he thought.

It was not an unusual thing for professors in the college at Union Valley to take students home to their houses. Hugh decided he would take the girl to his home. He thought about it several days and late one afternoon saw her going down the college hill ahead of him.

The girl's name was Mary Cochran and she had come to the school but a few months before from a place called Huntersburg, Illinois, no doubt just such another place as Union Valley. He knew nothing of her except that her father was dead, her mother too, perhaps. He walked rapidly down the hill to overtake her. "Miss Cochran," he called, and was surprised to find that his voice trembled a little. "What am I so eager about?" he asked himself.

A new life began in Hugh Walker's house. It was good for the man to have some one there who did not belong to him, and Winifred Walker and the children accepted the presence of the girl. Winifred urged her to come again. She did come several times a week.

To Mary Cochran it was comforting to be in the presence of a family of children. On winter afternoons she took Hugh's two sons and a sled and went to a small hill near the house. Shouts arose. Mary Cochran pulled the sled up the hill and the children followed. Then they all came tearing down together.

The girl, developing rapidly into womanhood, looked upon Hugh Walker as something that stood completely outside her own life. She and the man who had become suddenly and intensely interested in her had little to say to each other and Winifred seemed to have accepted her without question as an addition to the household. Often in the afternoon when the two negro women were busy she went away leaving the two older children in Mary's charge.

It was late afternoon and perhaps Hugh had walked home with Mary from the college. In the spring he worked in the neglected garden. It had been plowed and planted, but he took a hoe and rake and puttered about. The children played about the house with the college girl. Hugh did not look at them but at her. "She is one of the world of people with whom I live and with whom I am supposed to work here," he thought. "Unlike Winifred and these children she does not belong to me. I could go to her now, touch her fingers, look at her and then go away and never see her again."

That thought was a comfort to the distraught man. In the evening when he went out to walk the sense of distance that lay all about him did not tempt him to walk and walk, going half insanely forward for hours, trying to break through an intangible wall.

He thought about Mary Cochran. She was a girl from a country town. She must be like millions of American girls. He wondered what went on in her mind as she sat in his class-room, as she walked beside him along the streets of Union Valley, as she played with the children in the yard beside his house.

In the winter, when in the growing darkness of a late afternoon Mary and the children built a snow man in the yard, he went upstairs and stood in the darkness to look out a window. The tall straight figure of the girl, dimly seen, moved quickly about. "Well, nothing has happened to her. She may be anything or nothing. Her figure is like a young tree that has not borne fruit," he thought. He went away to his own room and sat for a long time in the darkness. That night when he left the house for his evening's walk he did not stay long but hurried home and went to his own room. He locked the door. Unconsciously he did not want Winifred to come to the door and disturb his thoughts. Sometimes she did that.

All the time she read novels. She read the novels of Robert Louis Stevenson. When she had read them all she began again.

Sometimes she came upstairs and stood talking by his door. She told some tale, repeated some wise saying that had fallen unexpectedly from the lips of the children. Occasionally she came into the room and turned out the light. There was a couch by a window. She went to sit on the edge of the couch. Something happened. It was as it had been before their marriage. New life came into her figure. He also went to sit on the couch and she put up her hand and touched his face.

Hugh did not want that to happen now. He stood within the room for a moment and then unlocked the door and went to the head of the stairs. "Be quiet when you come up, Winifred. I have a headache and am going to try to sleep," he lied.

When he had gone back to his own room and locked the door again he felt safe. He did not undress but threw himself on the couch and turned out the light.

He thought about Mary Cochran, the school girl, but was sure he thought about her in a quite impersonal way. She was like the woman going to milk cows he had seen across hills when he was a young fellow and walked far and wide over the country to cure the restlessness in himself. In his life she was like the man who threw the stone at dog.

"Well, she is unformed; she is like a young tree," he told himself again. "People are like that. They just grow up suddenly out of childhood. It will happen to my own children. My little Winifred that cannot yet say words will suddenly be like this girl. I have not selected her to think about for any particular reason. For some reason I have drawn away from life and she has brought me back. It might have happened when I saw a child playing in the street or an old man going up a stairway into a house. She does not belong to me. She will go away out of my sight. Winifred and the children will stay on and on here and I will stay on and on. We are imprisoned by the fact that we belong to each other. This Mary Cochran is free, or at least she is free as far as this prison is concerned. No doubt she will, after a while, make a prison of her own and live in it, but I will have nothing to do with the matter."

By the time Mary Cochran was in her third year in the college at Union Valley she had become almost a fixture in the Walker household. Still she did not know Hugh. She knew the children better than he did, perhaps better than their mother. In the fall she and the two boys went to the woods to gather nuts.

In the winter they went skating on a little pond near the house.

Winifred accepted her as she accepted everything, the service of the two negroes, the coming of the children, the habitual silence of her husband.

And then quite suddenly and unexpectedly Hugh's silence, that had lasted all through his married life, was broken up. He walked homeward with a German who had the chair of modern languages in the school and got into a violent quarrel. He stopped to speak to men on the street. When he went to putter about in the garden he whistled and sang.

One afternoon in the fall he came home and found the whole family assembled in the living room of the house. The children were playing on the floor and the negress sat in the chair by the window with his youngest child in her arms, crooning one of the negro songs. Mary Cochran was there. She sat reading a book.

Hugh walked directly toward her and looked over her shoulder. At that moment Winifred came into the room. He reached forward and snatched the book out of the girl's hands. She looked up startled. With an oath he threw it into the fire that burned in an open grate at the side of the room. A flood of words ran from him. He cursed books and people and schools. "Damn it all," he said. "What makes you want to read about life? What makes people want to think about life? Why don't they live? Why don't they leave books and thoughts and schools alone?"

He turned to look at his wife who had grown pale and stared at him with a queer fixed uncertain stare. The old negro woman got up and went quickly away. The two older children began to cry. Hugh was miserable. He looked at the startled girl in the chair who also had tears in her eyes, and at his wife. His fingers pulled nervously at his coat. To the two women he looked like a boy who had been caught stealing food in a pantry. "I am having one of my silly irritable spells," he said, looking at his wife but in reality addressing the girl. "You see I am more serious than I pretend to be. I was not irritated by your book but by something else. I see so much that can be done in life and I do so little."

He went upstairs to his own room wondering why he had lied to the two women, why he continually lied to himself.

Did he lie to himself? He tried to answer the question but couldn't. He was like one who walks in the darkness of the hallway of a house and comes to a blank wall. The old desire to run away from life, to wear himself out physically, came back upon him like a madness.

For a long time he stood in the darkness inside his own room. The children stopped crying and the house

became quiet again. He could hear his wife's voice
speaking softly and presently the back door of the
house banged and he knew the schoolgirl had gone
away.

Life in the house began again. Nothing happened.
Hugh ate his dinner in silence and went for a long
walk. For two weeks Mary Cochran did not come to
his house and then one day he saw her on the college
grounds. She was no longer one of his pupils. "Please
do not desert us because of my rudeness," he said.
The girl blushed and said nothing. When he got
home that evening she was in the yard beside the
house playing with the children. He went at once to
his own room. A hard smile came and went on his
face. "She isn't like a young tree any more. She is
almost like Winifred. She is almost like a person
who belongs here, who belongs to me and my life,"
he thought.

Mary Cochran's visits to the Walker household
came to an end very abruptly. One evening when
Hugh was in his room she came up the stairway with
the two boys. She had dined with the family and
was putting the two boys into their beds. It was a
privilege she claimed when she dined with the
Walkers.

Hugh had hurried upstairs immediately after din-
ing. He knew where his wife was. She was down-

stairs, sitting under a lamp, reading one of the books of Robert Louis Stevenson.

For a long time Hugh could hear the voices of his children on the floor above. Then the thing happened.

Mary Cochran came down the stairway that led past the door of his room. She stopped, turned back and climbed the stairs again to the room above. Hugh arose and stepped into the hallway. The schoolgirl had returned to the children's room because she had been suddenly overtaken with a hunger to kiss Hugh's oldest boy, now a lad of nine. She crept into the room and stood for a long time looking at the two boys, who unaware of her presence had gone to sleep. Then she stole forward and kissed the boy lightly. When she went out of the room Hugh stood in the darkness waiting for her. He took hold of her hand and led her down the stairs to his own room.

She was terribly afraid and her fright in an odd way pleased him. "Well," he whispered, "you can't understand now what's going to happen here but some day you will. I'm going to kiss you and then I'm going to ask you to go out of this house and never come back."

He held the girl against his body and kissed her upon the cheeks and lips. When he led her to the door she was so weak with fright and with new,

strange, trembling desires that she could with difficulty make her way down the stair and into his wife's
presence. "She will lie now," he thought, and heard
her voice coming up the stairs like an echo to his
thoughts. "I have a terrible headache. I must hurry
home," he heard her voice saying. The voice was dull
and heavy. It was not the voice of a young girl.

"She is no longer like a young tree," he thought.
He was glad and proud of what he had done. When
he heard the door at the back of the house close softly
his heart jumped. A strange quivering light came
into his eyes. "She will be imprisoned but I will have
nothing to do with it. She will never belong to me.
My hands will never build a prison for her," he
thought with grim pleasure.

THE NEW ENGLANDER

HER name was Elsie Leander and her girlhood was spent on her father's farm in Vermont. For several generations the Leanders had all lived on the same farm and had all married thin women, and so she was thin. The farm lay in the shadow of a mountain and the soil was not very rich. From the beginning and for several generations there had been a great many sons and few daughters in the family. The sons had gone west or to New York City and the daughters had stayed at home and thought such thoughts as come to New England women who see the sons of their fathers' neighbors slipping away, one by one, into the West.

Her father's house was a small white frame affair and when you went out at the back door, past a small barn and chicken house, you got into a path that ran up the side of a hill and into an orchard. The trees were all old and gnarled. At the back of the orchard the hill dropped away and bare rocks showed.

Inside the fence a large grey rock stuck high up out of the ground. As Elsie sat with her back to the rock, with a mangled hillside at her feet, she could see sev-

134

eral large mountains, apparently but a short distance away, and between herself and the mountains lay many tiny fields surrounded by neatly built stone walls. Everywhere rocks appeared. Large ones, too heavy to be moved, stuck out of the ground in the centre of the fields. The fields were like cups filled with a green liquid that turned grey in the fall and white in the winter. The mountains, far off but apparently near at hand, were like giants ready at any moment to reach out their hands and take the cups one by one and drink off the green liquid. The large rocks in the fields were like the thumbs of the giants.

Elsie had three brothers, born before her, but they had all gone away. Two of them had gone to live with her uncle in the West and her oldest brother had gone to New York City where he had married and prospered. All through his youth and manhood her father had worked hard and had lived a hard life, but his son in New York City had begun to send money home, and after that things went better. He still worked every day about the barn or in the fields but he did not worry about the future. Elsie's mother did house work in the mornings and in the afternoons sat in a rocking chair in her tiny living room and thought of her sons while she crocheted table covers and tidies for the backs of chairs. She was a silent woman, very thin and with very thin bony hands. She did not ease herself into a rocking chair but sat down and got up suddenly, and when she crocheted her back was as straight as the back of a drill sergeant.

The mother rarely spoke to the daughter. Sometimes in the afternoons as the younger woman went up the hillside to her place by the rock at the back of the orchard, her father came out of the barn and stopped her. He put a hand on her shoulder and asked her where she was going. "To the rock," she said and her father laughed. His laughter was like the creaking of a rusty barn door hinge and the hand he had laid on her shoulders was thin like her own hands and like her mother's hands. The father went into the barn shaking his head. "She's like her mother. She is herself like a rock," he thought. At the head of the path that led from the house to the orchard there was a great cluster of bayberry bushes. The New England farmer came out of his barn to watch his daughter go along the path, but she had disappeared behind the bushes. He looked away past his house to the fields and to the mountains in the distance. He also saw the green cup-like fields and the grim mountains. There was an almost imperceptible tightening of the muscles of his half worn-out old body. For a long time he stood in silence and then, knowing from long experience the danger of having thoughts, he went back into the barn and busied himself with the mending of an agricultural tool that had been mended many times before.

The son of the Leanders who went to live in New York City was the father of one son, a thin sensitive boy who looked like Elsie. The son died when he was twenty-three years old and some years later the father died and left his money to the old people on the New England farm. The two Leanders who had gone west had lived there with their father's brother, a farmer, until they grew into manhood. Then Will, the younger, got a job on a railroad. He was killed one winter morning. It was a cold snowy day and when the freight train he was in charge of as conductor left the city of Des Moines, he started to run over the tops of the cars. His feet slipped and he shot down into space. That was the end of him.

Of the new generation there was only Elsie and her brother Tom, whom she had never seen, left alive. Her father and mother talked of going west to Tom for two years before they came to a decision. Then it took another year to dispose of the farm and make preparations. During the whole time Elsie did not think much about the change about to take place in her life.

The trip west on the railroad train jolted Elsie out of herself. In spite of her detached attitude toward life she became excited. Her mother sat up very straight and stiff in the seat in the sleeping car and her father walked up and down in the aisle. After a night when the younger of the two women did not sleep but lay awake with red burning cheeks and with her thin fingers incessantly picking at the bed clothes in her berth while the train went through towns and cities, crawled up the sides of hills and fell down into forest-clad valleys, she got up and dressed to sit all day looking at a new kind of land. The train ran for a day and through another sleepless night in a flat land where every field was as large as a farm in her own country. Towns appeared and disappeared in a continual procession. The whole land was so unlike anything she had ever known that she began to feel unlike herself. In the valley where she had been born and where she had lived all her days everything had an air of finality. Nothing could be changed. The tiny fields were chained to the earth. They were fixed in their places and surrounded by aged stone walls. The fields like the mountains that looked down at them were as unchangeable as the passing days. She had a feeling they had always been so, would always be so.

Elsie sat like her mother, upright in the car seat and with a back like the back of a drill sergeant. The train ran swiftly along through Ohio and Indiana. Her thin hands like her mother's hands were crossed and locked. One passing casually through the car might have thought both women prisoners handcuffed and bound to their seats. Night came on and she again got into her berth. Again she lay awake and her thin cheeks became flushed, but she thought new thoughts. Her hands were no longer gripped together and she did not pick at the bed clothes. Twice during the night she stretched herself and yawned, a thing she had never in her life done before. The train stopped at a town on the prairies, and as there was something the matter with one of the wheels of the car in which she lay the trainsmen came with flaming torches to tinker it. There was a great pounding and shouting. When the train went on its way she wanted to get out of her berth and run up and down in the aisle of the car. The fancy had come to her that the men tinkering with the car wheel were new men out of the new land who with strong hammers had broken away the doors of her prison. They had destroyed forever the programme she had made for her life.

Elsie was filled with joy at the thought that the train was still going on into the West. She wanted to go on forever in a straight line into the unknown. She fancied herself no longer on a train and imagined she had become a winged thing flying through space. Her long years of sitting alone by the rock on the New England farm had got her into the habit of expressing her thoughts aloud. Her thin voice broke the silence that lay over the sleeping car and her father and mother, both also lying awake, sat up in their berth to listen.

Tom Leander, the only living male representative of the new generation of Leanders, was a loosely built man of forty inclined to corpulency. At twenty he had married the daughter of a neighboring farmer, and when his wife inherited some money she and Tom moved into the town of Apple Junction in Iowa where Tom opened a grocery. The venture prospered as did Tom's matrimonial venture. When his brother died in New York City and his father, mother, and sister decided to come west Tom was already the father of a daughter and four sons.

On the prairies north of town and in the midst of a vast level stretch of cornfields, there was a partly completed brick house that had belonged to a rich farmer named Russell who had begun to build the house intending to make it the most magnificent place in the county, but when it was almost completed he had found himself without money and heavily in debt. The farm, consisting of several hundred acres of corn land, had been split into three farms and sold. No one had wanted the huge unfinished brick house. For years it had stood vacant, its windows staring out over the fields that had been planted almost up to the door.

In buying the Russell house Tom was moved by two motives. He had a notion that in New England the Leanders had been rather magnificent people. His memory of his father's place in the Vermont valley was shadowy, but in speaking of it to his wife he became very definite. "We had good blood in us, we Leanders," he said, straightening his shoulders. "We lived in a big house. We were important people."

Wanting his father and mother to feel at home in the new place, Tom had also another motive. He was not a very energetic man and, although he had done well enough as keeper of a grocery, his success was largely due to the boundless energy of his wife. She did not pay much attention to her household and her children, like little animals, had to take care of themselves, but in any matter concerning the store her word was law.

To have his father the owner of the Russell place Tom felt would establish him as a man of consequence in the eyes of his neighbors. "I can tell you what, they're used to a big house," he said to his wife. "I tell you what, my people are used to living in style."

The exaltation that had come over Elsie on the train wore away in the presence of the grey empty Iowa fields, but something of the effect of it remained with her for months. In the big brick house life went on much as it had in the tiny New England house where she had always lived. The Leanders installed themselves in three or four rooms on the ground floor. After a few weeks the furniture that had been shipped by freight arrived and was hauled out from town in

one of Tom's grocery wagons. There were three or
four acres of ground covered with great piles of
boards the unsuccessful farmer had intended to use in
the building of stables. Tom sent men to haul the
boards away and Elsie's father prepared to plant a
garden. They had come west in April and as soon
as they were installed in the house ploughing and
planting began in the fields nearby. The habit of a
lifetime returned to the daughter of the house. In
the new place there was no gnarled orchard surrounded by a half-ruined stone fence. All of the
fences in all of the fields that stretched away out of
sight to the north, south, east, and west were made
of wire and looked like spider webs against the black-
ness of the ground when it had been freshly ploughed.

There was however the house itself. It was like
an island rising out of the sea. In an odd way the
house, although it was less than ten years old, was
very old. Its unnecessary bigness represented an old
impulse in men. Elsie felt that. At the east side
there was a door leading to a stairway that ran into
the upper part of the house that was kept locked.
Two or three stone steps led up to it. Elsie could sit
on the top step with her back against the door and
gaze into the distance without being disturbed. Almost at her feet began the fields that seemed to go on
and on forever. The fields were like the waters of a
sea. Men came to plough and plant. Giant horses

moved in a procession across the prairies. A young man who drove six horses came directly toward her. She was fascinated. The breasts of the horses as they came forward with bowed heads seemed like the breasts of giants. The soft spring air that lay over the fields was also like a sea. The horses were giants walking on the floor of a sea. With their breasts they pushed the waters of the sea before them. They were pushing the waters out of the basin of the sea. The young man who drove them also was a giant.

Elsie pressed her body against the closed door at the top of the steps. In the garden back of the house she could hear her father at work. He was raking dry masses of weeds off the ground preparatory to spading it for a family garden. He had always worked in a tiny confined place and would do the same thing here. In this vast open place he would work with small tools, doing little things with infinite care, raising little vegetables. In the house her mother would crochet little tidies. She herself would be small. She would press her body against the door of the house, try to get herself out of sight. Only the feeling that sometimes took possession of her, and that did not form itself into a thought would be large.

The six horses turned at the fence and the outside horse got entangled in the traces. The driver swore vigorously. Then he turned and started at the pale

New Englander and with another oath pulled the heads
of the horses about and drove away into the distance.
The field in which he was ploughing contained two
hundred acres. Elsie did not wait for him to return
but went into the house and sat with folded arms in a
room. The house she thought was a ship floating in a
sea on the floor of which giants went up and down.

May came and then June. In the great fields work
was always going on and Elsie became somewhat used
to the sight of the young man in the field that came
down to the steps. Sometimes when he drove his
horses down to the wire fence he smiled and nodded.

In the month of August, when it is very hot, the corn
in Iowa fields grows until the corn stalks resemble
young trees. The corn fields become forests. The
time for the cultivating of the corn has passed and
weeds grow thick between the corn rows. The men
with their giant horses have gone away. Over the
immense fields silence broods.

When the time of the laying-by of the crop came
that first summer after Elsie's arrival in the West her
mind, partially awakened by the strangeness of the
railroad trip, awakened again. She did not feel like
a staid thin woman with a back like the back of a drill
sergeant, but like something new and as strange as the
new land into which she had come to live. For a time
she did not know what was the matter. In the field

the corn had grown so high that she could not see into the distance. The corn was like a wall and the little bare spot of land on which her father's house stood was like a house built behind the walls of a prison. For a time she was depressed, thinking that she had come west into a wide open country, only to find herself locked up more closely than ever.

An impulse came to her. She arose and going down three or four steps seated herself almost on a level with the ground.

Immediately she got a sense of release. She could not see over the corn but she could see under it. The corn had long wide leaves that met over the rows. The rows became long tunnels running away into infinity. Out of the black ground grew weeds that made a soft carpet of green. From above light sifted down. The corn rows were mysteriously beautiful. They were warm passageways running out into life. She got up from the steps and, walking timidly to the wire fence that separated her from the field, put her hand between the wires and took hold of one of the corn stalks. For some reason after she had touched the strong young stalk and had held it for a moment firmly in her hand she grew afraid. Running quickly back to the step she sat down and covered her face with her hands. Her body trembled. She tried to imagine herself crawling through the fence and wandering along one of the passageways. The thought of trying the experiment fascinated but at the same time terrified. She got quickly up and went into the house.

One Saturday night in August Elsie found herself unable to sleep. Thoughts, more definite than any she had ever known before, came into her mind. It was a quiet hot night and her bed stood near a window. Her room was the only one the Leanders occupied on the second floor of the house. At midnight a little breeze came up from the south and when she sat up in bed the floor of corn tassels lying below her line of sight looked in the moonlight like the face of a sea just stirred by a gentle breeze.

A murmuring began in the corn and murmuring thoughts and memories awoke in her mind. The long wide succulent leaves had begun to dry in the intense heat of the August days and as the wind stirred the corn they rubbed against each other. A call, far away, as of a thousand voices arose. She imagined the voices were like the voices of children. They were not like her brother Tom's children, noisy boisterous little animals, but something quite different, tiny little things with large eyes and thin sensitive hands. One after another they crept into her arms. She became so excited over the fancy that she sat up in bed and taking a pillow into her arms held it against her breast. The figure of her cousin, the pale sensitive young Leander who had lived with his father in

New York City and who had died at the age of twenty-three, came into her mind. It was as though the young man had come suddenly into the room. She dropped the pillow and sat waiting, intense, expectant.

Young Harry Leander had come to visit his cousin on the New England farm during the late summer of the year before he died. He had stayed there for a month and almost every afternoon had gone with Elsie to sit by the rock at the back of the orchard. One afternoon when they had both been for a long time silent he began to talk. "I want to go live in the West," he said. "I want to go live in the West. I want to grow strong and be a man," he repeated. Tears came into his eyes.

They got up to return to the house, Elsie walking in silence beside the young man. The moment marked a high spot in her life. A strange trembling eagerness for something she had not realized in her experience of life had taken possession of her. They went in silence through the orchard but when they came to the bayberry bush her cousin stopped in the path and turned to face her. "I want you to kiss me," he said eagerly, stepping toward her.

A fluttering uncertainty had taken possession of Elsie and had been transmitted to her cousin. After he had made the sudden and unexpected demand and had stepped so close to her that his breath could be felt on her cheek, his own cheeks became scarlet and

his hand that had taken her hand trembled. "Well,
I wish I were strong. I only wish I were strong," he
said hesitatingly and turning walked away along the
path toward the house.

And in the strange new house, set like an island in its
sea of corn, Harry Leander's voice seemed to arise
again above the fancied voices of the children that had
been coming out of the fields. Elsie got out of bed
and walked up and down in the dim light coming
through the window. Her body trembled violently.
"I want you to kiss me," the voice said again and to
quiet it and to quiet also the answering voice in herself she went to kneel by the bed and taking the pillow
again into her arms pressed it against her face.

Tom Leander came with his wife and family to visit
his father and mother on Sundays. The family appeared at about ten o'clock in the morning. When
the wagon turned out of the road that ran past the
Russell place Tom shouted. There was a field between the house and the road and the wagon could
not be seen as it came along the narrow way through
the corn. After Tom had shouted, his daughter Elizabeth, a tall girl of sixteen, jumped out of the wagon.
All five children came tearing toward the house through
the corn. A series of wild shouts arose on the still
morning air.

The groceryman had brought food from the store.

When the horse had been unhitched and put into a shed he and his wife began to carry packages into the house. The four Leander boys, accompanied by their sister, disappeared into the near-by fields. Three dogs that had trotted out from town under the wagon accompanied the children. Two or three children and occasionally a young man from a neighboring farm had come to join in the fun. Elsie's sister-in-law dismissed them all with a wave of her hand. With a wave of her hand she also brushed Elsie aside. Fires were lighted and the house reeked with the smell of cooking. Elsie went to sit on the step at the side of the house. The corn fields that had been so quiet rang with shouts and with the barking of dogs.

Tom Leander's oldest child, Elizabeth, was like her mother, full of energy. She was thin and tall like the women of her father's house but very strong and alive. In secret she wanted to be a lady but when she tried her brothers, led by her father and mother, made fun of her. "Don't put on airs," they said. When she got into the country with no one but her brothers and two or three neighboring farm boys she herself became a boy. With the boys she went tearing through the fields, following the dogs in pursuit of rabbits. Sometimes a young man came with the children from a near-by farm. Then she did not know what to do with herself. She wanted to walk demurely along the rows through the corn but was afraid her brothers

would laugh and in desperation outdid the boys in roughness and noisiness. She screamed and shouted and running wildly tore her dress on the wire fences as she scrambled over in pursuit of the dogs. When a rabbit was caught and killed she rushed in and tore it out of the grasp of the dogs. The blood of the little dying animal dripped on her clothes. She swung it over her head and shouted.

The farm hand who had worked all summer in the field within sight of Elsie became enamoured of the young woman from town. When the groceryman's family appeared on Sunday mornings he also appeared but did not come to the house. When the boys and dogs came tearing through the fields he joined them. He also was self-conscious and did not want the boys to know the purpose of his coming and when he and Elizabeth found themselves alone together he became embarrassed. For a moment they walked together in silence. In a wide circle about them, in the forest of the corn, ran the boys and dogs. The young man had something he wanted to say, but when he tried to find words his tongue became thick and his lips felt hot and dry. "Well," he began, "let's you and me—"

Words failed him and Elizabeth turned and ran after her brothers and for the rest of the day he could not manage to get her out of their sight. When he went to join them she became the noisiest member of the party. A frenzy of activity took possession of her. With hair hanging down her back, with clothes torn and with cheeks and hands scratched and bleeding she led her brothers in the endless wild pursuit of the rabbits.

The Sunday in August that followed Elsie Leander's sleepless night was hot and cloudy. In the morning she was half ill and as soon as the visitors from town arrived she crept away to sit on the step at the side of the house. The children ran away into the fields. An almost overpowering desire to run with them, shouting and playing along the corn rows took possession of her. She arose and went to the back of the house. Her father was at work in the garden, pulling weeds from between rows of vegetables. Inside the house she could hear her sister-in-law moving about. On the front porch her brother Tom was asleep with his mother beside him. Elsie went back to the step and then arose and went to where the corn came down to the fence. She climbed awkwardly over and went a little way along one of the rows. Putting out her hand she touched the firm stalks and then, becoming afraid, dropped to her knees on the carpet of weeds that covered the ground. For a long time she stayed thus listening to the voices of the children in the distance.

An hour slipped away. Presently it was time for dinner and her sister-in-law came to the back door and shouted. There was an answering whoop from the

distance and the children came running through the fields. They climbed over the fence and ran shouting across her father's garden. Elsie also arose. She was about to attempt to climb back over the fence unobserved when she heard a rustling in the corn. Young Elizabeth Leander appeared. Beside her walked the ploughman who but a few months earlier had planted the corn in the field where Elsie now stood. She could see the two people coming slowly along the rows. An understanding had been established between them. The man reached through between the corn stalks and touched the hand of the girl who laughed awkwardly and running to the fence climbed quickly over. In her hand she held the limp body of a rabbit the dogs had killed.

The farm hand went away and when Elizabeth had gone into the house Elsie climbed over the fence. Her niece stood just within the kitchen door holding the dead rabbit by one leg. The other leg had been torn away by the dogs. At sight of the New England woman, who seemed to look at her with hard unsympathetic eyes, she was ashamed and went quickly into the house. She threw the rabbit upon a table in the parlor and then ran out of the room. Its blood ran out on the delicate flowers of a white crocheted table cover that had been made by Elsie's mother.

The Sunday dinner with all the living Leanders gathered about the table was gone through in a heavy lumbering silence. When the dinner was over and Tom and his wife had washed the dishes they went to sit with the older people on the front porch. Presently they were both asleep. Elsie returned to the step at the side of the house but when the desire to go again into the cornfields came sweeping over her she got up and went indoors.

The woman of thirty-five tip-toed about the big house like a frightened child. The dead rabbit that lay on the table in the parlour had become cold and stiff. Its blood had dried on the white table cover. She went upstairs but did not go to her own room. A spirit of adventure had hold of her. In the upper part of the house there were many rooms and in some of them no glass had been put into the windows. The windows had been boarded up and narrow streaks of light crept in through the cracks between the boards.

Elsie tip-toed up the flight of stairs past the room in which she slept and opening doors went into other rooms. Dust lay thick on the floors. In the silence she could hear her brother snoring as he slept in the chair on the front porch. From what seemed a far away place there came the shrill cries of the children. The cries became soft. They were like the cries of unborn children that had called to her out of the fields on the night before.

Into her mind came the intense silent figure of her mother sitting on the porch beside her son and waiting for the day to wear itself out into night. The thought brought a lump into her throat. She wanted something and did not know what it was. Her own mood frightened her. In a windowless room at the back of the house one of the boards over a window had been broken and a bird had flown in and become imprisoned.

The presence of the woman frightened the bird. It flew wildly about. Its beating wings stirred up dust that danced in the air. Elsie stood perfectly still ,also frightened, not by the presence of the bird but by the presence of life. Like the bird she was a prisoner. The thought gripped her. She wanted to go outdoors where her niece Elizabeth walked with the young ploughman through the corn, but was like the bird in the room—a prisoner. She moved restlessly about. The bird flew back and forth across the room. It alighted on the window sill near the place where the board was broken away. She stared into the frightened eyes of the bird that in turn stared into her eyes. Then the bird flew away, out through the window, and Elsie turned and ran nervously downstairs and out into the yard. She climbed over the wire fence and ran with stooped shoulders along one of the tunnels.

Elsie ran into the vastness of the cornfields filled with but one desire. She wanted to get out of her life and into some new and sweeter life she felt must be hidden away somewhere in the fields. After she had run a long way she came to a wire fence and crawled over. Her hair became unloosed and fell down over her shoulders. Her cheeks became flushed and for the moment she looked like a young girl. When she climbed over the fence she tore a great hole in the front of her dress. For a moment her tiny breasts were exposed and then her hand clutched and held nervously the sides of the tear. In the distance she could hear the voices of the boys and the barking of the dogs. A summer storm had been threatening for days and now black clouds had begun to spread themselves over the sky. As she ran nervously forward, stopping to listen and then running on again, the dry corn blades brushed against her shoulders and a fine shower of yellow dust from the corn tassels fell on her hair. A continued crackling noise accompanied her progress. The dust made a golden crown about her head. From the sky overhead a low rumbling sound, like the growling of giant dogs, came to her ears.

The thought that having at last ventured into the corn she would never escape became fixed in the mind of the running woman. Sharp pains shot through her body. Presently she was compelled to stop and sit on the ground. For a long time she sat with closed eyes. Her dress became soiled. Little insects that live in the ground under the corn came out of their holes and crawled over her legs.

Following some obscure impulse the tired woman threw herself on her back and lay still with closed eyes. Her fright passed. It was warm and close in the room-like tunnels. The pain in her side went away. She opened her eyes and between the wide green corn blades could see patches of a black threatening sky. She did not want to be alarmed and so closed her eyes again. Her thin hand no longer gripped the tear in her dress and her little breasts were exposed. They expanded and contracted in spasmodic jerks. She threw her hands back over her head and lay still.

It seemed to Elsie that hours passed as she lay thus, quiet and passive under the corn. Deep within her there was a feeling that something was about to happen, something that would lift her out of herself, that would tear her away from her past and the past of her people. Her thoughts were not definite. She lay still and waited as she had waited for days and months by the rock at the back of the orchard on the Vermont farm when she was a girl. A deep grumbling noise went on in the sky overhead but the sky and everything she had ever known seemed very far away, no part of herself.

After a long silence, when it seemed to her that she had gone out of herself as in a dream, Elsie heard a man's voice calling. "Aho, aho, aho," shouted the voice and after another period of silence there arose answering voices and then the sound of bodies crashing through the corn and the excited chatter of children. A dog came running along the row where she lay and stood beside her. His cold nose touched her face and she sat up. The dog ran away. The Leander boys passed. She could see their bare legs flashing in and out across one of the tunnels. Her brother had become alarmed by the rapid approach of the thunder storm and wanted to get his family to town. His voice kept calling from the house and the voices of the children answered from the fields.

Elsie sat on the ground with her hands pressed together. An odd feeling of disappointment had possession of her. She arose and walked slowly along in the general direction taken by the children. She came to a fence and crawled over, tearing her dress in a new place. One of her stockings had become unloosed and had slipped down over her shoe top. The long sharp weeds had scratched her leg so that it was criss-crossed with red lines, but she was not conscious of any pain.

The distraught woman followed the children until she came within sight of her father's house and then stopped and again sat on the ground. There was another loud crash of thunder and Tom Leander's voice called again, this time half angrily. The name of the girl Elizabeth was shouted in loud masculine tones that rolled and echoed like the thunder along the aisles under the corn.

And then Elizabeth came into sight accompanied by the young ploughman. They stopped near Elsie and the man took the girl into his arms. At the sound of their approach Elsie had thrown herself face downward on the ground and had twisted herself into a position where she could see without being seen. When their lips met her tense hands grasped one of the corn stalks. Her lips pressed themselves into the dust. When they had gone on their way she raised her head. A dusty powder covered her lips.

What seemed another long period of silence fell over the fields. The murmuring voices of unborn children, her imagination had created in the whispering fields, became a vast shout. The wind blew harder and harder. The corn stalks were twisted and bent. Elizabeth went thoughtfully out of the field and climbing the fence confronted her father. "Where you been? What you been a doing?" he asked. "Don't you think we got to get out of here?"

When Elizabeth went toward the house Elsie followed, creeping on her hands and knees like a little animal, and when she had come within sight of the fence surrounding the house she sat on the ground and put her hands over her face. Something within herself was being twisted and whirled about as the tops of the corn stalks were now being twisted and whirled by the wind. She sat so that she did not look toward the house and when she opened her eyes she could again see along the long mysterious aisles.

Her brother with his wife and children went away. By turning her head Elsie could see them driving at a trot out of the yard back of her father's house. With the going of the younger woman the farm house in the midst of the cornfield rocked by the winds seemed the most desolate place in the world.

Her mother came out at the back door of the house. She ran to the steps where she knew her daughter was in the habit of sitting and then in alarm began to call. It did not occur to Elsie to answer. The voice of the older woman did not seem to have anything to do with herself. It was a thin voice and was quickly lost in the wind and in the crashing sound that arose out of the fields. With her head turned toward the house Elsie stared at her mother who ran wildly around the house and then went indoors. The back door of the house went shut with a bang.

The storm that had been threatening broke with a roar. Broad sheets of water swept over the cornfields. Sheets of water swept over the woman's body. The storm that had for years been gathering in her also broke. Sobs arose out of her throat. She abandoned herself to a storm of grief that was only partially grief. Tears ran out of her eyes and made little furrows through the dust on her face. In the lulls that occasionally came in the storm she raised her head and heard, through the tangled mass of wet hair that covered her ears and above the sound of millions of rain-drops that alighted on the earthen floor inside the house of the corn, the thin voices of her mother and father calling to her out of the Leander house.

WAR

THE story came to me from a woman met on a train. The car was crowded and I took the seat beside her. There was a man in the offing who belonged with her—a slender girlish figure of a man in a heavy brown canvas coat such as teamsters wear in the winter. He moved up and down in the aisle of the car, wanting my place by the woman's side, but I did not know that at the time.

The woman had a heavy face and a thick nose. Something had happened to her. She had been struck a blow or had a fall. Nature could never have made a nose so broad and thick and ugly. She had talked to me in very good English. I suspect now that she was temporarily weary of the man in the brown canvas coat, that she had travelled with him for days, perhaps weeks, and was glad of the chance to spend a few hours in the company of some one else.

Everyone knows the feeling of a crowded train in the middle of the night. We ran along through western Iowa and eastern Nebraska. It had rained for days and the fields were flooded. In the clear night the moon came out and the scene outside the car-window was strange and in an odd way very beautiful.

161

You get the feeling: the black bare trees standing up in clusters as they do out in that country, the pools of water with the moon reflected and running quickly as it does when the train hurries along, the rattle of the car-trucks, the lights in isolated farm-houses, and occasionally the clustered lights of a town as the train rushed through it into the west.

The woman had just come out of war-ridden Poland, had got out of that stricken land with her lover by God knows what miracles of effort. She made me feel the war, that woman did, and she told me the tale that I want to tell you.

I do not remember the beginning of our talk, nor can I tell you of how the strangeness of my mood grew to match her mood until the story she told became a part of the mystery of the still night outside the car-window and very pregnant with meaning to me.

There was a company of Polish refugees moving along a road in Poland in charge of a German. The German was a man of perhaps fifty, with a beard. As I got him, he was much such a man as might be professor of foreign languages in a college in our country, say at Des Moines, Iowa, or Springfield, Ohio. He would be sturdy and strong of body and given to the eating of rather rank foods, as such men are. Also he would be a fellow of books and in his thinking inclined toward the ranker philosophies. He was dragged into the war because he was a German, and he had steeped his soul in the German philosophy of might. Faintly, I fancy, there was another notion in his head that kept bothering him, and so to serve his government with a whole heart he read books that would re-establish his feeling for the strong, terrible thing for which he fought. Because he was past fifty he was not on the battle line, but was in charge of the refugees, taking them out of their destroyed village to a camp near a railroad where they could be fed.

The refugees were peasants, all except the woman in the American train with me, her lover and her mother, an old woman of sixty-five. They had been small landowners and the others in their party had worked on their estate.

Along a country road in Poland went this party in charge of the German who tramped heavily along, urging them forward. He was brutal in his insistence, and the old woman of sixty-five, who was a kind of leader of the refugees, was almost equally brutal in her constant refusal to go forward. In the rainy night she stopped in the muddy road and her party gathered about her. Like a stubborn horse she shook her head and muttered Polish words. "I want to be let alone, that's what I want. All I want in the world is to be let alone," she said, over and over; and then the German came up and putting his hand on her back pushed her along, so that their progress through the dismal night was a constant repetition of the stopping, her muttered words, and his pushing. They hated each other with whole-hearted hatred, that old Polish woman and the German.

The party came to a clump of trees on the bank of a shallow stream and the German took hold of the old woman's arm and dragged her through the stream while the others followed. Over and over she said the words: "I want to be let alone. All I want in the world is to be let alone."

In the clump of trees the German started a fire. With incredible efficiency he had it blazing high in a few minutes, taking the matches and even some bits of dry wood from a little rubber-lined pouch carried in his inside coat pocket. Then he got out tobacco and, sitting down on the protruding root of a tree, smoked and stared at the refugees, clustered about the old woman on the opposite side of the fire.

The German went to sleep. That was what started his trouble. He slept for an hour and when he awoke the refugees were gone. You can imagine him jumping up and tramping heavily back through the shallow stream and along the muddy road to gather his party together again. He would be angry through and through, but he would not be alarmed. It was only a matter, he knew, of going far enough back along the road as one goes back along a road for strayed cattle.

And then, when the German came up to the party,

he and the old woman began to fight. She stopped muttering the words about being let alone and sprang at him. One of her old hands gripped his beard and the other buried itself in the thick skin of his neck.

The struggle in the road lasted a long time. The German was tired and not as strong as he looked, and there was that faint thing in him that kept him from hitting the old woman with his fist. He took hold of her thin shoulders and pushed, and she pulled. The struggle was like a man trying to lift himself by his boot straps. The two fought and were full of the determination that will not stop fighting, but they were not very strong physically.

And so their two souls began to struggle. The woman in the train made me understand that quite clearly, although it may be difficult to get the sense of it over to you. I had the night and the mystery of the moving train to help me. It was a physical thing, the fight of the two souls in the dim light of the rainy night on that deserted muddy road. The air was full of the struggle and the refugees gathered about and stood shivering. They shivered with cold and weariness, of course, but also with something else. In the air everywhere about them they could feel the vague something going on. The woman said that she would gladly have given her life to have it stopped, or to have someone strike a light, and that her man felt the same way. It was like two winds struggling, she said, like a soft yielding cloud become hard and trying vainly to push another cloud out of the sky.

Then the struggle ended and the old woman and the German fell down exhausted in the road. The refugees gathered about and waited. They thought something more was going to happen, knew in fact something more would happen. The feeling they had persisted, you see, and they huddled together and perhaps whimpered a little.

What happened is the whole point of the story. The woman in the train explained it very clearly. She said that the two souls, after struggling, went back into the two bodies, but that the soul of the old woman went into the body of the German and the soul of the German into the body of the old woman.

After that, of course, everything was quite simple. The German sat down by the road and began shaking his head and saying he wanted to be let alone, declared that all he wanted in the world was to be let alone, and the Polish woman took papers out of his pocket and began driving her companions back along the road, driving them harshly and brutally along, and when they grew weary pushing them with her hands.

There was more of the story after that. The woman's lover, who had been a school-teacher, took the papers and got out of the country, taking his sweetheart with him. But my mind has forgotten the

details. I only remember the German sitting by the
road and muttering that he wanted to be let alone,
and the old tired mother-in-Poland saying the harsh
words and forcing her weary companions to march
through the night back into their own country.

MOTHERHOOD

BELOW the hill there was a swamp in which cattails grew. The wind rustled the dry leaves of a walnut tree that grew on top of the hill.

She went beyond the tree to where the grass was long and matted. In the farmhouse a door bangs and in the road before the house a dog barked.

For a long time there was no sound. Then a wagon came jolting and bumping over the frozen road. The little noises ran along the ground to where she was lying on the grass and seemed like fingers playing over her body. A fragrance arose from her. It took a long time for the wagon to pass.

Then another sound broke the stillness. A young man from a neighboring farm came stealthily across a field and climbed a fence. He also came to the hill but for a time did not see her lying almost at his feet. He looked toward the house and stood with hands in pockets, stamping on the frozen ground like a horse.

Then he knew she was there. The aroma of her crept into his consciousness.

He ran to kneel beside her silent figure. Everything was different than it had been when they crept to the hill on the other evenings. The time of talking

and waiting was over. She was different. He grew
bold and put his hands on her face, her neck, her
breasts, her hips. There was a strange new firmness
and hardness to her body. When he kissed her lips
she did not move and for a moment he was afraid.
Then courage came and he went down to lie with her.

He had been a farm boy all his life and had plowed
many acres of rich black land.

He became sure of himself.

He plowed her deeply.

He planted the seeds of a son in the warm rich quivering soil.

*   *   *

She carried the seeds of a son within herself. On
winter evenings she went along a path at the foot of a
small hill and turned up the hill to a barn where she
milked cows. She was large and strong. Her legs
went swinging along. The son within her went swinging along.

He learned the rhythm of little hills.

He learned the rhythm of flat places.

He learned the rhythm of legs walking.

He learned the rhythm of firm strong hands pulling
at the teats of cows.

*   *   *

There was a field that was barren and filled with
stones. In the spring when the warm nights came and
when she was big with him she went to the fields. The

heads of little stones stuck out of the ground like the heads of buried children. The field, washed with moonlight, sloped gradually downward to a murmuring brook. A few sheep went among the stones nibbling the sparse grass.

A thousand children were buried in the barren field. They struggled to come out of the ground. They struggled to come to her. The brook ran over stones and its voice cried out. For a long time she stayed in the field, shaken with sorrow.

She arose from her seat on a large stone and went to the farmhouse. The voices of the darkness cried to her as she went along a lane and past a silent barn.

Within herself only the one child struggled. When she got into bed his heels beat upon the walls of his prison. She lay still and listened. Only one small voice seemed coming to her out of the silence of the night.

OUT OF NOWHERE INTO NOTHING.

I

ROSALIND WESCOTT, a tall strong looking woman of twenty-seven, was walking on the railroad track near the town of Willow Springs, Iowa. It was about four in the afternoon of a day in August, and the third day since she had come home to her native town from Chicago, where she was employed.

At that time Willow Springs was a town of about three thousand people. It has grown since. There was a public square with the town hall in the centre and about the four sides of the square and facing it were the merchandising establishments. The public square was bare and grassless, and out of it ran streets of frame houses, long straight streets that finally became country roads running away into the flat prairie country.

Although she had told everyone that she had merely come home for a short visit because she was a little homesick, and although she wanted in particular to have a talk with her mother in regard to a certain matter, Rosalind had been unable to talk with anyone. Indeed she had found it difficult to stay in the house with her mother and father and all the time, day and night, she was haunted by a desire to get out of town. As she went along the railroad tracks in the hot afternoon sunshine she kept scolding herself. "I've grown moody and no good. If I want to do it why don't I just go ahead and not make a fuss," she thought.

For two miles the railroad tracks, eastward out of Willow Springs, went through corn fields on a flat plain. Then there was a little dip in the land and a bridge over Willow Creek. The Creek was altogether dry now but trees grew along the edge of the grey streak of cracked mud that in the fall, winter and spring would be the bed of the stream. Rosalind left the tracks and went to sit under one of the trees. Her cheeks were flushed and her forehead wet. When she took off her hat her hair fell down in disorder and strands of it clung to her hot wet face. She sat in what seemed a kind of great bowl on the sides of which the corn grew rank. Before her and following the bed of the stream there was a dusty path along which cows came at evening from distant pastures. A great pancake formed of cow dung lay nearby. It was covered with grey dust and over it crawled shiny black beetles. They were rolling the dung into balls in preparation for the germination of a new generation of beetles.

Rosalind had come on the visit to her home town at a time of the year when everyone wished to escape from the hot dusty place. No one had expected her and she had not written to announce her coming. One hot morning in Chicago she had got out of bed and had suddenly begun packing her bag, and on that same evening there she was in Willow Springs, in the house where she had lived until her twenty-first year, among her own people. She had come up from the station in the hotel bus and had walked into the Wescott house unannounced. Her father was at the pump by the kitchen door and her mother came into the living room to greet her wearing a soiled kitchen apron. Everything in the house was just as it always had been. "I just thought I would come home for a few days," she said, putting down her bag and kissing her mother.

Ma and Pa Wescott had been glad to see their daughter. On the evening of her arrival they were excited and a special supper was prepared. After supper Pa Wescott went up town as usual, but he stayed only a few minutes. "I just want to run to the postoffice and get the evening paper," he said apologetically. Rosalind's mother put on a clean dress and they all sat in the darkness on the front porch. There was talk, of a kind. "Is it hot in Chicago now? I'm going to do a good deal of canning this fall. I thought later I would send you a box of canned fruit. Do you live in the same place on the North Side? It must be nice in the evening to be able to walk down to the park by the lake."

*   *   *

Rosalind sat under the tree near the railroad bridge two miles from Willow Springs and watched the tumble bugs at work. Her whole body was hot from the walk in the sun and the thin dress she wore clung to her legs. It was being soiled by the dust on the grass under the tree.

She had run away from town and from her mother's house. All during the three days of her visit she had been doing that. She did not go from house to house to visit her old schoolgirl friends, the girls who unlike herself had stayed in Willow Springs, had got married and settled down there. When she saw one of these women on the street in the morning, pushing a baby carriage and perhaps followed by a small child, she stopped. There was a few minutes of talk. "It's hot. Do you live in the same place in Chicago? My husband and I hope to take the children and go away for a week or two. It must be nice in Chicago where you are so near the lake." Rosalind hurried away.

All the hours of her visit to her mother and to her home town had been spent in an effort to hurry away.

From what? Rosalind defended herself. There was something she had come from Chicago hoping to be able to say to her mother. Did she really want to talk with her about things? Had she thought, by again breathing the air of her home town, to get strength to face life and its difficulties?

There was no point in her taking the hot uncomfortable trip from Chicago only to spend her days walking in dusty country roads or between rows of cornfields in the stifling heat along the railroad tracks.

"I must have hoped. There is a hope that cannot be fulfilled," she thought vaguely.

Willow Springs was a rather meaningless, dreary town, one of thousands of such towns in Indiana, Illinois, Wisconsin, Kansas, Iowa, but her mind made it more dreary.

She sat under the tree by the dry bed of Willow Creek thinking of the street in town where her mother and father lived, where she had lived until she had become a woman. It was only because of a series of circumstances she did not live there now. Her one brother, ten years older than herself, had married and moved to Chicago. He had asked her to come for a visit and after she got to the city she stayed. Her brother was a traveling salesman and spent a good deal of time away from home. "Why don't you stay here with Bess and learn stenography," he asked. "If you don't want to use it you don't have to. Dad can look out for you all right. I just thought you might like to learn."

*   *   *

"That was six years ago," Rosalind thought wearily. "I've been a city woman for six years." Her mind hopped about. Thoughts came and went. In the city, after she became a stenographer, something for a time awakened her. She wanted to be an actress and went in the evening to a dramatic school. In an office where she worked there was a young man, a clerk. They went out together, to the theatre or to walk in the park in the evening. They kissed.

Her thoughts came sharply back to her mother and father, to her home in Willow Springs, to the street in which she had lived until her twenty-first year.

It was but an end of a street. From the windows at the front of her mother's house six other houses could be seen. How well she knew the street and the people in the houses! Did she know them? From her eighteenth and until her twenty-first year she had stayed at home, helping her mother with the housework, waiting for something. Other young women in town waited just as she did. They like herself had graduated from the town highschool and their parents had no intention of sending them away to college. There was nothing to do but wait. Some of the young women—their mothers and their mothers' friends still spoke of them as girls—had young men friends who came to see them on Sunday and perhaps also on Wednesday or Thursday evenings. Others joined the church, went to prayer meetings, became active members of some church organization. They fussed about.

Rosalind had done none of these things. All through those three trying years in Willow Springs she had just waited. In the morning there was the work to do in the house and then, in some way, the day wore itself away. In the evening her father went up town and she sat with her mother. Nothing much was said. After she had gone to bed she lay awake, strangely nervous, eager for something to happen that never would happen. The noises of the Wescott house cut across her thoughts. What things went through her mind!

There was a procession of people always going away from her. Sometimes she lay on her belly at the edge of a ravine. Well it was not a ravine. It had two walls of marble and on the marble face of the walls strange figures were carved. Broad steps led down— always down and away. People walked along the steps, between the marble walls, going down and away from her.

What people! Who were they? Where did they come from? Where were they going? She was not asleep but wide awake. Her bedroom was dark. The walls and ceiling of the room receded. She seemed to hang suspended in space, above the ravine—the ravine with walls of white marble over which strange beautiful lights played.

The people who went down the broad steps and away into infinite distance—they were men and women. Sometime a young girl like herself but in some way sweeter and purer than herself, passed alone. The young girl walked with a swinging stride, going swiftly and freely like a beautiful young animal. Her legs and arms were like the slender top branches of trees swaying in a gentle wind. She also went down and away.

Others followed along the marble steps. Young boys walked alone. A dignified old man followed by a sweet faced woman passed. What a remarkable man! One felt infinite power in his old frame. There were deep wrinkles in his face and his eyes were sad. One felt he knew everything about life but had kept something very precious alive in himself. It was that precious thing that made the eyes of the woman who followed him burn with a strange fire. They also went down along the steps and away.

Down and away along the steps went others—how many others, men and women, boys and girls, single old men, old women who leaned on sticks and hobbled along.

In the bed in her father's house as she lay awake Rosalind's head grew light. She tried to clutch at something, understand something.

She couldn't. The noises of the house cut across her waking dream. Her father was at the pump by the kitchen door. He was pumping a pail of water. In a moment he would bring it into the house and put it on a box by the kitchen sink. A little of the water would slop over on the floor. There would be a sound like a child's bare foot striking the floor. Then her father would go to wind the clock. The day was done. Presently there would be the sound of his heavy feet on the floor of the bedroom above and he would get into bed to lie beside Rosalind's mother.

The night noises of her father's house had been in some way terrible to the girl in the years when she was becoming a woman. After chance had taken her to the city she never wanted to think of them again. Even in Chicago where the silence of nights was cut and slashed by a thousand noises, by automobiles whirling through the streets, by the belated footsteps of men homeward bound along the cement sidewalks after midnight, by the shouts of quarreling men drunk on summer nights, even in the great hubbub of noises there was comparative quiet. The insistent clanging noises of the city nights were not like the homely insistent noises of her father's house. Certain terrible truths about life did not abide in them, they did not cling so closely to life and did not frighten as did the noises in the one house on the quiet street in the town of Willow Springs. How often, there in the city, in the midst of the great noises she had fought to escape the little noises! Her father's feet were on the steps leading into the kitchen. Now he was putting the pail of water on the box by the kitchen sink. Upstairs her mother's body fell heavily into bed. The visions of the great marble-lined ravine down along which went the beautiful people flew away. There was the little slap of water on the kitchen floor. It was like a child's bare foot striking the floor. Rosalind wanted to cry out. Her father closed the kitchen door. Now he was winding the clock. In a moment his feet would be on the stairs——

There were six houses to be seen from the windows of the Wescott house. In the winter smoke from six brick chimneys went up into the sky. There was one house, the next one to the Wescott's place, a small frame affair, in which lived a man who was thirty-five years old when Rosalind became a woman of twenty-one and went away to the city. The man was unmarried and his mother, who had been his housekeeper, had died during the year in which Rosalind graduated from the high school. After that the man lived alone. He took his dinner and supper at the hotel, down town on the square, but he got his own breakfast, made his own bed and swept out his own house. Sometimes he walked slowly along the street past the Wescott house when Rosalind sat alone on the front porch. He raised his hat and spoke to her. Their eyes met. He had a long, hawk-like nose and his hair was long and uncombed.

Rosalind thought about him sometimes. It bothered her a little that he sometimes went stealing softly, as though not to disturb her, across her daytime fancies.

As she sat that day by the dry creek bed Rosalind thought about the bachelor, who had now passed the age of forty and who lived on the street where she had lived during her girlhood. His house was separated from the Wescott house by a picket fence. Sometimes in the morning he forgot to pull his blinds and Rosalind, busy with the housework in her father's house, had seen him walking about in his underwear. It was—uh, one could not think of it.

The man's name was Melville Stoner. He had a small income and did not have to work. On some days he did not leave his house and go to the hotel for his meals but sat all day in a chair with his nose buried in a book.

There was a house on the street occupied by a widow who raised chickens. Two or three of her hens were what the people who lived on the street called 'high flyers.' They flew over the fence of the chicken yard and escaped and almost always they came at once into the yard of the bachelor. The neighbors laughed about it. It was significant, they felt. When the hens had come into the yard of the bachelor, Stoner, the widow with a stick in her hand ran after them. Melville Stoner came out of his house and stood on a little porch in front. The widow ran through the front gate waving her arms wildly and the hens made a great racket and flew over the fence. They ran down the street toward the widow's house. For a moment she stood by the Stoner gate. In the summer time when the windows of the Wescott house were open Rosalind could hear what the man and woman said to each other. In Willow Springs it was not thought proper for an unmarried woman to stand talking to an unmarried man near the door of his bachelor establishment. The widow wanted to observe the conventions. Still she did linger a moment, her bare arm resting on the gate post. What bright eager little eyes she had! "If those hens of mine bother you I wish you would catch them and kill them," she said fiercely. "I am always glad to see them coming along the road," Melville Stoner replied, bowing. Rosalind thought he was making fun of the widow. She liked him for that. "I'd never see you if you did not have to come here after your hens. Don't let anything happen to them," he said, bowing again.

For a moment the man and woman lingered looking into each other's eyes. From one of the windows of the Wescott house Rosalind watched the woman. Nothing more was said. There was something about the woman she had not understood—well the widow's senses were being fed. The developing woman in the house next door had hated her.

*   *   *

Rosalind jumped up from under the tree and climbed up the railroad embankment. She thanked the gods she had been lifted out of the life of the town of Willow Springs and that chance had set her down to live in a city. "Chicago is far from beautiful. People say it is just a big noisy dirty village and perhaps that's what it is, but there is something alive there," she thought. In Chicago, or at least during the last two or three years of her life there, Rosalind felt she had learned a little something of life. She had read books for one thing, such books as did not come to Willow Springs, books that Willow Springs knew nothing about, she had gone to hear the Symphony Orchestra, she had begun to understand something of the possibility of line and color, had heard intelligent, understanding men speak of these things. In Chicago, in the midst of the twisting squirming millions of men and women there were voices. One occasionally saw men or at least heard of the existence of men who, like the beautiful old man who had walked away down the marble stairs in the vision of her girlhood nights, had kept some precious thing alive in themselves.

And there was something else—it was the most important thing of all. For the last two years of her life in Chicago she had spent hours, days in the presence of a man to whom she could talk. The talks had awakened her. She felt they had made her a woman, had matured her.

"I know what these people here in Willow Springs are like and what I would have been like had I stayed here," she thought. She felt relieved and almost happy. She had come home at a crisis of her own life hoping to be able to talk a little with her mother, or if talk proved impossible hoping to get some sense of sisterhood by being in her presence. She had thought there was something buried away, deep within every woman, that at a certain call would run out to other women. Now she felt that the hope, the dream, the desire she had cherished was altogether futile. Sitting in the great flat bowl in the midst of the corn lands two miles from her home town where no breath of air stirred and seeing the beetles at their work of preparing to propagate a new generation of beetles, while she thought of the town and its people, had settled something for her. Her visit to Willow Springs had come to something after all.

Rosalind's figure had still much of the spring and swing of youth in it. Her legs were strong and her shoulders broad. She went swinging along the railroad track toward town, going westward. The sun had begun to fall rapidly down the sky. Away over the tops of the corn in one of the great fields she could see in the distance to where a man was driving a motor along a dusty road. The wheels of the car kicked up dust through which the sunlight played. The floating cloud of dust became a shower of gold that settled down over the fields. "When a woman most wants what is best and truest in another woman, even in her own mother, she isn't likely to find it," she thought grimly. "There are certain things every woman has to find out for herself, there is a road she must travel alone. It may only lead to some more ugly and terrible place, but if she doesn't want death to overtake her and live within her while her body is still alive she must set out on that road."

Rosalind walked for a mile along the railroad track and then stopped. A freight train had gone eastward as she sat under the tree by the creek bed and now, there beside the tracks, in the grass was the body of a man. It lay still, the face buried in the deep burned grass. At once she concluded the man had been struck and killed by the train. The body had been thrown thus aside. All her thoughts went away and she turned and started to tiptoe away, stepping carefully along the railroad ties, making no noise. Then she stopped again. The man in the grass might not be dead, only hurt, terribly hurt. It would not do to leave him there. She imagined him mutilated but still struggling for life and herself trying to help him. She crept back along the ties. The man's legs were not twisted and beside him lay his hat. It was as though he had put it there before lying down to sleep, but a man did not sleep with his face buried in the grass in such a hot uncomforable place. She drew nearer. "O, you Mister," she called, "O, you—are you hurt?"

The man in the grass sat up and looked at her. He laughed. It was Melville Stoner, the man of whom she had just been thinking and in thinking of whom she had come to certain settled conclusions regarding the futility of her visit to Willow Springs. He got to his feet and picked up his hat. "Well, hello, Miss Rosalind Wescott," he said heartily. He climbed a small embankment and stood beside her. "I knew you were at home on a visit but what are you doing out here?" he asked and then added, "What luck this is! Now I shall have the privilege of walking home with you. You can hardly refuse to let me walk with you after shouting at me like that."

They walked together along the tracks he with his hat in his hand. Rosalind thought he looked like a gigantic bird, an aged wise old bird, "perhaps a vulture" she thought. For a time he was silent and then he began to talk, explaining his lying with his face buried in the grass. There was a twinkle in his eyes and Rosalind wondered if he was laughing at her as she had seen him laugh at the widow who owned the hens.

He did not come directly to the point and Rosalind thought it strange that they should walk and talk together. At once his words interested her. He was so much older than herself and no doubt wiser. How vain she had been to think herself so much more knowing than all the people of Willow Springs. Here was this man and he was talking and his talk did not sound like anything she had ever expected to hear from the lips of a native of her home town. "I want to explain myself but we'll wait a little. For years I've been wanting to get at you, to talk with you, and this is my chance. You've been away now five or six years and have grown into womanhood.

"You understand it's nothing specially personal, my wanting to get at you and understand you a little," he added quickly. "I'm that way about everyone. Perhaps that's the reason I live alone, why I've never married or had personal friends. I'm too eager. It isn't comfortable to others to have me about."

Rosalind was caught up by this new view point of the man. She wondered. In the distance along the tracks the houses of the town came into sight. Melville Stoner tried to walk on one of the iron rails but after a few steps lost his balance and fell off. His long arms whirled about. A strange intensity of mood and feeling had come over Rosalind. In one moment Melville Stoner was like an old man and then he was like a boy. Being with him made her mind, that had been racing all afternoon, race faster than ever.

When he began to talk again he seemed to have forgotten the explanation he had intended making. "We've lived side by side but we've hardly spoken to each other," he said. "When I was a young man and you were a girl I used to sit in the house thinking of you. We've really been friends. What I mean is we've had the same thoughts."

He began to speak of life in the city where she had been living, condemning it. "It's dull and stupid here but in the city you have your own kind of stupidity too," he declared. "I'm glad I do not live there."

In Chicago when she had first gone there to live a thing had sometimes happened that had startled Rosalind. She knew no one but her brother and his wife and was sometimes very lonely. When she could no longer bear the eternal sameness of the talk in her brother's house she went out to a concert or to the theatre. Once or twice when she had no money to buy a theatre ticket she grew bold and walked alone in the streets, going rapidly along without looking to the right or left. As she sat in the theatre or walked in the street an odd thing sometimes happened. Someone spoke her name, a call came to her. The thing happened at a concert and she looked quickly about. All the faces in sight had that peculiar, half bored, half expectant expression one grows accustomed to seeing on the faces of people listening to music. In the entire theatre no one seemed aware of her. On the street or in the park the call had come when she was utterly alone. It seemed to come out of the air, from behind a tree in the park.

And now as she walked on the railroad tracks with Melville Stoner the call seemed to come from him. He walked along apparently absorbed with his own thoughts, the thoughts he was trying to find words to express. His legs were long and he walked with a queer loping gait. The idea of some great bird, per-

haps a sea-bird stranded far inland, stayed in Rosalind's mind but the call did not come from the bird part
of him. There was something else, another personality hidden away. Rosalind fancied the call came this
time from a young boy, from such another clear-eyed
boy as she had once seen in her waking dreams at night
in her father's house, from one of the boys who walked
on the marble stairway, walked down and away. A
thought came that startled her. "The boy is hidden
away in the body of this strange bird-like man," she
told herself. The thought awoke fancies within her.
It explained much in the lives of men and women. An
expression, a phrase, remembered from her childhood
when she had gone to Sunday School in Willow
Springs, came back to her mind. "And God spoke to
me out of a burning bush." She almost said the words
aloud.

Melville Stoner loped along, walking on the railroad
ties and talking. He seemed to have forgotten the incident of his lying with his nose buried in the grass and
was explaining his life lived alone in the house in town.
Rosalind tried to put her own thoughts aside and to
listen to his words but did not succeed very well. "I
came home here hoping to get a little closer to life, to
get, for a few days, out of the company of a man so I
could think about him. I fancied I could get what I
wanted by being near mother, but that hasn't worked.
It would be strange if I got what I am looking for by

this chance meeting with another man," she thought. Her mind went on recording thoughts. She heard the spoken words of the man beside her but her own mind went on, also making words. Something within herself felt suddenly relaxed and free. Ever since she had got off the train at Willow Springs three days before there had been a great tenseness. Now it was all gone. She looked at Melville Stoner who occasionally looked at her. There was something in his eyes, a kind of laughter—a mocking kind of laughter. His eyes were grey, of a cold greyness, like the eyes of a bird.

"It has come into my mind—I have been thinking—well you see you have not married in the six years since you went to live in the city. It would be strange and a little amusing if you are like myself, if you cannot marry or come close to any other person," he was saying.

Again he spoke of the life he led in his house. "I sometimes sit in my house all day, even when the weather is fine outside," he said. "You have no doubt seen me sitting there. Sometimes I forget to eat. I read books all day, striving to forget myself and then night comes and I cannot sleep.

"If I could write or paint or make music, if I cared at all about expressing what goes on in my mind it would be different. However, I would not write as others do. I would have but little to say about what people do. What do they do? In what way does it matter? Well you see they build cities such as you live in and towns like Willow Springs, they have built this railroad track on which we are walking, they marry and raise children, commit murders, steal, do kindly acts. What does it matter? You see we are walking here in the hot sun. In five minutes more we will be in town and you will go to your house and I to mine. You will eat supper with your father and mother. Then your father will go up town and you and your mother will sit together on the front porch. There will be little said. Your mother will speak of her intention to can fruit. Then your father will come home and you will all go to bed. Your father will pump a pail of water at the pump by the kitchen door. He will carry it indoors and put it on a box by the kitchen sink. A little of the water will be spilled. It will make a soft little slap on the kitchen floor—"

"Ha!"

Melville Stoner turned and looked sharply at Rosalind who had grown a little pale. Her mind raced madly, like an engine out of control. There was a kind of power in Melville Stoner that frightened her. By the recital of a few commonplace facts he had suddenly invaded her secret places. It was almost as though he had come into the bedroom in her father's house where she lay thinking. He had in fact got into her bed. He laughed again, an unmirthful laugh. "I'll tell you what, we know little enough here in

America, either in the towns or in the cities," he said
rapidly. "We are all on the rush. We are all for
action. I sit still and think. If I wanted to write I'd
do something. I'd tell what everyone thought. It
would startle people, frighten them a little, eh? I
would tell you what you have been thinking this afternoon while you walked here on this railroad track
with me. I would tell you what your mother has been
thinking at the same time and what she would like to
say to you."

Rosalind's face had grown chalky white and her
hands trembled. They got off the railroad tracks and
into the streets of Willow Springs. A change came
over Melville Stoner. Of a sudden he seemed just a
man of forty, a little embarrassed by the presence of
the younger woman, a little hesitant. "I'm going to
the hotel now and I must leave you here," he said.
His feet made a shuffling sound on the sidewalk. "I
intended to tell you why you found me lying out there
with my face buried in the grass," he said. A new
quality had come into his voice. It was the voice of
the boy who had called to Rosalind out of the body of
the man as they walked and talked on the tracks.
"Sometimes I can't stand my life here," he said almost
fiercely and waved his long arms about. "I'm alone
too much. I grow to hate myself. I have to run out
of town."

The man did not look at Rosalind but at the ground.

His big feet continued shuffling nervously about. "Once in the winter time I thought I was going insane," he said. "I happened to remember an orchard, five miles from town where I had walked one day in the late fall when the pears were ripe. A notion came into my head. It was bitter cold but I walked the five miles and went into the orchard. The ground was frozen and covered with snow but I brushed the snow aside. I pushed my face into the grass. In the fall when I had walked there the ground was covered with ripe pears. A fragrance arose from them. They were covered with bees that crawled over them, drunk, filled with a kind of ecstacy. I had remembered the fragrance. That's why I went there and put my face into the frozen grass. The bees were in an ecstasy of life and I had missed life. I have always missed life. It always goes away from me. I always imagined people walking away. In the spring this year I walked on the railroad track out to the bridge over Willow Creek. Violets grew in the grass. At that time I hardly noticed them but today I remembered. The violets were like the people who walk away from me. A mad desire to run after them had taken possession of me. I felt like a bird flying through space. A conviction that something had escaped me and that I must pursue it had taken possession of me."

Melville Stoner stopped talking. His face also had grown white and his hands also trembled. Rosalind had an almost irresistible desire to put out her hand and touch his hand. She wanted to shout, crying—"I am here. I am not dead. I am alive." Instead she stood in silence, staring at him, as the widow who owned the high flying hens had stared. Melville Stoner struggled to recover from the ecstasy into which he had been thrown by his own words. He bowed and smiled. "I hope you are in the habit of walking on railroad tracks," he said. "I shall in the future know what to do with my time. When you come to town I shall camp on the railroad tracks. No doubt, like the violets, you have left your fragrance out there." Rosalind looked at him. He was laughing at her as he had laughed when he talked to the widow standing at his gate. She did not mind. When he had left her she went slowly through the streets. The phrase that had come into her mind as they walked on the tracks came back and she said it over and over. "And God spoke to me out of a burning bush." She kept repeating the phrase until she got back into the Wescott house.

* * *

Rosalind sat on the front porch of the house where her girlhood had been spent. Her father had not come home for the evening meal. He was a dealer in coal and lumber and owned a number of unpainted sheds facing a railroad siding west of town. There was a tiny office with a stove and a desk in a corner by a window. The desk was piled high with unanswered letters and with circulars from mining and lumber companies. Over them had settled a thick layer of coal dust. All day he sat in his office looking like an animal in a cage, but unlike a caged animal he was apparently not discontented and did not grow restless. He was the one coal and lumber dealer in Willow Springs. When people wanted one of these commodities they had to come to him. There was no other place to go. He was content. In the morning as soon as he got to his office he read the Des Moines paper and then if no one came to disturb him he sat all day, by the stove in winter and by an open window through the long hot summer days, apparently unaffected by the marching change of seasons pictured in the fields, without thought, without hope, without regret that life was becoming an old worn out thing for him.

In the Wescott house Rosalind's mother had already begun the canning of which she had several times spoken. She was making gooseberry jam. Rosalind could hear the pots boiling in the kitchen. Her mother walked heavily. With the coming of age she was beginning to grow fat.

The daughter was weary from much thinking. It had been a day of many emotions. She took off her hat and laid it on the porch beside her. Melville Stoner's house next door had windows that were like eyes staring at her, accusing her. "Well now, you see, you have gone too fast," the house declared. It sneered at her. "You thought you knew about people. After all you knew nothing." Rosalind held her head in her hands. It was true she had misunderstood. The man who lived in the house was no doubt like other people in Willow Springs. He was not, as she had smartly supposed, a dull citizen of a dreary town, one who knew nothing of life. Had he not said words that had startled her, torn her out of herself?

Rosalind had an experience not uncommon to tired nervous people. Her mind, weary of thinking, did not stop thinking but went on faster than ever. A new plane of thought was reached. Her mind was like a flying machine that leaves the ground and leaps into the air.

It took hold upon an idea expressed or implied in something Melville Stoner had said. "In every human being there are two voices, each striving to make itself heard."

A new world of thought had opened itself before her. After all human beings might be understood. It might be possible to understand her mother and her mother's life, her father, the man she loved, herself. There was the voice that said words. Words came forth from lips. They conformed, fell into a certain mold. For the most part the words had no life of their own. They had come down out of old times and many of them were no doubt once strong living words, coming out of the depth of people, out of the bellies of people. The words had escaped out of a shut-in place. They had once expressed living truth. Then they had gone on being said, over and over, by the lips of many people, endlessly, wearily.

She thought of men and women she had seen together, that she had heard talking together as they sat in the street cars or in apartments or walked in a Chicago park. Her brother, the traveling salesman, and his wife had talked half wearily through the long evenings she had spent with them in their apartment. It was with them as with the other people. A thing happened. The lips said certain words but the eyes of the people said other words. Sometimes the lips expressed affection while hatred shone out of the eyes. Sometimes it was the other way about. What a confusion!

It was clear there was something hidden away within people that could not get itself expressed except accidentally. One was startled or alarmed and then the words that fell from the lips became pregnant words, words that lived.

The vision that had sometimes visited her in her girlhood as she lay in bed at night came back. Again she saw the people on the marble stairway, going down and away, into infinity. Her own mind began to make words that struggled to get themselves expressed through her lips. She hungered for someone to whom to say the words and half arose to go to her mother, to where her mother was making gooseberry jam in the kitchen, and then sat down again. "They were going down into the hall of the hidden voices," she whispered to herself. The words excited and intoxicated her as had the words from the lips of Melville Stoner. She thought of herself as having quite suddenly grown amazingly, spiritually, even physically. She felt relaxed, young, wonderfully strong. She imagined herself as walking, as had the young girl she had seen in the vision, with swinging arms and shoulders, going down a marble stairway—down into the hidden places in people, into the hall of the little voices. "I shall understand after this, what shall I not understand?" she asked herself.

Doubt came and she trembled a little. As she walked with him on the railroad track Melville Stoner had gone down within herself. Her body was a house, through the door of which he had walked. He had known about the night noises in her father's house— her father at the well by the kitchen door, the slap of the spilled water on the floor. Even when she was a young girl and had thought herself alone in the bed in the darkness in the room upstairs in the house before which she now sat, she had not been alone. The strange bird-like man who lived in the house next door had been with her, in her room, in her bed. Years later he had remembered the terrible little noises of the house and had known how they had terrified her.

There was something terrible in his knowledge too. He had spoken, given forth his knowledge, but as he did so there was laughter in his eyes, perhaps a sneer.

In the Wescott house the sounds of housekeeping went on. A man who had been at work in a distant field, who had already begun his fall plowing, was unhitching his horses from the plow. He was far away, beyond the street's end, in a field that swelled a little out of the plain. Rosalind stared. The man was hitching the horses to a wagon. She saw him as through the large end of a telescope. He would drive the horses away to a distant farmhouse and put them into a barn. Then he would go into a house where there was a woman at work. Perhaps the woman like her mother would be making gooseberry jam. He would grunt as her father did when at evening he came home from the little hot office by the railroad siding. "Hello," he would say, flatly, indifferently, stupidly. Life was like that.

Rosalind became weary of thinking. The man in the distant field had got into his wagon and was driving away. In a moment there would be nothing left of him but a thin cloud of dust that floated in the air. In the house the gooseberry jam had boiled long enough. Her mother was preparing to put it into glass jars. The operation produced a new little side current of sounds. She thought again of Melville

Stoner. For years he had been sitting, listening to sounds. There was a kind of madness in it.

She had got herself into a half frenzied condition. "I must stop it," she told herself. "I am like a stringed instrument on which the strings have been tightened too much." She put her face into her hands, wearily.

And then a thrill ran through her body. There was a reason for Melville Stoner's being what he had become. There was a locked gateway leading to the marble stairway that led down and away, into infinity, into the hall of the little voices and the key to the gateway was love. Warmth came back into Rosalind's body. "Understanding need not lead to weariness," she thought. Life might after all be a rich, a triumphant thing. She would make her visit to Willow Springs count for something significant in her life. For one thing she would really approach her mother, she would walk into her mother's life. "It will be my first trip down the marble stairway," she thought and tears came to her eyes. In a moment her father would be coming home for the evening meal but after supper he would go away. The two women would be alone together. Together they would explore a little into the mystery of life, they would find sisterhood. The thing she had wanted to talk about with another understanding woman could be talked about then. There might yet be a beautiful outcome to her visit to Willow Springs and to her mother.

II

The story of Rosalind's six years in Chicago is the story of thousands of unmarried women who work in offices in the city. Necessity had not driven her to work nor kept her at her task and she did not think of herself as a worker, one who would always be a worker. For a time after she came out of the stenographic school she drifted from office to office, acquiring always more skill, but with no particular interest in what she was doing. It was a way to put in the long days. Her father, who in addition to the coal and lumber yards owned three farms, sent her a hundred dollars a month. The money her work brought was spent for clothes so that she dressed better than the women she worked with.

Of one thing she was quite sure. She did not want to return to Willow Springs to live with her father and mother, and after a time she knew she could not continue living with her brother and his wife. For the first time she began seeing the city that spread itself out before her eyes. When she walked at the noon hour along Michigan Boulevard or went into a restaurant or in the evening went home in the street car she saw men and women together. It was the same when on Sunday afternoons in the summer she walked in the park or by the lake. On a street car she saw a small round-faced woman put her hand into the hand of her male companion. Before she did it she looked cautiously about. She wanted to assure herself of something. To the other women in the car, to Rosalind and the others the act said something. It was as though the woman's voice had said aloud, "He is mine. Do not draw too close to him."

There was no doubt that Rosalind was awakening out of the Willow Springs torpor in which she had lived out her young womanhood. The city had at least done that for her. The city was wide. It flung itself out. One had but to let his feet go thump, thump upon the pavements to get into strange streets, see always new faces.

On Saturday afternoon and all day Sunday one did not work. In the summer it was a time to go to places —to the park, to walk among the strange colorful crowds in Halsted Street, with a half dozen young people from the office, to spend a day on the sand dunes at the foot of Lake Michigan. One got excited and was hungry, hungry, always hungry—for companionship. That was it. One wanted to possess something—a man—to take him along on jaunts, be sure of him, yes—own him.

She read books—always written by men or by man-like women. There was an essential mistake in the viewpoint of life set forth in the books. The mistake was always being made. In Rosalind's time it grew more pronounced. Someone had got hold of a key with which the door to the secret chamber of life could be unlocked. Others took the key and rushed in. The secret chamber of life was filled with a noisy vulgar crowd. All the books that dealt with life at all dealt with it through the lips of the crowd that had newly come into the sacred place. The writer had hold of the key. It was his time to be heard. "Sex," he cried. "It is by understanding sex I will untangle the mystery."

It was all very well and sometimes interesting but one grew tired of the subject.

She lay abed in her room at her brother's house on a Sunday night in the summer. During the afternoon she had gone for a walk and on a street on the Northwest Side had come upon a religious procession. The Virgin was being carried through the streets. The houses were decorated and women leaned out at the windows of houses. Old priests dressed in white gowns waddled along. Strong young men carried the platform on which the Virgin rested. The procession stopped. Someone started a chant in a loud clear voice. Other voices took it up. Children ran about gathering in money. All the time there was a loud hum of ordinary conversation going on. Women shouted across the street to other women. Young girls walked on the sidewalks and laughed softly as the young men in white, clustered about the Virgin, turned to stare at them. On every street corner merchants sold candies, nuts, cool drinks—

In her bed at night Rosalind put down the book she had been reading. "The worship of the Virgin is a form of sex expression," she read.

"Well what of it? If it be true what does it matter?"

She got out of bed and took off her nightgown. She was herself a virgin. What did that matter? She turned herself slowly about, looking at her strong young woman's body. It was a thing in which sex lived. It was a thing upon which sex in others might express itself. What did it matter?

There was her brother sleeping with his wife in another room near at hand. In Willow Springs, Iowa, her father was at just this moment pumping a pail of water at the well by the kitchen door. In a moment he would carry it into the kitchen to set it on the box by the kitchen sink.

Rosalind's cheeks were flushed. She made an odd and lovely figure standing nude before the glass in her room there in Chicago. She was so much alive and yet not alive. Her eyes shone with excitement. She continued to turn slowly round and round twisting her head to look at her naked back. "Perhaps I am learning to think," she decided. There was some sort of essential mistake in people's conception of life. There was something she knew and it was of as much importance as the things the wise men knew and put into books. She also had found out something about life. Her body was still the body of what was called a virgin. What of it? "If the sex impulse within it had been gratified in what way would my problem be solved? I am lonely now. It is evident that after that had happened I would still be lonely."

III

Rosalind's life in Chicago had been like a stream that apparently turns back toward its source. It ran forward, then stopped, turned, twisted. At just the time when her awakening became a half realized thing she went to work at a new place, a piano factory on the Northwest Side facing a branch of the Chicago River. She became secretary to a man who was treasurer of the company. He was a slender, rather small man of thirty-eight with thin white restless hands and with gray eyes that were clouded and troubled. For the first time she became really interested in the work that ate up her days. Her employer was charged with the responsibility of passing upon the credit of the firm's customers and was unfitted for the task. He was not shrewd and within a short time had made two costly mistakes by which the company had lost money. "I have too much to do. My time is too much taken up with details. I need help here," he had explained, evidently irritated, and Rosalind had been engaged to relieve him of details.

Her new employer, named Walter Sayers, was the only son of a man who in his time had been well known in Chicago's social and club life. Everyone had thought him wealthy and he had tried to live up to

people's estimate of his fortune. His son Walter had
wanted to be a singer and had expected to inherit a
comfortable fortune. At thirty he had married and
three years later when his father died he was already
the father of two children.

And then suddenly he had found himself quite pen-
niless. He could sing but his voice was not large.
It wasn't an instrument with which one could make
money in any dignified way. Fortunately his wife had
some money of her own. It was her money, invested
in the piano manufacturing business, that had secured
him the position as treasurer of the company. With
his wife he withdrew from social life and they went
to live in a comfortable house in a suburb.

Walter Sayers gave up music, apparently surrendered even his interest in it. Many men and women
from his suburb went to hear the orchestra on Friday
afternoons but he did not go. "What's the use of tor-
turing myself and thinking of a life I cannot lead?"
he said to himself. To his wife he pretended a growing interest in his work at the factory. "It's really
fascinating. It's a game, like moving men back and
forth on a chess board. I shall grow to love it," he
said.

He had tried to build up interest in his work but
had not been successful. Certain things would not get
into his consciousness. Although he tried hard he
could not make the fact that profit or loss to the com-

pany depended upon his judgment seem important to himself. It was a matter of money lost or gained and money meant nothing to him. "It's father's fault," he thought. "While he lived money never meant anything to me. I was brought up wrong. I am ill prepared for the battle of life." He became too timid and lost business that should have come to the company quite naturally. Then he became too bold in the extension of credit and other losses followed.

His wife was quite happy and satisfied with her life. There were four or five acres of land about the suburban house and she became absorbed in the work of raising flowers and vegetables. For the sake of the children she kept a cow. With a young negro gardener she puttered about all day, digging in the earth, spreading manure about the roots of bushes and shrubs, planting and transplanting. In the evening when he had come home from his office in his car she took him by the arm and led him eagerly about. The two children trotted at their heels. She talked glowingly. They stood at a low spot at the foot of the garden and she spoke of the necessity of putting in tile. The prospect seemed to excite her. "It will be the best land on the place when it's drained," she said. She stooped and with a trowel turned over the soft black soil. An odor arose. "See! Just see how rich and black it is!" she exclaimed eagerly. "It's a little sour now because water has stood on it." She seemed to be apologizing as for a wayward child. "When it's drained I shall use lime to sweeten it," she added. She was like a mother leaning over the cradle of a sleeping babe. Her enthusiasm irritated him.

When Rosalind came to take the position in his office the slow fires of hatred that had been burning beneath the surface of Walter Sayers' life had already eaten away much of his vigor and energy. His body sagged in the office chair and there were heavy sagging lines at the corners of his mouth. Outwardly he remained always kindly and cheerful but back of the clouded, troubled eyes the fires of hatred burned slowly, persistently. It was as though he was trying to awaken from a troubled dream that gripped him, a dream that frightened a little, that was unending. He had contracted little physical habits. A sharp paper cutter lay on his desk. As he read a letter from one of the firm's customers he took it up and jabbed little holes in the leather cover of his desk. When he had several letters to sign he took up his pen and jabbed it almost viciously into the inkwell. Then before signing he jabbed it in again. Sometimes he did the thing a dozen times in succession.

Sometimes the things that went on beneath the surface of Walter Sayers frightened him. In order to do what he called "putting in his Saturday afternoons and Sundays" he had taken up photography. The camera took him away from his own house and the sight of the garden where his wife and the negro were busy digging, and into the fields and into stretches of woodland at the edge of the suburban village. Also it took him away from his wife's talk, from her eternal planning for the garden's future. Here by the house tulip bulbs were to be put in in the fall. Later there would be a hedge of lilac bushes shutting off the house from the road. The men who lived in the other houses along the suburban street spent their Saturday afternoons and Sunday mornings tinkering with motor cars. On Sunday afternoons they took their families driving, sitting up very straight and silent at the driving wheel. They consumed the afternoon in a swift dash over country roads. The car ate up the hours. Monday morning and the work in the city was there, at the end of the road. They ran madly toward it.

For a time the use of the camera made Walter Sayers almost happy. The study of light, playing on the trunk of a tree or over the grass in a field appealed to some instinct within. It was an uncertain delicate business. He fixed himself a dark room upstairs in the house and spent his evenings there. One dipped the films into the developing liquid, held them to the light and then dipped them again. The little nerves that controlled the eyes were aroused. One felt oneself being enriched, a little—

One Sunday afternoon he went to walk in a strip of woodland and came out upon the slope of a low hill. He had read somewhere that the low hill country southwest of Chicago, in which his suburb lay, had once been the shore of Lake Michigan. The low hills sprang out of the flat land and were covered with forests. Beyond them the flat lands began again. The prairies went on indefinitely, into infinity. People's lives went on so. Life was too long. It was to be spent in the endless doing over and over of an unsatisfactory task. He sat on the slope and looked out across the land.

He thought of his wife. She was back there, in the suburb in the hills, in her garden making things grow. It was a noble sort of thing to be doing. One shouldn't be irritated.

Well he had married her expecting to have money of his own. Then he would have worked at something else. Money would not have been involved in the matter and success would not have been a thing one must seek. He had expected his own life would be motivated. No matter how much or how hard he worked he would not have been a great singer. What did that matter? There was a way to live—a way of life in which such things did not matter. The delicate shades of things might be sought after. Before his eyes, there on the grass covered flat lands, the afternoon light was playing. It was like a breath, a vapor of color blown suddenly from between red lips out over the grey dead burned grass. Song might be like that. The beauty might come out of himself, out of his own body.

Again he thought of his wife and the sleeping light in his eyes flared up, it became a flame. He felt himself being mean, unfair. It didn't matter. Where did the truth lie? Was his wife, digging in her garden, having always a succession of small triumphs, marching forward with the seasons—well, was she becoming a little old, lean and sharp, a little vulgarized?

It seemed so to him. There was something smug in the way in which she managed to fling green growing flowering things over the black land. It was obvious the thing could be done and that there was satisfaction in doing it. It was a little like running a business and making money by it. There was a deep seated vulgarity involved in the whole matter. His wife put her hands into the black ground. They felt about, caressed the roots of the growing things. She laid hold of the slender trunk of a young tree in a certain way—as though she possessed it.

One could not deny that the destruction of beautiful things was involved. Weeds grew in the garden, delicate shapely things. She plucked them out without thought. He had seen her do it.

As for himself, he also had been pulled out of something. Had he not surrendered to the fact of a wife and growing children? Did he not spend his days doing work he detested? The anger within him burned bright. The fire came into his conscious self. Why should a weed that is to be destroyed pretend to a vegetable existence? As for puttering about with a camera—was it not a form of cheating? He did not want to be a photographer. He had once wanted to be a singer.

He arose and walked along the hillside, still watching the shadows play over the plains below. At night —in bed with his wife—well, was she not sometimes with him as she was in the garden? Something was plucked out of him and another thing grew in its place—something oho wanted to have grow. Their love making was like his puttering with a camera —to make the the weekends pass. She came at him a little too determinedly—sure. She was plucking delicate weeds in order that things she had determined upon—"vegetables," he exclaimed in disgust—in order that vegetables might grow. Love was a fragrance, the shading of a tone over the lips, out of the throat. It was like the afternoon light on the burned grass. Keeping a garden and making flowers grow had nothing to do with it.

Walter Sayers' fingers twitched. The camera hung by a strap over his shoulder. He took hold of the strap and walked to a tree. He swung the box above his head and brought it down with a thump against the tree trunk. The sharp breaking sound—the delicate parts of the machine being broken—was sweet to his ears. It was as though a song had come suddenly from between his lips. Again he swung the box and again brought it down against the tree trunk.

IV

Rosalind at work in Walter Sayers' office was from the beginning something different, apart from the young woman from Iowa who had been drifting from office to office, moving from rooming house to rooming house on Chicago's North Side, striving feebly to find out something about life by reading books, going to the theatre and walking alone in the streets. In the new place her life at once began to have point and purpose, but at the same time the perplexity that was later to send her running to Willow Springs and to the presence of her mother began to grow in her.

Walter Sayers' office was a rather large room on the third floor of the factory whose walls went straight up from the river's edge. In the morning Rosalind arrived at eight and went into the office and closed the door. In a large room across a narrow hallway and shut off from her retreat by two thick, clouded-glass partitions was the company's general office. It contained the desks of salesmen, several clerks, a bookkeeper and two stenographers. Rosalind avoided becoming acquainted with these people. She was in a mood to be alone, to spend as many hours as possible alone with her own thoughts.

She got to the office at eight and her employer did

not arrive until nine-thirty or ten. For an hour or two in the morning and in the late afternoon she had the place to herself. Immediately she shut the door into the hallway and was alone she felt at home. Even in her father's house it had never been so. She took off her wraps and walked about the room touching things, putting things to rights. During the night a negro woman had scrubbed the floor and wiped the dust off her employer's desk but she got a cloth and wiped the desk again. Then she opened the letters that had come in and after reading arranged them in little piles. She wanted to spend a part of her wages for flowers and imagined clusters of flowers arranged in small hanging baskets along the grey walls. "I'll do that later, perhaps," she thought.

The walls of the room enclosed her. "What makes me so happy here?" she asked herself. As for her employer—she felt she scarcely knew him. He was a shy man, rather small—

She went to a window and stood looking out. Near the factory a bridge crossed the river and over it went a stream of heavily loaded wagons and motor trucks. The sky was grey with smoke. In the afternoon, after her employer had gone for the day, she would stand again by the window. As she stood thus she faced westward and in the afternoon saw the sun fall down the sky. It was glorious to be there alone during the late hours of the afternoon. What a tremendous thing this city in which she had come to live! For some reason after she went to work for Walter Sayers the city seemed, like the room in which she worked, to have accepted her, taken her into itself. In the late afternoon the rays of the departing sun fell across great banks of clouds. The whole city seemed to reach upwards. It left the ground and ascended into the air. There was an illusion produced. Stark grim factory chimneys, that all day were stiff cold formal things sticking up into the air and belching forth black smoke, were now slender upreaching pencils of light and wavering color. The tall chimneys detached themselves from the buildings and sprang into the air. The factory in which Rosalind stood had such a chimney. It also was leaping upward. She felt herself being lifted, an odd floating sensation was achieved. With what a stately tread the day went away, over the city! The city, like the factory chimneys yearned after it, hungered for it.

In the morning gulls came in from Lake Michigan to feed on the sewage floating in the river below. The river was the color of chrysoprase. The gulls floated above it as sometimes in the evening the whole city seemed to float before her eyes. They were graceful, living, free things. They were triumphant. The getting of food, even the eating of sewage was done thus gracefully, beautifully. The gulls turned and twisted in the air. They wheeled and floated and then fell downward to the river in a long curve, just touching, caressing the surface of the water and then rising again.

Rosalind raised herself on her toes. At her back beyond the two glass partitions were other men and women, but there, in that room, she was alone. She belonged there. What an odd feeling she had. She also belonged to her employer, Walter Sayers. She scarcely knew the man and yet she belonged to him. She threw her arms above her head, trying awkwardly to imitate some movement of the birds.

Her awkwardness shamed her a little and she turned and walked about the room. "I'm twenty-five years old and it's a little late to begin trying to be a bird, to be graceful," she thought. She resented the slow stupid heavy movements of her father and mother, the movements she had imitated as a child. "Why was I not taught to be graceful and beautiful in mind and body, why in the place I came from did no one think it worth while to try to be graceful and beautiful?" she whispered to herself.

How conscious of her own body Rosalind was becoming! She walked across the room, trying to go lightly and gracefully. In the office beyond the glass partitions someone spoke suddenly and she was startled. She laughed foolishly. For a long time after she went to work in the office of Walter Sayers she thought the desire in herself to be physically more graceful and beautiful and to rise also out of the mental stupidity and sloth of her young womanhood was due to the fact that the factory windows faced the river and the western sky, and that in the morning she saw the gulls feeding and in the afternoon the sun going down through the smoke clouds in a riot of colors.

V

On the August evening as Rosalind sat on the porch before her father's house in Willow Springs, Walter Sayers came home from the factory by the river and to his wife's suburban garden. When the family had dined he came out to walk in the paths with the two children, boys, but they soon tired of his silence and went to join their mother. The young negro came along a path by the kitchen door and joined the party. Walter went to sit on a garden seat that was concealed behind bushes. He lighted a cigarette but did not smoke. The smoke curled quietly up through his fingers as it burned itself out.

Closing his eyes Walter sat perfectly still and tried not to think. The soft evening shadows began presently to close down and around him. For a long time he sat thus motionless, like a carved figure placed on the garden bench. He rested. He lived and did not live. The intense body, usually so active and alert, had become a passive thing. It was thrown aside, on to the bench, under the bush, to sit there, waiting to be reinhabited.

This hanging suspended between consciousness and unconsciousness was a thing that did not happen often. There was something to be settled between himself and a woman and the woman had gone away. His whole plan of life had been disturbed. Now he wanted to rest. The details of his life were forgotten. As for the woman he did not think of her, did not want to think of her. It was ridiculous that he needed her so much. He wondered if he had ever felt that way about Cora, his wife. Perhaps he had. Now she was near him, but a few yards away. It was almost dark but she with the negro remained at work, digging in the ground—somewhere near—caressing the soil, making things grow.

When his mind was undisturbed by thoughts and lay like a lake in the hills on a quiet summer evening little thoughts did come. "I want you as a lover—far away. Keep yourself far away." The words trailed through his mind as the smoke from the cigarette trailed slowly upwards through his fingers. Did the words refer to Rosalind Wescott? She had been gone from him three days. Did he hope she would never come back or did the words refer to his wife?

His wife's voice spoke sharply. One of the children in playing about, had stepped on a plant. "If you are not careful I shall have to make you stay out of the garden altogether." She raised her voice and called, "Marian!" A maid came from the house and took the children away. They went along the path toward the house protesting. Then they ran back to kiss their mother. There was a struggle and then acceptance. The kiss was acceptance of their fate—to obey. "O, Walter," the mother's voice called, but the man on the bench did not answer. Tree toads began to cry. "The kiss is acceptance. Any physical contact with another is acceptance," he reflected.

The little voices within Walter Sayers were talking away at a great rate. Suddenly he wanted to sing. He had been told that his voice was small, not of much account, that he would never be a singer. It was quite true no doubt but here, in the garden on the quiet summer night, was a place and a time for a small voice. It would be like the voice within himself that whispered sometimes when he was quiet, relaxed. One evening when he had been with the woman, Rosalind, when he had taken her into the country in his car, he had suddenly felt as he did now. They sat together in the car that he had run into a field. For a long time they had remained silent. Some cattle came and stood nearby, their figures soft in the night. Suddenly he had felt like a new man in a new world and had begun to sing. He sang one song over and over, then sat in silence for a time and after that drove out of the field and through a gate into the road. He took the woman back to her place in the city.

In the quiet of the garden on the summer evening he opened his lips to sing the same song. He would sing with the tree toad hidden away in the fork of a tree somewhere. He would lift his voice up from the earth, up into the branches, of trees, away from the ground in which people were digging, his wife and the young negro.

The song did not come. His wife began speaking and the sound of her voice took away the desire to sing. Why had she not, like the other woman, remained silent?

He began playing a game. Sometimes, when he was alone the thing happened to him that had now happened. His body became like a tree or a plant. Life ran through it unobstructed. He had dreamed of being a singer but at such a moment he wanted also to be a dancer. That would have been sweetest of all things—to sway like the tops of young trees when a wind blew, to give himself as grey weeds in a sunburned field gave themself to the influence of passing shadows, changing color constantly, becoming every moment something new, to live in life and in death too, always to live, to be unafraid of life, to let it flow through his body, to let the blood flow through his body, not to struggle, to offer no resistance, to dance.

Walter Sayers' children had gone into the house with the nurse girl Marian. It had become too dark for his wife to dig in the garden. It was August and the fruitful time of the year for farms and gardens had come, but his wife had forgotten fruitfulness. She was making plans for another year. She came along the garden path followed by the negro. "We will set out strawberry plants there," she was saying. The soft voice of the young negro murmured his assent. It was evident the young man lived in her conception of the garden. His mind sought out her desire and gave itself.

The children Walter Sayers had brought into life through the body of his wife Cora had gone into the house and to bed. They bound him to life, to his wife, to the garden where he sat, to the office by the riverside in the city.

They were not his children. Suddenly he knew that quite clearly. His own children were quite different things. "Men have children just as women do. The children come out of their bodies. They play about," he thought. It seemed to him that children, born of his fancy, were at that very moment playing about the bench where he sat. Living things that dwelt within him and that had at the same time the power to depart out of him were now running along paths, swinging from the branches of trees, dancing in the soft light.

His mind sought out the figure of Rosalind Wescott. She had gone away, to her own people in Iowa. There had been a note at the office saying she might be gone for several days. Between himself and Rosalind the conventional relationship of employer and employee had long since been swept quite away. It needed

something in a man he did not possess to maintain
that relationship with either men or women.

At the moment he wanted to forget Rosalind. In
her there was a struggle going on. The two people
had wanted to be lovers and he had fought against
that. They had talked about it. "Well," he said, "it
will not work out. We will bring unnecessary un-
happiness upon ourselves."

He had been honest enough in fighting off the in-
tensification of their relationship. "If she were here
now, in this garden with me, it wouldn't matter. We
could be lovers and then forget about being lovers,"
he told himself.

IIis wife came along the path and stopped nearby.
She continued talking in a low voice, making plans for
another year of gardening. The negro stood near
her, his figure making a dark wavering mass against
the foliage of a low growing bush. His wife wore a
white dress. He could see her figure quite plainly.
In the uncertain light it looked girlish and young.
She put her hand up and took hold of the body of
a young tree. The hand became detached from her
body. The pressure of her leaning body made the
young tree sway a little. The white hand moved
slowly back and forth in space.

Rosalind Wescott had gone home to tell her mother
of her love. In her note she had said nothing of that
but Walter Sayers knew that was the object of her

visit to the Iowa town. It was on odd sort of thing to try to do—to tell people of love, to try to explain it to others.

The night was a thing apart from Walter Sayers, the male being sitting in silence in the garden. Only the children of his fancy understood it. The night was a living thing. It advanced upon him, enfolded him. "Night is the sweet little brother of Death," he thought.

His wife stood very near. Her voice was soft and low and the voice of the negro when he answered her comments on the future of the garden was soft and low. There was music in the negro's voice, perhaps a dance in it. Walter remembered about him.

The young negro had been in trouble before he came to the Sayers. He had been an ambitious young black and had listened to the voices of people, to the voices that filled the air of America, rang through the houses of America. He had wanted to get on in life and had tried to educate himself. The black had wanted to be a lawyer.

How far away he had got from his own people, from the blacks of the African forests! He had wanted to be a lawyer in a city in America. What a notion!

Well he had got into trouble. He had managed to get through college and had opened a law office. Then one evening he went out to walk and chance led him into a street where a woman, a white woman, had been murdered an hour before. The body of the woman was found and then he was found walking in the street. Mrs. Sayers' brother, a lawyer, had saved him from being punished as a murderer and after the trial, and the young negro's acquittal, had induced his sister to take him as gardener. His chances as a professional man in the city were no good. "He has had a terrible experience and has just escaped by a fluke" the brother had said. Cora Sayers had taken the young man. She had bound him to herself, to her garden.

It was evident the two people were bound together. One cannot bind another without being bound. His wife had no more to say to the negro who went away along the path that led to the kitchen door. He had a room in a little house at the foot of the garden. In the room he had books and a piano. Sometimes in the evening he sang. He was going now to his place. By educating himself he had cut himself off from his own people.

Cora Sayers went into the house and Walter sat alone. After a time the young negro came silently down the path. He stopped by the tree where a moment before the white woman had stood talking to him. He put his hand on the trunk of the young tree where her hand had been and then went softly away. His feet made no sound on the garden path.

An hour passed. In his little house at the foot of

the garden the negro began to sing softly. He did that sometimes in the middle of the night. What a life he had led too! He had come away from his black people, from the warm brown girls with the golden colors playing through the blue black of their skins and had worked his way through a Northern college, had accepted the patronage of impertinent people who wanted to uplift the black race, had listened to them, had bound himself to them, had tried to follow the way of life they had suggested.

Now he was in the little house at the foot of the Sayers' garden. Walter remembered little things his wife had told him about the man. The experience in the court room had frightened him horribly and he did not want to go off the Sayers' place. Education, books had done something to him. He could not go back to his own people. In Chicago, for the most part, the blacks lived crowded into a few streets on the South Side. "I want to be a slave," he had said to Cora Sayers. "You may pay me money if it makes you feel better but I shall have no use for it. I want to be your slave. I would be happy if I knew I would never have to go off your place."

The black sang a low voiced song. It ran like a little wind on the surface of a pond. It had no words. He had remembered the song from his father who had got it from his father. In the South, in Alabama and Mississippi the blacks sang it when they rolled cotton bales onto the steamers in the rivers. They had got it from other rollers of cotton bales long since dead. Long before there were any cotton bales to roll black men in boats on rivers in Africa had sung it. Young blacks in boats floated down rivers and came to a town they intended to attack at dawn. There was bravado in singing the song then. It was addressed to the women in the town to be attacked and contained both a caress and a threat. "In the morning your husbands and brothers and sweethearts we shall kill. Then we shall come into your town to you. We shall hold you close. We shall make you forget. With our hot love and our strength we shall make you forget." That was the old significance of the song.

Walter Sayers remembered many things. On other nights when the negro sang and when he lay in his room upstairs in the house, his wife came to him. There were two beds in their room. She sat upright in her bed. "Do you hear, Walter?" she asked. She came to sit on his bed, sometimes she crept into his arms. In the African villages long ago when the song floated up from the river men arose and prepared for battle. The song was a defiance, a taunt. That was all gone now. The young negro's house was at the foot of the garden and Walter with his wife lay upstairs in the larger house situated on high ground. It was a sad song, filled with race sadness. There was something in the ground that wanted to

grow, buried deep in the ground. Cora Sayers understood that. It touched something instinctive in her.
Her hand went out and touched, caressed her husband's face, his body. The song made her want to
hold him tight, possess him.

The night was advancing and it grew a little cold
in the garden. The negro stopped singing. Walter
Sayers arose and went along the path toward the house
but did not enter. Instead he went through a gate into
the road and along the suburban streets until he got
into the open country. There was no moon but the
stars shone brightly. For a time he hurried along
looking back as though afraid of being followed, but
when he got out into a broad flat meadow he went more
slowly. For an hour he walked and then stopped and
sat on a tuft of dry grass. For some reason he knew
he could not return to his house in the suburb that
night. In the morning he would go to the office and
wait there until Rosalind came. Then? He did not
know what he would do then. "I shall have to make
up some story. In the morning I shall have to telephone Cora and make up some silly story," he thought.
It was an absurd thing that he, a grown man, could
not spend a night abroad, in the fields without the
necessity of explanations. The thought irritated him
and he arose and walked again. Under the stars in
the soft night and on the wide flat plains the irritation
soon went away and he began to sing softly, but the

song he sang was not the one he had repeated over and over on that other night when he sat with Rosalind in the car and the cattle came. It was the song the negro sang, the river song of the young black warriors that slavery had softened and colored with sadness. On the lips of Walter Sayers the song had lost much of its sadness. He walked almost gaily along and in the song that flowed from his lips there was a taunt, a kind of challenge.

VI

At the end of the short street on which the Wescotts lived in Willow Springs there was a cornfield. When Rosalind was a child it was a meadow and beyond was an orchard.

On summer afternoons the child often went there to sit alone on the banks of a tiny stream that wandered away eastward toward Willow Creek, draining the farmer's fields on the way. The creek had made a slight depression in the level contour of the land and she sat with her back against an old apple tree and with her bare feet almost touching the water. Her mother did not permit her to run bare footed through the streets but when she got into the orchard she took her shoes off. It gave her a delightful naked feeling.

Overhead and through the branches the child could see the great sky. Masses of white clouds broke into fragments and then the fragments came together again. The sun ran in behind one of the cloud masses and grey shadows slid silently over the face of distant fields. The world of her child life, the Wescott household, Melville Stoner sitting in his house, the cries of other children who lived in her street, all the life she knew went far away. To be there in that silent place was like lying awake in bed at night only in some way sweeter and better. There were no dull household sounds and the air she breathed was sweeter, cleaner. The child played a little game. All the apple trees in the orchard were old and gnarled and she had given all the trees names. There was one fancy that frightened her a little but was delicious too. She fancied that at night when she had gone to bed and was asleep and when all the town of Willow Springs had gone to sleep the trees came out of the ground and walked about. The grasses beneath the trees, the bushes that grew beside the fence—all came out of the ground and ran madly here and there. They danced wildly. The old trees, like stately old men, put their heads together and talked. As they talked their bodies swayed slightly—back and forth, back and forth. The bushes and flowering weeds ran in great circles among the little grasses. The grasses hopped straight up and down.

Sometimes when she sat with her back against the tree on warm bright afternoons the child Rosalind had played the game of dancing-life until she grew afraid and had to give it up. Nearby in the fields men were cultivating corn. The breasts of the horses and their wide strong shoulders pushed the young corn aside and made a low rustling sound. Now and then a man's voice was raised in a shout. "Hi, there you Joe! Get in there Frank!" The widow of the hens owned a little woolly dog that occasionally broke into a spasm

of barking, apparently without cause, senseless, eager,
barking. Rosalind shut all the sounds out. She closed
her eyes and struggled, trying to get into the place
beyond human sounds. After a time her desire was
accomplished. There was a low sweet sound like
the murmuring of voices far away. Now the thing
was happening. With a kind of tearing sound the
trees came up to stand on top of the ground. They
moved with stately tread toward each other. Now
the mad bushes and the flowering weeds came running, dancing madly, now the joyful grasses hopped.
Rosalind could not stay long in her world of fancy.
It was too mad, too joyful. She opened her eyes and
jumped to her feet. Everything was all right. The
trees stood solidly rooted in the ground, the weeds
and bushes had gone back to their places by the fence,
the grasses lay asleep on the ground. She felt that
her father and mother, her brother, everyone she
knew would not approve of her being there among
them. The world of dancing life was a lovely but a
wicked world. She knew. Sometimes she was a little
mad herself and then she was whipped or scolded.
The mad world of her fancy had to be put away. It
frightened her a little. Once after the thing appeared
she cried, went down to the fence crying. A man who
was cultivating corn came along and stopped his
horses. "What's the matter?" he asked sharply. She
couldn't tell him so she told a lie. "A bee stung me,"

she said. The man laughed. "It'll get well. Better put on your shoes," he advised.

The time of the marching trees and the dancing grasses was in Rosalind's childhood. Later when she had graduated from the Willow Springs High School and had the three years of waiting about the Wescott house before she went to the city she had other experiences in the orchard. Then she had been reading novels and had talked with other young women. She knew many things that after all she did not know. In the attic of her mother's house there was a cradle in which she and her brother had slept when they were babies. One day she went up there and found it. Bedding for the cradle was packed away in a trunk and she took it out. She arranged the cradle for the reception of a child. Then after she did it she was ashamed. Her mother might come up the attic stairs and see it. She put the bedding quickly back into the trunk and went down stairs, her cheeks burning with shame.

What a confusion! One day she went to the house of a schoolgirl friend who was about to be married. Several other girls came and they were all taken into a bedroom where the bride's trousseau was laid out on a bed. What soft lovely things! All the girls went forward and stood over them, Rosalind among them. Some of the girls were shy, others bold. There was one, a thin girl who had no breasts. Her body was flat like a door and she had a thin sharp voice and a thin sharp face. She began to cry out strangely. "How sweet, how sweet, how sweet," she cried over and over. The voice was not like a human voice. It was like something being hurt, an animal in the forest, far away somewhere by itself, being hurt. Then the girl dropped to her knees beside the bed and began to weep bitterly. She declared she could not bear the thought of her schoolgirl friend being married. "Don't do it! O, Mary don't do it!" she pleaded. The other girls laughed but Rosalind couldn't stand it. She hurried out of the house.

That was one thing that had happened to Rosalind and there were other things. Once she saw a young man on the street. He clerked in a store and Rosalind did not know him. However her fancy played with the thought that she had married him. Her own thoughts made her ashamed.

Everything shamed her. When she went into the orchard on summer afternoons she sat with her back against the apple tree and took off her shoes and stockings just as she had when she was a child, but the world of her childhood fancy was gone, nothing could bring it back.

Rosalind's body was soft but all her flesh was firm and strong. She moved away from the tree and lay on the ground. She pressed her body down into the grass, into the firm hard ground. It seemed to her that her mind, her fancy, all the life within her, except just her physical life, went away. The earth pressed upwards against her body. Her body was pressed against the earth. There was darkness. She was imprisoned. She pressed against the walls of her prison. Everything was dark and there was in all the earth silence. Her fingers clutched a handful of the grasses, played in the grasses.

Then she grew very still but did not sleep. There was something that had nothing to do with the ground beneath her or the trees or the clouds in the sky, that seemed to want to come to her, come into her, a kind of white wonder of life.

The thing couldn't happen. She opened her eyes and there was the sky overhead and the trees standing silently about. She went again to sit with her back against one of the trees. She thought with dread of the evening coming on and the necessity of going out of the orchard and to the Wescott house. She was weary. It was the weariness that made her appear to others a rather dull stupid young women. Where was the wonder of life? It was not within herself, not in the ground. It must be in the sky overhead. Presently it would be night and the stars would come out. Perhaps the wonder did not really exist in life. It had something to do with God. She wanted to ascend upwards, to go at once up into God's house, to be there among the light strong men and women who had died and left dullness and heaviness behind them on the earth. Thinking of them took some of her weariness away and sometimes she went out of the orchard in the late afternoon walking almost lightly. Something like grace seemed to have come into her tall strong body.

* * *

Rosalind had gone away from the Wescott house and from Willow Springs, Iowa, feeling that life was essentially ugly. In a way she hated life and people. In Chicago sometimes it was unbelievable how ugly the world had become. She tried to shake off the feeling but it clung to her. She walked through the crowded streets and the buildings were ugly. A sea of faces floated up to her. They were the faces of dead people. The dull death that was in them was in her also. They too could not break through the walls of themselves to the white wonder of life. After all perhaps there was no such thing as the white wonder of life. It might be just a thing of the mind. There was something essentially dirty about life. The dirt was on her and in her. Once as she walked at evening over the Rush Street bridge to her room on the North Side she looked up suddenly and saw the chrysoprase river running inland from the lake. Near at hand stood a soap factory. The men of the city had turned the river about, made it flow inland from the lake. Someone had erected a great soap factory

there near the river's entrance to the city, to the land
of men. Rosalind stopped and stood looking along
the river toward the lake. Men and women, wagons,
automobiles rushed past her. They were dirty. She
was dirty. "The water of an entire sea and millions of
cakes of soap will not wash me clean," she thought.
The dirtiness of life seemed a part of her very being
and an almost overwhelming desire to climb upon the
railing of the bridge and leap down into the chrysoprase river swept over her. Her body trembled
violently and putting down her head and staring at
the flooring of the bridge she hurried away.

And now Rosalind, a grown woman, was in the
Wescott house at the supper table with her father
and mother. None of the three people ate. They
fussed about with the food Ma Wescott had prepared.
Rosalind looked at her mother and thought of what
Melville Stoner had said.

"If I wanted to write I'd do something. I'd tell
what everyone thought. It would startle people,
frighten them a little, eh? I would tell what you have
been thinking this afternoon while you walked here on
this railroad track with me. I would tell what your
mother has been thinking at the same time and what
she would like to say to you."

What had Rosalind's mother been thinking all
through the three days since her daughter had so un-

expectedly come home from Chicago? What did
mothers think in regard to the lives led by their
daughters? Had mothers something of importance
to say to daughters and if they did when did the time
come when they were ready to say it?

She looked at her mother sharply. The older
woman's face was heavy and sagging. She had grey
eyes like Rosalind's but they were dull like the eyes
of a fish lying on a slab of ice in the window of a city
meat market. The daughter was a little frightened by
what she saw in her mother's face and something
caught in her throat. There was an embarrassing
moment. A strange sort of tenseness came into the
air of the room and all three people suddenly got up
from the table.

Rosalind went to help her mother with the dishes
and her father sat in a chair by a window and read a
paper. The daughter avoided looking again into her
mother's face. "I must gather myself together if I
am to do what I want to do," she thought. It was
strange—in fancy she saw the lean bird-like face of
Melville Stoner and the eager tired face of Walter
Sayers floating above the head of her mother who
leaned over the kitchen sink, washing the dishes. Both
of the men's faces sneered at her. "You think you
can but you can't. You are a young fool," the men's
lips seemed to be saying.

Rosalind's father wondered how long his daughter's

visit was to last. After the evening meal he wanted to
clear out of the house, go up town, and he had a
guilty feeling that in doing so he was being dis-
courteous to his daughter. While the two women
washed the dishes he put on his hat and going into
the back yard began chopping wood. Rosalind went
to sit on the front porch. The dishes were all washed
and dried but for a half hour her mother would putter
about in the kitchen. She always did that. She would
arrange and rearrange, pick up dishes and put them
down again. She clung to the kitchen. It was as
though she dreaded the hours that must pass before she
could go upstairs and to bed and asleep, to fall into
the oblivion of sleep.

When Henry Wescott came around the corner of
the house and confronted his daughter he was a little
startled. He did not know what was the matter but
he felt uncomfortable. For a moment he stopped and
looked at her. Life radiated from her figure. A fire
burned in her eyes, in her grey intense eyes. Her hair
was yellow like cornsilk. She was, at the moment, a
complete, a lovely daughter of the cornlands, a being
to be loved passionately, completely by some son of the
cornlands—had there been in the land a son as alive
as this daughter it had thrown aside. The father had
hoped to escape from the house unnoticed. "I'm going up town a little while," he said hesitatingly. Still
he lingered a moment. Some old sleeping thing awoke

in him, was awakened in him by the startling beauty of his daughter. A little fire flared up among the charred rafters of the old house that was his body. "You look pretty, girly," he said sheepishly and then turned his back to her and went along the path to the gate and the street.

Rosalind followed her father to the gate and stood looking as he went slowly along the short street and around a corner. The mood induced in her by her talk with Melville Stoner had returned. Was it possible that her father also felt as Melville Stoner sometimes did? Did loneliness drive him to the door of insanity and did he also run through the night seeking some lost, some hidden and half forgotten loveliness?

When her father had disappeared around the corner she went through the gate and into the street. "I'll go sit by the tree in the orchard until mother has finished puttering about the kitchen," she thought.

Henry Wescott went along the streets until he came to the square about the court house and then went into Emanuel Wilson's Hardware Store. Two or three other men presently joined him there. Every evening he sat among these men of his town saying nothing. It was an escape from his own house and his wife. The other men came for the same reason. A faint perverted kind of male fellowship was achieved. One of the men of the party, a little old man who followed the housepainters trade, was unmarried and lived with his mother. He was himself nearing the age of sixty but his mother was still alive. It was a thing to be wondered about. When in the evening the house painter was a trifle late at the rendezvous a mild flurry of speculation arose, floated in the air for a moment and then settled like dust in an empty house. Did the old house painter do the housework in his own house, did he wash the dishes, cook the food, sweep and make the beds or did his feeble old mother do these things? Emanuel Wilson told a story he had often told before. In a town in Ohio where he had lived as a young man he had once heard a tale. There was an old man like the house painter whose mother was also still alive and lived with him. They were very poor and in the winter had not enough bedclothes to keep them both warm. They crawled into a bed together. It was an innocent enough matter, just like a mother taking her child into her bed.

Henry Wescott sat in the store listening to the tale Emanuel Wilson told for the twentieth time and thought about his daughter. Her beauty made him feel a little proud, a little above the men who were his companions. He had never before thought of his daughter as a beautiful woman. Why had he never before noticed her beauty? Why had she come from Chicago, there by the lake, to Willow Springs, in the hot month of August? Had she come home from

Chicago because she really wanted to see her father and mother? For a moment he was ashamed of his own heavy body, of his shabby clothes and his unshaven face and then the tiny flame that had flared up within him burned itself out. The house painter came in and the faint flavor of male companionship to which he clung so tenaciously was reestablished.

In the orchard Rosalind sat with her back against the tree in the same spot where her fancy had created the dancing life of her childhood and where as a young woman graduate of the Willow Springs High School she had come to try to break through the wall that separated her from life. The sun had disappeared and the grey shadows of night were creeping over the grass, lengthening the shadows cast by the trees. The orchard had long been neglected and many of the trees were dead and without foliage. The shadows of the dead branches were like long lean arms that reached out, felt their way forward over the grey grass. Long lean fingers reached and clutched. There was no wind and the night would be dark and without a moon, a hot dark starlit night of the plains.

In a moment more it would be black night. Already the creeping shadows on the grass were barely discernible. Rosalind felt death all about her, in the orchard, in the town. Something Walter Sayers had once said to her came sharply back into her mind. "When you are in the country alone at night sometime try giving yourself to the night, to the darkness, to the shadows cast by trees. The experience, if you really give yourself to it, will tell you a startling story. You will find that, although the white men have owned the land for several generations now and although they have built towns everywhere, dug coal out of the ground, covered the land with railroads, towns and cities, they do not own an inch of the land in the whole continent. It still belongs to a race who in their physical life are now dead. The red men, although they are practically all gone still own the American continent. Their fancy has peopled it with ghosts, with gods and devils. It is because in their time they loved the land. The proof of what I say is to be seen everywhere. We have given our towns no beautiful names of our own because we have not built the towns beautifully. When an American town has a beautiful name it was stolen from another race, from a race that still owns the land in which we live. We are all strangers here. When you are alone at night in the country, anywhere in America, try giving yourself to the night. You will find that death only resides in the conquering whites and that life remains in the red men who are gone."

The spirits of the two men, Walter Sayers and Melville Stoner, dominated the mind of Rosalind. She felt that. It was as though they were beside her, sitting beside her on the grass in the orchard. She was quite certain that Melville Stoner had come back to his house and was now sitting within sound of her voice, did she raise her voice to call. What did they want her of her? Had she suddenly begun to love two men, both older than herself? The shadows of the branches of trees made a carpet on the floor of the orchard, a soft carpet spun of some delicate material on which the footsteps of men could make no sound. The two men were coming toward her, advancing over the carpet. Melville Stoner was near at hand and Walter Sayers was coming from far away, out of the distance. The spirit of him was creeping toward her. The two men were in accord. They came bearing some male knowledge of life, something they wanted to give her.

She arose and stood by the tree, trembling. Into what a state she had got herself! How long would it endure? Into what knowledge of life and death was she being led? She had come home on a simple mission. She loved Walter Sayers, wanted to offer herself to him but before doing so had felt the call to come home to her mother. She had thought she would be bold and would tell her mother the story of her love. She would tell her and then take what the older woman offered. If her mother understood and sympathized, well that would be a beautiful thing to have happen. If her mother did not understand—at any rate she would have paid some old debt, would have been true to some old, unexpressed obligation.

The two men—what did they want of her? What had Melville Stoner to do with the matter? She put the figure of him out of her mind. In the figure of the other man, Walter Sayers, there was something less aggressive, less assertive. She clung to that.

She put her arm about the trunk of the old apple tree and laid her cheek against its rough bark. Within herself she was so intense, so excited that she wanted to rub her cheeks against the bark of the tree until the blood came, until physical pain came to counteract the tenseness within that had become pain.

Since the meadow between the orchard and the street end had been planted to corn she would have to reach the street by going along a lane, crawling under a wire fence and crossing the yard of the widowed chicken raiser. A profound silence reigned over the orchard and when she had crawled under the fence and reached the widow's back yard she had to feel her way through a narrow opening between a chicken house and a barn by running her fingers forward over the rough boards.

Her mother sat on the porch waiting and on the narrow porch before his house next door sat Melville Stoner. She saw him as she hurried past and shivered slightly. "What a dark vulture-like thing he is! He lives off the dead, off dead glimpses of beauty, off dead old sounds heard at night," she thought. When she got to the Wescott house she threw herself down on the porch and lay on her back with her arms stretched above her head. Her mother sat on a rocking chair beside her. There was a street lamp at the corner at the end of the street and a little light came through the branches of trees and lighted her mother's face. How white and still and death-like it was. When she had looked Rosalind closed her eyes. "I mustn't. I shall lose courage," she thought.

There was no hurry about delivering the message she had come to deliver. It would be two hours before her father came home. The silence of the village street was broken by a hubbub that arose in the house across the street. Two boys playing some game ran from room to room through the house, slamming doors, shouting. A baby began to cry and then a woman's voice protested. "Quit it! Quit it!" the voice called. "Don't you see you have wakened the baby? Now I shall have a time getting him to sleep again."

Rosalind's fingers closed and her hands remained clenched. "I came home to tell you something. I have fallen in love with a man and can't marry him. He is a good many years older than myself and is already married. He has two children. I love him and I think he loves me—I know he does. I want him to have me too. I wanted to come home and tell you before it happened," she said speaking in a low clear voice. She wondered if Melville Stoner could hear her declaration.

Nothing happened. The chair in which Rosalind's mother sat had been rocking slowly back and forth and making a slight creaking sound. The sound continued. In the house across the street the baby stopped crying. The words Rosalind had come from Chicago to say to her mother were said and she felt relieved and almost happy. The silence between the two women went on and on. Rosalind's mind wandered away. Presently there would be some sort of reaction from her mother. She would be condemned. Perhaps her mother would say nothing until her father came home and would then tell him. She would be condemned as a wicked woman, ordered to leave the house. It did not matter.

Rosalind waited. Like Walter Sayers, sitting in his garden, her mind seemed to float away, out of her body. It ran away from her mother to the man she loved.

One evening, on just such another quiet summer evening as this one, she had gone into the country with Walter Sayers. Before that he had talked to her, at her, on many other evenings and during long hours in the office. He had found in her someone to whom he could talk, to whom he wanted to talk. What doors of life he had opened for her! The talk had gone on and on. In her presence the man was relieved, he relaxed out of the tenseness that had become the habit of his body. He had told her of how he had wanted to be a singer and had given up the notion. "It isn't my wife's fault nor the children's fault," he had said. "They could have lived without me. The trouble is I could not have lived without them. I am a defeated man, was intended from the first to be a defeated man and I needed something to cling to, something with which to justify my defeat. I realize that now. I am a dependent. I shall never try to sing now because I am one who has at least one merit. I know defeat. I can accept defeat."

That is what Walter Sayers had said and then on the summer evening in the country as she sat beside him in his car he had suddenly begun to sing. He had opened a farm gate and had driven the car silently along a grass covered lane and into a meadow. The lights had been put out and the car crept along. When it stopped some cattle came and stood nearby.

Then he began to sing, softly at first and with increasing boldness as he repeated the song over and over. Rosalind was so happy she had wanted to cry out. "It is because of myself he can sing now," she had thought proudly. How intensely, at the moment she loved the man, and yet perhaps the thing she felt was not love after all. There was pride in it. It was for her a moment of triumph. He had crept up to her out of a dark place, out of the dark cave of defeat. It had been her hand reached down that had given him courage.

She lay on her back, at her mother's feet, on the porch of the Wescott house trying to think, striving to get her own impulses clear in her mind. She had just told her mother that she wanted to give herself to the man, Walter Sayers. Having made the statement she already wondered if it could be quite true. She was a woman and her mother was a woman. What would her mother have to say to her? What did mothers say to daughters? The male element in life —what did it want? Her own desires and impulses were not clearly realized within herself. Perhaps what she wanted in life could be got in some sort of communion with another woman, with her mother. What a strange and beautiful thing it would be if mothers could suddenly begin to sing to their daughters, if out of the darkness and silence of old women song could come.

Men confused Rosalind, they had always confused her. On that very evening her father for the first time in years had really looked at her. He had stopped before her as she sat on the porch and there had been something in his eyes. A fire had burned in his old eyes as it had sometimes burned in the eyes of Walter. Was the fire intended to consume her quite?

Was it the fate of women to be consumed by men and of men to be consumed by women?

In the orchard, an hour before she had distinctly felt the two men, Melville Stoner and Walter Sayers coming toward her, walking silently on the soft carpet made of the dark shadows of trees.

They were again coming toward her. In their thoughts they approached nearer and nearer to her, to the inner truth of her. The street and the town of Willow Springs were covered with a mantle of silence. Was it the silence of death? Had her mother died? Did her mother sit there now a dead thing in the chair beside her?

The soft creaking of the rocking chair went on and on. Of the two men whose spirits seemed hovering about one, Melville Stoner, was bold and cunning. He was too close to her, knew too much of her. He was unafraid. The spirit of Walter Sayers was merciful. He was gentle, a man of understanding. She grew afraid of Melville Stoner. He was too close to her, knew too much of the dark, stupid side of her life. She turned on her side and stared into the darkness toward the Stoner house remembering her girlhood. The man was too physically close. The faint light from the distant street lamp that had lighted her mother's face crept between branches of trees and over the tops of bushes and she could see dimly the figure of Melville Stoner sitting before his house. She wished it were possible with a thought to destroy him, wipe him out, cause him to cease to exist. He was waiting. When her mother had gone to bed and when she had gone upstairs to her own room to lie awake he would invade her privacy. Her father would come home, walking with dragging footsteps along the sidewalk. He would come into the Wescott house and through to the back door. He would pump the pail of water at the pump and bring it into the house to put it on the box by the kitchen sink. Then he would wind the clock. He would—

Rosalind stirred uneasily. Life in the figure of Melville Stoner had her, it gripped her tightly. She could not escape. He would come into her bedroom and invade her secret thoughts. There was no escape for her. She imagined his mocking laughter ringing through the silent house, the sound rising above the dreadful commonplace sounds of everyday life there. She did not want that to happen. The sudden death of Melville Stoner would bring sweet silence. She wished it possible with a thought to destroy him, to destroy all men. She wanted her mother to draw close to her. That would save her from the men. Surely, before the evening had passed her mother would have something to say, somthing living and true.

Rosalind forced the figure of Melville Stoner out of her mind. It was as though she had got out of her bed in the room upstairs and had taken the man by the

254 THE TRIUMPH OF THE EGG

arm to lead him to the door. She had put him out of
the room and had closed the door.

Her mind played her a trick. Melville Stoner had
no sooner gone out of her mind than Walter Sayers
came in. In imagination she was with Walter in the
car on the summer evening in the pasture and he was
singing. The cattle with their soft broad noses and
the sweet grass-flavored breaths were crowding in
close.

There was sweetness in Rosalind's thoughts now.
She rested and waited, waited for her mother to speak.
In her presence Walter Sayers had broken his long
silence and soon the old silence between mother and
daughter would also be broken.

The singer who would not sing had begun to sing
because of her presence. Song was the true note of
life, it was the triumph of life over death.

What sweet solace had come to her that time when
Walter Sayers sang! How life had coursed through
her body! How alive she had suddenly become! It
was at that moment she had decided definitely, finally,
that she wanted to come closer to the man, that she
wanted with him the ultimate physical closeness—to
find in physical expression through him what in his
song he was finding through her.

It was in expressing physically her love of the man
she would find the white wonder of life, the wonder
of which, as a clumsy and crude girl, she had dreamed

as she lay on the grass in the orchard. Through the
body of the singer she would approach, touch the
white wonder of life. "I shall willingly sacrifice
everything else on the chance that may happen," she
thought.

How peaceful and quiet the summer night had become! How clearly now she understood life! The
song Walter Sayers had sung in the field, in the
presence of the cattle was in a tongue she had not
understood, but now she understood everything, even
the meaning of the strange foreign words.

The song was about life and death. What else
was there to sing about? The sudden knowledge of
the content of the song had not come out of her own
mind. The spirit of Walter was coming toward her.
It had pushed the mocking spirit of Melville Stoner
aside. What things had not the mind of Walter
Sayers already done to her mind, to the awakening
woman within her. Now it was telling her the story
of the song. The words of the song itself seemed to
float down the silent street of the Iowa town. They
described the sun going down in the smoke clouds of
a city and the gulls coming from a lake to float over
the city.

Now the gulls floated over a river. The river was
the color of chrysoprase. She, Rosalind Wescott,
stood on a bridge in the heart of the city and she had
become entirely convinced of the filth and ugliness of

life. She was about to throw herself into the river, to destroy herself in an effort to make herself clean.

It did not matter. Strange sharp cries came from the birds. The cries of the birds were like the voice of Melville Stoner. They whirled and turned in the air overhead. In a moment more she would throw herself into the river and then the birds would fall straight down in a long graceful line. The body of her would be gone, swept away by the stream, carried away to decay but what was really alive in herself would arise with the birds, in the long graceful upward line of the flight of the birds.

Rosalind lay tense and still on the porch at her mother's feet. In the air above the hot sleeping town, buried deep in the ground beneath all towns and cities, life went on singing, it persistently sang. The song of life was in the humming of bees, in the calling of tree toads, in the throats of negroes rolling cotton bales on a boat in a river.

The song was a command. It told over and over the story of life and of death, life forever defeated by death, death forever defeated by life.

* * *

The long silence of Rosalind's mother was broken and Rosalind tried to tear herself away from the spirit of the song that had begun to sing itself within her—

The sun sank down into the western sky over
a city—
> Life defeated by death,
> Death defeated by life.

The factory chimneys had become pencils of
light—
> Life defeated by death,
> Death defeated by life.

The rocking chair in which Rosalind's mother sat
kept creaking. Words came haltingly from between
her white lips. The test of Ma Wescott's life had
come. Always she had been defeated. Now she must
triumph in the person of Rosalind, the daughter who
had come out of her body. To her she must make
clear the fate of all women. Young girls grew up
dreaming, hoping, believing. There was a conspiracy.
Men made words, they wrote books and sang songs
about a thing called love. Young girls believed. They
married or entered into close relationships with men
without marriage. On the marriage night there was
a brutal assault and after that the woman had to try
to save herself as best she could. She withdrew
within herself, further and further within herself. Ma
Wescott had stayed all her life hidden away within
her own house, in the kitchen of her house. As the
years passed and after the children came her man had
demanded less and less of her. Now this new trouble

had come. Her daughter was to have the same experience, to go through the experience that had spoiled
life for her.

How proud she had been of Rosalind, going out into
the world, making her own way. Her daughter dressed
with a certain air, walked with a certain air. She was
a proud, upstanding, triumphant thing. She did not
need a man.

"God, Rosalind, don't do it, don't do it," she muttered over and over.

How much she had wanted Rosalind to keep clear
and clean! Once she also had been a young woman,
proud, upstanding. Could anyone think she had ever
wanted to become Ma Wescott, fat, heavy and old?
All through her married life she had stayed in her own
house, in the kitchen of her own house, but in her own
way she had watched, she had seen how things went
with women. Her man had known how to make
money, he had always housed her comfortably. He
was a slow, silent man but in his own way he was as
good as any of the men of Willow Springs. Men
worked for money, they ate heavily and then at night
they came home to the woman they had married.

Before she married, Ma Wescott had been a farmer's daughter. She had seen things among the beasts,
how the male pursued the female. There was a certain hard insistence, cruelty. Life perpetuated itself
that way. The time of her own marriage was a dim,

terrible time. Why had she wanted to marry? She
tried to tell Rosalind about it. "I saw him on the
Main Street of town here, one Saturday evening when
I had come to town with father, and two weeks after
that I met him again at a dance out in the country,"
she said. She spoke like one who has been running a
long distance and who has some important, some im-
mediate message to deliver. "He wanted me to marry
him and I did it. He wanted me to marry him and I
did it."

She could not get beyond the fact of her marriage.
Did her daughter think she had no vital thing to say
concerning the relationship of men and women? All
through her married life she had stayed in her husband's house, working as a beast might work, washing
dirty clothes, dirty dishes, cooking food.

She had been thinking, all through the years she
had been thinking. There was a dreadful lie in life,
the whole fact of life was a lie.

She had thought it all out. There was a world
somewhere unlike the world in which she lived. It
was a heavenly place in which there was no marrying
or giving in marriage, a sexless quiet windless place
where mankind lived in a state of bliss. For some unknown reason mankind had been thrown out of that
place, had been thrown down upon the earth. It was
a punishment for an unforgivable sin, the sin of sex.

The sin had been in her as well as in the man she

had married. She had wanted to marry. Why else did she do it? Men and women were condemned to commit the sin that destroyed them. Except for a few rare sacred beings no man or woman escaped.

What thinking she had done! When she had just married and after her man had taken what he wanted of her he slept heavily but she did not sleep. She crept out of bed and going to a window looked at the stars. The stars were quiet. With what a slow stately tread the moon moved across the sky. The stars did not sin. They did not touch one another. Each star was a thing apart from all other stars, a sacred inviolate thing. On the earth, under the stars everything was corrupt, the trees, flowers, grasses, the beasts of the field, men and women. They were all corrupt. They lived for a moment and then fell into decay. She herself was falling into decay. Life was a lie. Life perpetuated itself by the lie called love. The truth was that life itself came out of sin, perpetuated itself only by sin.

"There is no such thing as love. The word is a lie. The man you are telling me about wants you for the purpose of sin," she said and getting heavily up went into the house.

Rosalind heard her moving about in the darkness. She came to the screen door and stood looking at her daughter lying tense and waiting on the porch. The passion of denial was so strong in her that she felt choked. To the daughter it seemed that her mother standing in the darkness behind her had become a great spider, striving to lead her down into some web of darkness. "Men only hurt women," she said, "they can't help wanting to hurt women. They are made that way. The thing they call love doesn't exist. It's a lie."

"Life is dirty. Letting a man touch her dirties a woman." Ma Wescott fairly screamed forth the words. They seemed torn from her, from some deep inner part of her being. Having said them she moved off into the darkness and Rosalind heard her going slowly toward the stairway that led to the bedroom above. She was weeping in the peculiar half choked way in which old fat women weep. The heavy feet that had begun to mount the stair stopped and there was silence. Ma Wescott had said nothing of what was in her mind. She had thought it all out, what she wanted to say to her daughter. Why would the words not come? The passion for denial within her was not satisfied. "There is no love. Life is a lie. It leads to sin, to death and decay," she called into the darkness.

A strange, almost uncanny thing happened to Rosalind. The figure of her mother went out of her mind and she was in fancy again a young girl and had gone with other young girls to visit a friend about to be married. With the others she stood in a room where white dresses lay on a bed. One of her companions, a thin, flat breasted girl fell on her knees beside the bed. A cry arose. Did it come from the girl or from the old tired defeated woman within the Wescott house? "Don't do it. O, Rosalind don't do it," pleaded a voice broken with sobs.

The Wescott house had become silent like the street outside and like the sky sprinkled with stars into which Rosalind gazed. The tenseness within her relaxed and she tried again to think. There was a thing that balanced, that swung backward and forward. Was it merely her heart beating? Her mind cleared.

The song that had come from the lips of Walter Sayers was still singing within her—

> Life the conqueror over death,
> Death the conqueror over life.

She sat up and put her head into her hands. "I came here to Willow Springs to put myself to a test. Is it the test of life and death?" she asked herself. Her mother had gone up the stairway, into the darkness of the bedroom above.

The song singing within Rosalind went on—

> Life the conquerer over death,
> Death the conquerer over life.

Was the song a male thing, the call of the male to the female, a lie, as her mother had said? It did not sound like a lie. The song had come from the lips of the man Walter and she had left him and had come to her mother. Then Melville Stoner, another male, had come to her. In him also was singing the song of life and death. When the song stopped singing within one did death come? Was death but denial? The song was singing within herself. What a confusion!

After her last outcry Ma Wescott had gone weeping up the stairs and to her own room and to bed. After a time Rosalind followed. She threw herself onto her own bed without undressing. Both women lay waiting. Outside in the darkness before his house sat Melville Stoner, the male, the man who knew of all that had passed between mother and daughter. Rosalind thought of the bridge over the river near the factory in the city and of the gulls floating in the air high above the river. She wished herself there, standing on the bridge. "It would be sweet now to throw my body down into the river," she thought. She imagined herself falling swiftly and the swifter fall of the birds down out of the sky. They were swooping down to pick up the life she was ready to drop, sweeping swiftly and beautifully down. That was what the song Walter had sung was about.

Henry Wescott came home from his evening at Emanuel Wilson's store. He went heavily through the house to the back door and the pump. There was the slow creaking sound of the pump working and then he came into the house and put the pail of water on the box by the kitchen sink. A little of the water spilled. There was a soft little slap—like a child's bare feet striking the floor—

Rosalind arose. The dead cold weariness that had settled down upon her went away. Cold dead hands had been gripping her. Now they were swept aside. Her bag was in a closet but she had forgotten it. Quickly she took off her shoes and holding them in her hands went out into the hall in her stockinged feet. Her father came heavily up the stairs past her as she stood breathless with her body pressed against the wall in the hallway.

How quick and alert her mind had become! There was a train Eastward bound toward Chicago that passed through Willow Springs at two in the morning. She would not wait for it. She would walk the eight miles to the next town to the east. That would get her out of town. It would give her something to do. "I need to be moving now," she thought as she ran down the stairs and went silently out of the house.

She walked on the grass beside the sidewalk to the gate before Melville Stoner's house and he came down to the gate to meet her. He laughed mockingly. "I fancied I might have another chance to walk with you before the night was gone," he said bowing. Rosa-

lind did not know how much of the conversation between herself and her mother he had heard. It did not
matter. He knew all Ma Wescott had said, all she
could say and all Rosalind could say or understand.
The thought was infinitely sweet to Rosalind. It was
Melville Stoner who lifted the town of Willow Springs
up out of the shadow of death. Words were unnecessary. With him she had established the thing beyond
words, beyond passion—the fellowship in living, the
fellowship in life.

They walked in silence to the town's edge and then
Melville Stoner put out his hand. "You'll come with
me?" she asked, but he shook his head and laughed.
"No," he said, "I'll stay here. My time for going
passed long ago. I'll stay here until I die. I'll stay
here with my thoughts."

He turned and walked away into the darkness beyond the round circle of light cast by the last street
lamp on the street that now became a country road
leading to the next town to the east. Rosalind stood
to watch him go and something in his long loping gait
again suggested to her mind the figure of a gigantic
bird. "He is like the gulls that float above the river in
Chicago," she thought. "His spirit floats above the
town of Willow Springs. When the death in life comes
to the people here he swoops down, with his mind,
plucking out the beauty of them."

She walked at first slowly along the road between

corn fields. The night was a vast quiet place into which she could walk in peace. A little breeze rustled the corn blades but there were no dreadful significant human sounds, the sounds made by those who lived physically but who in spirit were dead, had accepted death, believed only in death. The corn blades rubbed against each other and there was a low sweet sound as though something was being born, old dead physical life was being torn away, cast aside. Perhaps new life was coming into the land.

Rosalind began to run. She had thrown off the town and her father and mother as a runner might throw off a heavy and unnecessary garment. She wished also to throw off the garments that stood between her body and nudity. She wanted to be naked, new born. Two miles out of town a bridge crossed Willow Creek. It was now empty and dry but in the darkness she imagined it filled with water, swift running water, water the color of chrysoprase. She had been running swiftly and now she stopped and stood on the bridge her breath coming in quick little gasps.

After a time she went on again, walking until she had regained her breath and then running again. Her body tingled with life. She did not ask herself what she was going to do, how she was to meet the problem she had come to Willow Springs half hoping to have solved by a word from her mother. She ran. Before her eyes the dusty road kept coming up to her out of darkness. She ran forward, always forward into a faint streak of light. The darkness unfolded before her. There was joy in the running and with every step she took she achieved a new sense of escape. A delicious notion came into her mind. As she ran she thought the light under her feet became more distinct. It was, she thought, as though the darkness had grown afraid in her presence and sprang aside, out of her path. There was a sensation of boldness. She had herself become something that within itself contained light. She was a creator of light. At her approach darkness grew afraid and fled away into the distance. When that thought came she found herself able to run without stopping to rest and half wished she might run on forever, through the land, through towns and cities, driving darkness away with her presence.

THE MAN WITH THE TRUMPET

I STATED it as definitely as I could.
I was in a room with them.
They had tongues like me, and hair and eyes.
I got up out of my chair and said it as definitely as I could.
Their eyes wavered. Something slipped out of their grasp. Had I been white and strong and young enough I might have plunged through walls, gone outward into nights and days, gone into prairies, into distances —gone outward to the doorstep of the house of God, gone to God's throne room with their hands in mine.
What I am trying to say is this—
By God I made their minds flee out of them.
Their minds came out of them as clear and straight as anything could be.
I said they might build temples to their lives.
I threw my words at faces floating in a street.
I threw my words like stones, like building stones.
I scattered words in alleyways like seeds.
I crept at night and threw my words in empty rooms of houses in a street.
I said that life was life, that men in streets and cities might build temples to their souls.

I whispered words at night into a telephone.

I told my people life was sweet, that men might live.

I said a million temples might be built, that door-steps might be cleansed.

At their fleeing harried minds I hurled a stone.

I said they might build temples to themselves.

THE SOUND OF THE STREAM

I HAVE already mentioned that my house stands by a mountain stream. It is a stream of sounds, and at night, ever since I had completed the building of my house and had moved into it, the stream has talked to me.

On how many nights have I lain in my bed in my house, the doors and windows that faced the stream all open and the sounds coming in.

The stream runs over rocks. It runs under a bridge, and somewhere I have written telling how, on dark nights, the sounds change and become strangely significant.

There was the sound of the feet of children running on the floor of the bridge. A horse galloped, soldiers marched. I heard at night the footsteps of old friends, the voices of women I had loved.

There was a crippled girl I have spoken of to whom I had once made love, in the rain, under a bush in a city park. She had cried, and I heard the haunting sound of her feet, the curious broken rhythm on the bridge over the stream by my house at night . . . the voices of Fred, of Mary, of Tom, of Esther, and a hundred others, loved and lost in what I called my real life, and always, above these voices, the sound also of the footsteps and the voices of those of my imaginative world.

The long slow stride of Hugh McVey. These mingled let us say with the footsteps of Carl Sandburg or Ben Hecht. My friend John Emerson or Maurice Long walking beside my Doctor Parcival. The footsteps of the naked man in the room with his daughter in *Many Marriages*, soft beside the footsteps of some dear one in the life I had led away from my desk.

These sounds from the stream whispering to me, sometimes crying out, through many nights, making nights alive . . .

It was in the early summer and I had gotten a letter from my literary agent. It may be that I had been writing to him. He had certain stories I had sent him to sell.

'Can't you, sir, sell one of the stories to some magazine? I am needing money.'

He answered my letter. He is a sensible man, knows his business.

'I admit that the stories you have sent me are good stories. But,' he said, 'you are always getting something into all of your stories that spoils the sale.'

He did not go further, but I know what he meant.

'Look here,' he once said to me, 'why don't you, for the time at least, drop this rather intimate style of yours?'

He smiled when he said it and I also smiled.

'Let us say, now, that you are yourself the editor of one of our big American magazines. You have yourself been in business. When you first began to write, even after you had published some of your earlier books, you had to go on for years, working in an advertising place. You must know that all of our large American magazines are business ventures. It costs a great deal of money to print and distribute hundreds of thousands of copies. Often, as you know, the price received for the magazine, when sold on the newsstand, does not pay for the paper on which it is printed.'

'Yes, I know.'

'They have to have stories that please people.'

'Yes. I know.'

We had stopped to have a drink at a bar. But a few weeks before he had written me a letter. 'There is a certain large magazine that would like to have a story from you. It should be, let us say, a story of about ten thousand words. Do not attempt to write the story. Make an outline, I should say a three- or four-page outline. I can sell the story for you.'

I made the outline and sent it to him.

'It is splendid,' he wrote. 'Now you can go ahead. I can get such and such a sum.'

'Oh!' the sum mentioned would get me out of my difficulties.

'I will get busy,' I said to myself. 'In a week I will dash off the story.'

Some two or three weeks before, a man friend had come to me one evening. He is a man to whom I am deeply attached.

'Come and walk with me,' he said, and we set out afoot, leaving the town where he lived. I had gone to the town to see him, but, when I got to his town, there was a sudden illness in his house. The man has children and two of them were in bed with a contagious disease.

I stayed at a hotel. He came there. We walked beyond the town, got into a dirt road, passed farmhouses, dogs barked at us. We got into a moonlit meadow.

We had walked for a long time in silence. At the hotel I had noticed that my friend was in a tense, excited mood.

'You are in some sort of trouble. Is it the children? Has the disease taken a turn for the worse?'

'No,' he said, 'the children are better. They are all right.'

We were in the moonlit meadow, standing by a fence, some sheep grazing nearby and it was a delicious night of the early summer.

'There is something I have to tell to someone,' he said. 'I wrote to you, begged you to come here.'

My friend is a highly respected man in his town.

He began talking. He talked for hours. He told me a story of a secret life he had been living.

My friend is a man of fifty. He is employed as an experimental scientist by a large manufacturing company.

But I might as well confess at once that I am, as you the reader may have guessed, covering the trail of my friend. I am a man rather fortunate in life. I have a good many men friends. If I make this one an experimental scientist working for a large manufacturing company, it will do.

His story was, on the whole, strange. It was like so many stories, not invented but coming directly out of life. It was a story having in it certain so-called sordid touches, strange impulses come to a man of fifty in the grip of an odd passion.

'I have been doing this.

'I have been doing that.

'I have to unload, to tell someone.

'I have been suffering.'

My friend did unload his story, getting a certain relief talking to me of a turn in his life that threatened to destroy the position he had achieved in his community. He had got a sudden passion for a woman of his town, the sort of thing always happening in towns. 'Three years ago,' he said to me, 'there was another man here, a friend, a man, as I am, of standing in our community, who did what I am doing now. He became enamored of a woman here, the wife of a friend, and began to meet her secretly.

'At least he thought, or hoped, he was meeting her secretly.

'He did as I have been doing. In the evening when darkness came, he got into his car. She had walked out along a street and in some dark place along the street he picked her up. He drove with her out along little side roads, went to distant towns, but soon everyone knew.

'And how I blamed him. I went to him. "What a fool you are being," I said to him.

'"Yes, but I cannot help it. This is the great love of my life."

'"What nonsense," I said. I pled with him, quarreled with him, but it did no good. I thought him an utter fool and now I am being just such another.'

I had taken the man with whom I talked in the field, and his story, as the basis for the story I was to write for one of the popular magazines, had made an outline that was pronounced splendid by my agent.

But what rough places I had smoothed out.

'No, I cannot say that such a figure holding such a respectable place in my life did that. There must not be anything unpleasant. There must be nothing that will remind readers of certain sordid moments, thoughts, passions, acts, in their own lives if I am to get this money—and, oh, how I need it.'

I am no Shakespeare, but did not even Shakespeare write a play he called *As You Like It*?

'When you are writing to please people you must not touch certain secret, often dark little recesses, that are in all humans.

'Keep in the clear, man. Go gaily along.

'It will be all right to startle them a little.

'You must get a certain dramatic force into your story.'

But that night the man, upon whose story I have based the story I am about to write, was, as he talked, simply broken. He even put his face down upon the top rail of the fence, there in that moonlit meadow, and cried. I went to him. I put my arms about his shoulders, said words to him.

'This passion that has come to you at this time in your life, that now threatens to tear down all you have so carefully built up, that threatens to destroy the lives of others you love, will pass.

'At our age everything passes.'

I do not remember just what I did say to him.

And so I began to write, but alas . . .

Our difficulty is that as we write we become interested, absorbed, often a little in love with these characters of our stories that seem to be growing here, under our hand.

I have begun this story, taking off, as it were, from the story told me in the meadow by my friend; but now, as I write, he has disappeared.

There is a new man, coming to life, here. He seems to be here in this room where I work.

'You must do me right now,' he seems to be saying to me.

'There is a certain morality involved,' he says.

'Now you must tell everything, put it all down. Do not hesitate. I want it all put down.'

At this point there was a series of letters concerning a story to be written that lay on my desk. I had had them brought to me from my files.

'If you are to write the story for us, it would be well for you to keep certain things in mind.

'The story should be concerned with the lives of people who are in what might be called comfortable circumstances.

'Above all, it should not be too gloomy.

'We want you to understand that we do not wish, in any way, to dictate to you.'

I had sat down to write the tale, for which I had made an outline, in bitter need of the money it might bring. After twenty-five years of writing, some twenty to twenty-five books published, my name up as one of the outstanding American writers of my

day, my books translated into many languages, after
all of this, I was always in need of money, always just
two jumps ahead of the sheriff.

'Well, I will do it. I will. I will.'

For two days, three, a week, I wrote doggedly, with
dogged determination.

'I will give them just what they want. I had been
told, it had been impressed deeply upon my mind,
that, above all things, to be popular, successful, I must
first of all observe the "don'ts."'

A friend, another American writer, came to see me.
He mentioned a certain, at present, very popular
woman writer.

'Boy, she is cleaning up,' he said.

However it seemed that she, one who knew her
trade and was safe, occasionally slipped.

It may be that here, in telling of this incident, I
have got the story of what happened to the woman
writer confused with many such stories I have heard.

However, it lies in my mind that the writer was
making, for the movies, an adaptation of a very popular novel of a past generation. In it there was a child
who, eating candy before breakfast, was reproved by
his mother.

'Put that stuff aside. It will ruin your health.'

Something of that sort must have been written. It
was unnoticed, got by. What, and with the candy
people spending millions in advertising! What, the

suggestion that candy could ruin the health of a child, candy called 'stuff'!

My friend told some tale of a big damage suit, of indignant candy manufacturers.

'Why, there must be thousands of these "don'ts,"' I said to myself.

'It would be better, in your story, if your people be in what might be called comfortable positions in life.'

I had got that sentence from someone. I wrote it out, tucked it up over my desk.

And so I wrote for a week, and there was a great sickness in me. I who had always loved the pile of clean white sheets on my desk, who had been for years obsessed with the notion that some day, by chance, I would find myself suddenly overtaken by a passion for writing and would find myself without paper, pencils, pens, or ink so that I was always stealing fountain pens and pencils from my friends, storing them away as a squirrel stores nuts, who, upon going for even a short trip away from home, always put into my car enough paper to write at least five long novels, who kept bottles of ink stored in all sorts of odd places about the house, found myself suddenly hating the smell of ink.

There were the white sheets and I wanted to throw them all out of the window.

Days of this, a week. It may have gone on for two weeks. There were the days, something strangely gone out of life, and there were the nights. Why, I dare say that to those who do not write or paint or in any way work in the arts, all of this will seem nonsense indeed.

'When it comes to that,' they will be saying, 'our own work is not always so pleasant. Do you think it's always a joy to be a lawyer, wrangling over other people's ugly quarrels in courts, or being a doctor, always and forever with the sick, or a factory owner, with all this new unrest among workers, or a worker, getting nowhere working your life out for the profit of others?'

But there I was, having what is called literary fame. And I was no longer young. 'Presently I will be old. The pen will fall from my hand. There will come the time of long afternoons sitting in the sun, or under the shade of a tree. I will no longer want to write. It may be that I will have my fill of people, their problems, the tangle of life, and will want only to look at sheep grazing on distant hillsides, to watch the waters of a stream rolling over rocks, or just follow with my aging eyes the wandering of a country road winding away among hills,' I thought.

'It would be better for me to turn aside, make money now. I must. I must.'

I remembered the advice always being given me when I was a young writer. 'Go in for it,' my friends said. At that time the movies had just become a gold mine for writers.

'Take it on for a time,' my friends were saying to
me. 'You can change. Get yourself a stake. Make
yourself secure and then, when you are quite safe, you
can go abroad. Then you can write as you want to
write.'

'It may not have been good advice then but it is
now,' I said to myself. Formerly when I was writing
all of my earlier books, I was very strong. I could work
all day in the advertising place or in the factory I once
owned. I could go home to my rooms. I took a cold
plunge. Always, it seemed to me there was something
that had to be washed away. When I was writing the
Winesburg tales and, later, the novel, *Poor White*, I
couldn't get tired, and often after working all day
wrote all night. I have never been one who can
correct, fill in, rework his stories. I must try, and
when I fail must throw away. Some of my best stories
have been written ten or twelve times.

An odd thing happens to a man, a writer. Perhaps I
am saying all of this, not at all for those who do not
write but for the young American writers. Nowadays
they are always coming to me. They write me letters.
'You are our father,' they say to me.

'One day I picked up a book of stories of yours, or it
was one of your novels, and a great door seemed to
swing open for me.'

There are such sentences written to me by young writers in letters. Sometimes they even put such sentences into the autobiographical novels with which almost all new writers begin.

And it is so they should begin too. First the learning to use the experiences, the words and hungers of their own lives and then, gradually, the reaching out into other lives.

And so I am addressing here our young American writers, the beginners, but what am I trying to say to them?

Perhaps I am only trying to say that the struggle in which we are engaged has no end; that we in America have, all of us, been led into a blind alley. We have always before us, we keep before us, the mythical thing we call 'success,' but for us there is, there can be, no success, for while this belief in the mythical thing called success remains among us, always in the minds of others about us, we shall be in danger of infection. I am trying to prove all of this to you by showing here how I, a veteran now among you, for a long time thinking myself safe from the contagion, was also taken with the disease.

And so I sat in my room, trying and trying.

I was in one of my frightened moods. Soon now my money would all be gone. I am a man who has always had, in the matter of finance, a line that, when crossed, made me begin to tremble. Anything above five hundred dollars in the bank has always seemed to me riches, but when my bank account goes below that amount, the fears come.

Soon I shall have but four hundred dollars, then three, two, one. I live in the country on a farm and in the house built by my one successful book. Bills come, so many pounds of grass seed for a field, a ton of lime, a new plow. Great God, will I be compelled to return to the advertising agency?

I have three or four short stories in my agent's hands. Once a magazine called *Pictorial Review* paid me seven hundred and fifty dollars for a short story. I had given the story the title, 'There She is, She is Taking Her Bath,' but after the story had been got into type and illustrations made for it, the editor of the magazine grew doubtful. 'We are doubtful about the title,' he wired. 'Can't you suggest another?' and I replied, saying, 'Roll Your Own,' but got from him a second wire, saying that he didn't think that that title fitted the story, and in the end he never published it.

'Will he be demanding back my seven hundred and fifty dollars?' I asked myself, knowing nothing of my own legal rights. But then a thought came, a very comforting thought.

'He may demand but how can he get it?' I had spent the money for an automobile, had got a new overcoat, a new suit of clothes.

'Just let him try. What can he do? I am dustproof,' I
muttered; but I had misjudged the man. He must
really have been a splendid fellow, for in the end and
without protest, and after some four or five years, he
sent the story back to me, saying nothing at all of all
that money given me for it. He said, if I remember
correctly, that, while he personally liked the story, in
fact thought it splendid, a magnificent achievement,
etc., etc., also that he had always greatly admired my
work, this story did not really fit into the tone of the
magazine. There was in it, as I now remember, a little
business man, timid and absurdly jealous of his wife.
He had got it into his head that she was having
affairs with other men and had determined to have it
out with her, but, when he worked himself up to it
and rushed home, always fearing he would lose his
courage, it happened that invariably she was taking
her bath. A man couldn't, of course, stand outside the
door of a bathroom, his wife splashing in the tub, and
through the door accuse her of unfaithfulness.

In my story the wife was, to be sure, quite innocent.
As a detective he hired to watch her assured him, she
was as innocent as a little flower . . . if I remember
correctly that was the expression used . . . but, also, as
in so many of my stories, there was a business man
made to appear a little ridiculous.

Why, I am told there are men and women who
receive, for a single short story, as much as a thou-

sand, fifteen hundred, even two thousand dollars. I am also told that I have had a profound effect upon the art of short-story writing.

'And so, what's wrong?' I more than a hundred times have asked myself; but at last I have come to a conclusion.

'You are just a little too apt, Sherwood, my boy, to find the business man a little ridiculous,' I have told myself.

'Yes, and there is just your trouble, my boy. The business man, as he is represented in our picture, as he must be represented, is, above all things, a shrewd and knowing man. It would be better to represent him as very resolute, very courageous. He should have really what is called "an iron jaw." This is to indicate resolution, courage, determination.

'And you are to bear in mind that earlier in life he was an athlete. He was a star football player, a triple threat, whatever that is, or he was of the team at Yale.

'He is older now, but he has kept himself in trim. He is like the first Roosevelt, the Teddy one. Every day he goes to his club to box. The man who is to succeed in business cannot . . . keep that in mind . . . let himself grow fat. Do not ever make him fat, watery-eyed, bald. Do not let him have a kidney complaint.

'The trouble with you,' I told myself, 'is just the years you spent in business,' and I began to remember the

men, hundreds of them, some of them known inter-
nationally, often sensitive fellows, at bottom kindly,
who were puzzled as I was puzzled, always breaking
out into odd confessions, telling intimate little stories
of their loves, their hopes, their disappointments.

'How did I get where I am? What brought me
here?'

'This is something I never wanted to do. Why am I
doing it?'

Something of that sort and then also, so often,
something naïve, often wistful and also a little ridiculous.

I could not shake off the fact that, in the fifteen or
twenty years during which I was in business as advertising writer, as manufacturer, five men among my
personal acquaintances killed themselves.

So there was tragedy too, plenty of it.

'But, my dear fellow, you must bear in mind that
this is a country ruled by business. Only yesterday,
when you were driving on the highway, you saw a
huge sign. "What is good for business is good for
you," the sign said.

'So there, you see, we are one great brotherhood.'

All of this said to myself, over and over. 'Now you
are below the line, the five-hundred-dollar line. Keep
that in mind.'

There were these days, my struggle to write in
a new vein, to keep persistently cheerful, letting

nothing reflecting on the uprightness, the good intent, the underlying courage of business, creep into
my story.

'Above all do not put into your story a business
man who is by chance shy, sensitive, who does occasionally ridiculous things. Even if, at bottom, the
fellow is gentle, lovable, do not do that.

'But, you see, my man is not in business. I have
made him a judge.

'But, you fool, don't you see . . . my God, man, a
judge!

'Is there not also a pattern, a mold made, for the
judge?'

And so you see me arguing, fighting with myself,
through the days, through the nights. The nights
were the worst.

'But can't you sleep, my dear?'

'No, my darling, I cannot sleep.'

'But what is on your mind?'

You see, I cannot tell my wife. She would rebel. She
would begin talking about a job. 'We can give up this
house, this farm,' she would say. 'You are always
spending your money on it,' she would add. She
would call attention to the absurd notion I have that,
in the end, I can make our farm pay. We would get
into an argument, with me pointing out that it is a
dishonorable thing to live on land and not work
constantly to make it more productive.

'It would be better for me to surrender everything else before my love of the land itself,' I would say, and this would set me off. As she is a Southern woman, I would begin on the South, pointing out to her how the masters of the land and the slaves of the old South, claiming as they did an aristocratic outlook on life, had been, nevertheless, great land destroyers; and from that I would go on, declaring that no man could make claim to aristocracy who destroyed the land under his feet.

It is a favorite subject of mine and it gets us nowhere.

'I think I have been smoking too many cigarettes,' I said, and she agreed with me. She spoke again, as she had so often, of her fear of the habit-forming danger of a certain drug I sometimes take; but—'You had better take one,' she said.

And so I did, but it did not help.

'But why should you be afraid?' I asked myself. Even after I had taken the drug, I was wide awake and remained so night after night.

But why go on? We story-tellers, and I am writing all of this solely for story-tellers, all know, we must know, it is the beginning of knowledge of our craft, that the unreal is more real than the real, that there is no real other than the unreal; and I say this here because, first of all, I presume to re-establish my own faith—badly shaken recently by an experience—and I say it a little because as a veteran story-teller I want to strengthen the faith in other and younger American men.

Now I have remembered that once, some five or ten years ago . . . I was living in New Orleans at the time . . . I had been in the evening to the movies and had seen a picture, written by a man of talent, who had once been my friend, and having seen it had been shocked by what seemed to me a terrible selling out of all life, and, having got out of the movie theater and into the street, I went along, growing constantly more and more angry, so that when I got to my room I sat down at my desk and wrote for the rest of the night, and what I wrote was a kind of American 'I Accuse.'

I had written the words, 'I Accuse,' at the head of the first of a great pile of sheets on the desk before me and, as I wrote that night, I called the roll. I made a great list of the names, of American actors, American writers, who, having had a quick and often temporary success in New York, or who, having written a novel or a story that had caught the popular fancy, had walked off to Hollywood.

There was the temptation and I knew it must be a terrible one: . . . five hundred, a thousand a week.

'I will do it for a time. I will store up my money.

'When I have got rich I will be free.'

'But, my dear fellow, do you not understand that the complete selling out of the imaginations of the men and women of America, by the artists, of the stage, by the artist story-tellers, is completely and wholly an acceptance of harlotry?'

I had written all of this very bitterly, on a certain night in New Orleans, naming the men who had done it, some of them my personal friends. A good many of them were also radicals. They wanted, or thought they wanted, a new world. They thought that a new world could be made by depending on the economists . . . it was a time when the whole world was, seemingly, dominated by the economists. A new world was to arise, dominated by a new class, the proletariat. A good many of them had turned to the writing of so-called proletarian stories. It was the fashion.

'If I go to Hollywood, write there, get money by it, and if I give that money to the cause?'

'But please, what cause?'

'Why, to the overthrowing of capitalism, the making of a new and better world.'

'But, don't you see that what you are doing . . . the suffering of the world, the most bitter suffering, does not come primarily from physical suffering. It is by the continual selling out of the imaginative lives of people that the great suffering comes. There the most bitter harm is done.'

I accuse.

I accuse.

I had accused my fellow artists of America, had named names. I wrote for hours and hours, and when I had finished writing, had poured out all of the bitterness in me, brought on by the picture I had seen, I leaned back in my chair and laughed at myself.

'How can you accuse others when you yourself have not been tempted?'

Once, being in California, I had gone to Hollywood to see a friend working in one of the great studios; and as we walked through a hallway in one of the buildings, now often a row of little offices like the offices we used to sit in in the advertising agency, I saw the name of a writer I knew; the writer came out to me.

'And have they got you too?'

'No,' I said, 'I am just looking about.'

'Well, they have not got you yet, but they will get to you.'

I had even written two or three times to agents in New York or Hollywood.

'Cannot you sell, to the pictures, such and such a story of mine?'

There had been no offers. I had not been tempted.

'Let us say,' I remarked to myself that night in New Orleans after the outbreak of writing against others, accusations hurled on their heads, 'that you had been

offered . . . let us be generous . . . let us say twenty-
five thousand for the best of all of your Winesburg
stories, or, for that matter, for the whole series.

'Would you have turned the offer down? If you did
such a thing, everyone who knew you and who knew
of your constant need of money would call you a fool.
Would you do it?'

I had to admit that I did not know and so, laughing
at myself, I was compelled to tear up, to throw in the
wastebasket, the thousands of words of my American
'I Accuse.'

You were, on that night in New Orleans, asking
yourself whether you, the pure and holy one, would
have the courage to turn down an offer of twenty-five
thousand just to let someone sentimentalize one of
your stories, twist the characters of the stories about;
yet now, because you are again nearly broke, because
you are beginning to fear old age, an old age perhaps
of poverty, you are at work doing the thing for which
you were about to publicly accuse others and doing it
for a few hundred dollars.

The above thought jumping into my head at night,
I got out of bed. The moon was shining and sending
so bright a path of light through an open door into
the room that I thought a lamp must have been left
burning in a near-by room. I went to look.

I returned to where my wife lay, curled into a little
ball at the bed's edge, the light coming through the

door falling on her face. I had told her nothing of the new temptation that had come to me. She was one who, like my mother, would have gladly worked herself into the grave, as my mother had done, rather than that I should be trying to do what I had been trying to do.

And what was the fear that had come upon me, the fear of old age, an old age of poverty?

But you will not starve. At the worst you will have more than your mother ever had during her whole life. You will wear better clothes, eat better food. You may be even able to retain this beautiful house a book of yours built.

I stood that night by my wife's bed, having this argument with myself, the whole matter being one that will interest only other artists, realizing dimly, as I stood thus, that the fear in me that night, of which my wife knew nothing . . . it would have shocked her profoundly to be told of it . . . the fear perhaps came up into me from a long line of men and women . . . I remembered that night how my father, in his occasional sad moods . . . he was, most of the time rather a gay dog . . . used to go sit in the darkness of our house in a street of workingmen's houses, and sitting there, the rest of us suddenly silent, sing in a low voice a song called 'Over the Hill to the Poor-House.'

The fear in him, too, perhaps into him from his father and his father's father and on back and back, all perhaps men who had lived, as I had always lived, precariously.

It is what gets a man. In the artist there must always be this terrible contradiction. It is in all of us. We want passionately the luxuries of life, the things we produce—our books, paintings, statues, the songs we make, the music we make—these are all luxuries.

We want luxuries, for who but his fellow artists can really love the work of the artist while at the same time knowing, deep down in us, that if we give way to this passion for the possession of beautiful things about us, getting them by cheapening our own work, all understanding of beauty must go out of us.

'And so why all this silly struggle? Why this absurd fear?'

I left the moonlit room where my wife lay asleep . . . there is something grows very close between people who have lived long together, who have really achieved a marriage . . . as I had stood at the foot of the bed in which my wife lay, I had seen little waves of pain run across her sleeping face as waves run across a lake in a wind . . .

Barefooted I went out of my house, clad in my pajamas . . . they are of silk . . . my wife insists on buying them for me with money she herself earns . . . she is constantly, persistently buying me expensive shirts, expensive ties, shoes, hats, overcoats . . . I speak here of poverty, but, on a rack in a closet off my

sleeping room there are dozens, perhaps even a
hundred ties that have cost at least two dollars each.

Absurdity and more absurdity. What children we
are. I went and stood by an apple tree in the orchard
back of my house and then, going around the house,
climbed a little hill where I could see the front of the
house.

'It is one of the most beautiful houses in all America,' I said to myself, and for a time that night I sat
absorbed, forgetting entirely the absurd struggle that
had been going on in me for a week, for two weeks,
my eye following the line of the wall rising out of the
ground and then following along the roof. 'Oh, how
perfect the proportion; and there is where beauty
lies.'

Only a few of the many people who had come to
visit me had been able to realize the extreme beauty
of my achievement in building the house. It was true
that there had been an architect who had made the
drawings for me, but I had not followed the drawings.
For two years and while the house was building, all
the money made for me by Horace Liveright going
into it, myself once having to stop building for two
years while I went delivering silly lectures to get
more money, I had done no writing. It didn't matter.
A friend had once walked up the hill with me, to sit
with me on the top of a cement tank that went down
into the ground, where I sat that night in my paja-

mas, it also being a moonlight night, had said that my house was as beautiful to him as a poem. 'Cling to it,' he said. 'Live all the rest of your days in it.' He went on at length, saying that the house was as beautiful as my story 'Brother Death.' He named those other stories, 'The Untold Lie,' 'The New Englander,' and 'A Man's Story.' 'It has the quality they have.'

He said that and I giggled with pleasure, enjoying his praise of the beauty of my house more than any praise I had ever got from my writing.

On that night I walked down the hill past my house and to a bridge over a stream and stood, still arguing with myself.

'But I have a right now to put money first. I have got to begin now thinking of money. I have got to begin making money. I will—I will. These people of my story shall behave as I wish. For years I have been a slave to these people of my imagination, but I will be a slave no longer. For years I have served them and now they shall serve me.'

Here I was, standing in silence on the bridge over the stream. . . . And there again were the sounds in the stream. They crept into me, invaded me. I heard again the sound of the feet of children, horses galloping, soldiers marching, the sob of that crippled girl. I heard the voices of old friends. The sounds went on for a time. Of a sudden the sounds all changed.

There were no more voices, only laughter. The laughter began. It increased in volume. It seemed to become a roar.

'See, the very stream is laughing at me,' I cried, and began to run along the country road that goes past my house. I ran and ran. I ran until I was exhausted. I ran up hill and down. I hurt my bare feet. I had come out of my house wearing bedroom slippers, but I had lost them. I ran until I was out of breath, exhausted. I had hurt one of my feet on a sharp stone. It bled. I stopped running that night at the brow of a low hill, after all not far from my house . . . a man of my age, who has spent so much of his life at a desk, who has smoked so many hundreds of thousands, it may be near millions, of cigarettes, does not run far.

I ran until I was exhausted and then, hobbling along, as once a cripple girl in Chicago had hobbled sobbing beside me in a rainswept Chicago street, I went back over the road along which I had been running and to my cabin by the creek.

I let myself into my cabin and getting the manuscript on which I had been at work I took it out to a little open grassy place beside the stream and sitting there on the grass I burned it page by page.

The burning took a long time and it was a job. It was, I knew, an absurd performance; and I knew that I was, as all such men as myself must ever be, a child.

But later, as you see, I have wanted to write of it, to see if in words I can catch the mood of it.

'It will be a joy to other writers, other artists, to know that I also, a veteran among them, am also as they are, a child,' I thought.

I did all of this—as I have here set it down, going at great length, as you will see, to catch the mood of it, to give it background—and then, being very careful with my cut foot, I went back to my house and to my bed.

However, I went first to the bathroom. I put disinfectant on the cut on my foot and my wife awoke.

'What are you doing?' she asked me, speaking sleepily, and, 'Oh, I just got up to go to the bathroom,' I said. And so she slept again, and before again getting into bed I stood for a time looking at her asleep.

'I dare say that all men, artists and others, are, as I am, children, at bottom,' I thought; and I wondered a little if it were true that only a few women among all the millions of women got, by the pain of living with us, a little mature.

I was again in my bed and I thought that the voices in the stream by my house had stopped laughing at me and that again they talked and whispered to me; and on the next morning my shoe hurt my foot so that, when I was out of my wife's sight, I hobbled painfully along. I went to my cabin and to the black spot on the grass by the creek where I had burned the attempt I had made to impose my own will on the people of my imaginative world. I began to laugh at myself.

It had, I thought, been an absurd and silly experience through which I had passed but, God knows, I told myself, I may have to pass through it again, time after time. I knew as I sat down at my desk that morning, determined again not to impose myself, to let the story I was trying to write write itself, to be again what I had always been, a slave to the people of my imaginary world if they would do it, making their own story of their own loves, my pen merely forming the words on the paper . . . I knew that what I had been through, in such an absurd and childish form, letting myself again be a victim to old fears, was nevertheless the story of like experiences in the life of all artists, no doubt throughout time.

BOOKS FROM
FOUR WALLS EIGHT WINDOWS

Algren, Nelson. NEVER COME MORNING.
ISBN: 0–941423–00–X (paper) $7.95

Anderson, Sherwood. TRIUMPH OF THE EGG.
ISBN: 0–941423–11–5 (paper) $8.95

Brodsky, Michael. XMAN
ISBN: 0–941423–01–8 (cloth) $21.95
ISBN: 0–941423–02–6 (paper) $11.95

Codrescu, Andrei, ed.
AMERICAN POETRY SINCE 1970: UP LATE
ISBN: 0–941423–03–4 (cloth) $23.95
ISBN: 0–941423–04–2 (paper) $12.95

Dubuffet, Jean.
ASPHYXIATING CULTURE AND OTHER WRITINGS.
ISBN: 0–941423–09–3 (cloth) $17.95

Johnson, Phyllis, and Martin, David, eds.
FRONTLINE SOUTHERN AFRICA:
DESTRUCTIVE ENGAGEMENT
ISBN: 0–941423–08–5 (paper) $14.95

Null, Gary. THE EGG PROJECT:
GARY NULL'S COMPLETE GUIDE TO GOOD EATING.
ISBN: 0–941423–05–0 (cloth) $21.95
ISBN: 0–941423–06–9 (paper) $12.95

Sokolov, Sasha. A SCHOOL FOR FOOLS.
ISBN: 0–941423–07–7 (paper) $9.95